TLHALEFO

ROSI MOLEFE

TLHALEFO

A Novel

THE WHISPER OF HOPE BEYOND BROKENNESS

INSPIRED
PUBLISHING

TLHAFELO
The Whisper Of Hope Beyond Brokenness

First Edition, First Impression 2025
ISBN: 978-0-6398535-1-2
Copyright © Rosi Molefe

Published by: Inspired Publishing

PO Box 82058 | Southdale | 2135, Johannesburg, South Africa
Email: info@inspiredpublishing.co.za | www.inspiredpublishing.co.za

Edited by: Eloise Scoble

To My Reader

I hope this beloved masterpiece of mine finds you well. And if it doesn't, I hope it gives you enough inspiration to conquer whatever you are going through.

I hope you see and find yourself in at least one of the characters in this book, even if it is only one tiny quality that might be highlighted, good or bad, just know that you are the realest of them all.

This piece of writing hopes to inspire you to stand tall throughout whatever this monster called 'life' may throw at you. May you use all those stones thrown at you, big or small, and build an empire with them. If possible, tame that so-called monster – 'life'.

I wrote this book with nothing but my reader in mind.

Have a wonderful time reading this art piece that is dedicated to you.

It is as real as it gets.

With love,
Rosi Molefe

Table of Contents

CHAPTER ONE

I found myself in a dark, cold place, unable to see or hear anything. The silence was heavy, broken only by the rough wind whispering something sorrowful. Suddenly, it stopped. Silence. Then, a voice pierced through the quiet, "Tlaya! Tlaya mosetsana wame!" I knew that voice; I had yearned to hear it for the past eight years. I moved toward it, heart pounding. "Tlaya!" it called again, and I ran. But before I could reach it, I stumbled and fell into a deep, dark hole.

"Ms. Khama! They're here! Are you ready?" Themba's voice jolted me awake. I'd fallen asleep on my desk, and as always, Themba, my ever-reliable assistant, had come to the rescue. It hit me—I had a meeting with a high-profile potential client, one that could give my agency the boost it desperately needed.

"Themba, yes! I'm ready, just resting a bit to calm my nerves," I replied, trying to sound convincing. This meeting was critical—do or die.

"You okay? You look like you've seen a ghost," Themba said, concern in his eyes.

"I'm perfect, Themba. Just send them in."

I wasn't fine, but I had no choice. I straightened myself out and prepared to ace this pitch. Themba brought in a young, slim woman in her mid-twenties, followed by a tall, commanding man—Mr. Mogorosi, owner of Mogorosi Incorporated. His presence filled the room; he didn't need words to command respect.

"Mr. Mogorosi, I'm glad you could come. Please, take a seat," I said, extending a hand.

The young woman shook my hand, her tone sharp. "Linda. But to you, it's Ms. Khumalo. Thank you."

"Noted," I replied, staying professional as Mr. Mogorosi took his seat with a slight frown, perhaps at Ms. Khumalo's attitude or the situation.

Nerves surged at the start of my pitch, but soon I found my rhythm. Mr. Mogorosi's nods and approving smile boosted my confidence, and ideas began flowing freely, even beyond what I had planned. I avoided looking at Ms. Khumalo, who seemed uninterested, checking her expensive watch with an air of impatience. But Mr. Mogorosi's engagement kept me going.

"Impressive," he said, breaking into a rare smile. "You've got a fresh, dynamic perspective—exactly what my company needs."

I was elated. But Ms. Khumalo interrupted, "Can we go? We'll be in touch, lady."

"Tlhalefo. But to you, it's Ms. Khama," I replied with a smirk, relishing the moment as Mr. Mogorosi stifled a chuckle.

"Noted," she replied, forcing a smile.

"Thank you, Ms. Khama," Mr. Mogorosi said, smiling as he walked to the elevator. Just before the doors closed, he glanced back with a slight smile again.

After they left, Themba burst in, his eyes wide with excitement.

"Well?!"

"Actually, really well," I said, grinning. "I didn't think I'd pull it off, but I did."

Themba suggested celebrating, though he was avoiding his own strained situation at home. I declined, not wanting to celebrate prematurely. I still had work piling up, and running an agency wasn't as glamorous as I'd imagined. But it was my passion for marketing and sales that kept me going.

I took a taxi home, exhausted. Once there, I collapsed onto my bed, grateful for its comfort. Not wanting to cook, I ordered takeout for my little sister and myself, along with a bottle of red wine—a perfect nightcap after a long day.

After eating, I returned to work, determined. A girl's gotta do what a girl's gotta do. By 2 a.m., I finally gave in, my body begging for rest. I put on my pink nightie and climbed into bed, but sleep eluded me. The dream lingered, the voice echoing in my mind. Hearing him had brought joy, but not seeing or reaching him had left a void. I cried myself to sleep, secretly hoping I'd dream of him again and finally get close enough to see him, touch him.

But there was only silence. No dream. No voice.

CHAPTER TWO

My name is Tlhalefo Khama. I'm a twenty-three-year-old Motswana woman from Rustenburg, now living in Johannesburg after finishing varsity. A qualified Marketing Communications Practitioner, I recently left my role as a Junior Communications Practitioner to start my own agency, *New-Age Marketing Intellects*. Being self-employed has always been my dream, and after years of saving, I finally had enough to take the leap. I also care for my seventeen-year-old sister, Botlhale, ever since our father, Goitsimang Khama, passed away eight years ago. She's the light of my life, even though she considers me the most boring person she's ever met. As for our mother, I only have faint memories—she remarried when Botlhale was just a year old, and we've never heard from her since.

It's Friday morning, and I'm already counting down to the end of the workday. My alarm pulls me from sleep at 5:30 a.m., much to my body's displeasure—probably thanks to the wine I had last night. I slip into my morning routine: a quick bath, a light brown, knee-length dress that hugs my hourglass figure, nude heels, a sleek ponytail, and a pop of maroon lipstick against my fair skin. I prefer to keep my look natural, though today, I have to admit, it's a killer.

Before heading out, I stop by Botlhale's room to hand her some money for lunch and transport.

"Wow, ausi! You look amazing today!" she says with a rare compliment. My heart warms, but I sense a 'but' coming.

"But, seriously, that hair? Can't you put on a weave or something? Who even does afro these days, ausi?" she quips.

"Thanks, Mosetsana, but I love my hair as it is. I'm running late. And don't skip school, Ms. Fashion Police," I say with a smirk. What a sister I have!

At the taxi rank, the line is terrifyingly long. Thankfully, I manage to catch a taxi to work in time to grab a coffee and catch up with Themba, on the latest gossip. Still, I'm anxious; two days have passed since I pitched to Mogorosi Incorporated, and I haven't heard back. I hope I didn't sour things with Ms. Khumalo. This deal could be everything for my agency.

Just as I'm reviewing documents, my phone rings. The caller ID is unknown.

"Good day," I answer.

"Ms. Khama. How have you been?" says a calm, unfamiliar voice.

"Not to sound rude, but who is this?"

"Oh, my manners. It's Tsebo," the caller says.

"Tsebo?" I pause. "I'm sorry, I don't know of any Tsebo. Must be a wrong number."

"Ms. Khama, it's Mr. Mogorosi from Mogorosi Incorporated. I wanted to keep it less formal."

Oh no! The last thing I want is for him to think I'm rude.

"Oh, Mr. Mogorosi! My apologies, sir. I didn't recognise your voice. I'm well, thank you. How have you been?" I ask, scrambling to cover my misstep.

"Doing fine. I called regarding your pitch. Could you stop by my office around 5 p.m. for feedback?" he asks.

"Of course, sir. I'll see you at five."

The call leaves me uncertain. Why use my personal number? And he sounded so calm—good or bad sign? I shake it off and focus on brainstorming with my team on a new client portfolio. Hours pass, and by 4:10p.m, I'm ready to head to Mogorosi Incorporated.

At the reception, the elderly receptionist smiles as I introduce myself. "Finally, I get to see you. Mr. Mogorosi hasn't stopped talking about your pitch. He's been counting down the hours to this appointment."

Well, that's... unexpected. I chuckle nervously as she leads me to Mr Mogorosi's office, not knowing what to say.

In his office, Mr. Mogorosi greets me with a piercing gaze, ignoring my outstretched hand.

"Please call me Tsebo, it's less formal," he utters as he's looking directly into my eyes. Sounds a bit unprofessional but what the client wants, the client gets, right?

"Tsebo," I manage, feeling shy.

"That's more like it," he says with a smile, revealing his strikingly white teeth. I can't help but notice his neatly groomed moustache and strong features. He laughs as I shift uncomfortably, his laughter unexpectedly warm.

"We'll be working closely together, so we can keep it informal," he says, seemingly reading my thoughts. "I've chosen your agency to assist with a new strategy for my company. Here's a copy of the contract; review it and let me know when you're ready."

I'm stunned. Tsebo Mogorosi himself? I'm ready to burst with excitement, but I try to stay professional.

He grins, "Isn't this the part where you're supposed to jump for joy?"

"I'm honoured to be working with Mogorosi Incorporated; I promise I won't disappoint." I said in my most professional voice, trying to hide my excitement.

Tsebo: "How about we go and celebrate at your favourite spot, The Zone? It's Friday anyway and we've got every reason to pop the bottles."

"How did you know The Zone is my favourite chill spot now?" I asked, with shock.

Tsebo: "I have my ways lady. Now, shall we?"

He hands me the contract and off we go. I must admit, I don't know how the conversation in his car would take place as we don't even know each other. He plays some house music, and I think he notices my discomfort.

Tsebo: "Don't like House music?"

Me: "Not really, I'm more of a Lionel Richie and Luther Vandross fan... that kind of music."

He smiles and plays "Precious Lady" by Lionel Richie. I can't help but blush; he laughs out loud. This guy is not mentally stable, I've concluded.

We arrive at The Zone and it's a chilled vibe as usual. We order some food and drinks.

Tsebo: "So, Tlhalefo Khama. Why did you leave Optimistic Marketing? You looked like you were doing pretty well there. And your departure was a very great loss to the company, trust me I know."

"It was time," I say. "I've always wanted to build something of my own, and New-Age Marketing Intellects has been my dream for as long as I can remember. No regrets so far. But how do you know so much about me?"

He just chuckles, brushing off the question, and the evening goes on. At 8:30 p.m, I finally tell him it's time for me to head home—my sister's alone, and I want to be there.

"Don't be silly; I'll take you home," he insists, and I don't argue.

He pays the bill, and we make our way to the parking lot and as soon as he starts driving, I fall asleep. I guess I underestimated my level of fatigue. Before I know it, we are at the front of my apartment's gate. How he knew where I stayed, I have no idea. I don't even have the energy to question him.

"Thank you." I say in a sleepy tone.

"You look like a small baby when you are sleepy," he says while laughing. At this point, I honestly wish I have some psychologist friends to sort this guy out. But I believe he's beyond repair.

Me: "Whatever. Goodnight Tsebo. O tla tsamaya sentle"

Tsebo: "O robale sentle kgosatsana"

Inside, Botlhale is awake, watching music videos. The smell of food fills the air—she cooked, just as our dad taught us. Cooking is our only shared passion.

"Where have you been?" she asks with an accusing look.

"It's none of your business," I tease as I head to bed, content knowing the weekend ahead is lighter. I'll review Tsebo's contract and work on the MacroMedics presentation, but for now, sleep is calling.

I am in a vast, empty desert. My throat is parched, my knees ache from crawling. I try to scream, but my voice is gone. I turn and see a tap and cup. I crawl toward it, twisting the tap, but only blood flows. Then, a voice echoes: "O matla mosetsana wame, ntwa e ke ya gago."

I try to find him, to see him. But all I see are his footprints in the sand, disappearing into the distance. I scream, but there's only silence.

* * * * * * *

It's a beautiful Saturday morning—the sun shines warmly, and birds fill the air with cheerful songs. I feel fantastic; my spirit light and carefree. After a long, refreshing shower, I slip into my red summer dress and comb out my afro, which sits like a crown. I look pretty cute, if I say so myself, and the mirror agrees.

Today, I've decided to indulge my sweet tooth by baking my favourite chocolate muffins. But first, I need to go to the mall to gather ingredients.

"Ngwana ko gae, let's go to the mall for some baking supplies. I want to make muffins," I call out to Botlhale.

"No problem! I'm bored anyway. Let me just grab my sandals," she says with a smile.

I know how this goes—with Botlhale tagging along, I'm bound to overspend. She never misses a chance to add a few "essentials" to the list. But I can't resist her charm. She reminds me so much of myself at her age, always knowing just how to melt Dad's heart (and wallet) with her requests. He always called us his "two little angels," and I still feel his warmth in moments like these.

Once we're at the mall, we fall right into our usual routine. First stop? Seafood at Botlhale's favourite restaurant. Afterwards, we browse the jewellery store, where I let her pick out a small piece before we finally get around to buying the baking ingredients. We catch a taxi home, bags in hand, ready for our baking adventure.

In less than an hour, the muffin batter is in the oven, filling the kitchen with the sweet aroma of chocolate. While they bake, I settle down with my phone, catching up on social media. Then, a message pops up from Tsebo. My heart skips a beat, hoping he hasn't changed his mind about partnering with N-AMI.

Hey, saw you with the younger version of yourself at the mall. You looked beautiful in that red dress, and I love your crown. Enjoy the rest of your weekend. - T

People always say Botlhale and I look alike, so his comment doesn't surprise me. But a smile sneaks onto my face—maybe it's the way he noticed my natural hair, calling it my "crown." I decide not to reply; I've got bigger things to focus on, like reviewing that contract.

Before long, the muffins are ready, perfectly baked. I outdid myself, as usual.

"Ausi, we have a school trip next month to Gold Reef City, and I'd really love to go. You know, one can never be too old for that!" Botlhale says, her eyes twinkling with excitement.

"I don't know why you're putting on this innocent act... We've been to Gold Reef City a thousand times! But sure, if you want to go again, I'll pay. Just keep up your grades and stay on track with your dreams of becoming a lawyer," I reply with a grin.

"Consider it done, Ausi wame o montle!" she says, beaming. We both burst out laughing. This child!

Later, I review the presentation my team has prepared for a prospective client. Only a few minor adjustments are needed—they've done excellent work, as always.

The next morning, I'm barely awake at 7 a.m. when Botlhale rushes in, full of energy.

"Ausi! When are we going to church? It's been years, and I miss it. Today feels like the perfect day! Then we can come back and cook a big Sunday meal, just like Dad used to show us," she says, bouncing with enthusiasm.

Half asleep, I mumble, "Next time, girl. I need a restful weekend."

The truth is, the last time we went to church was eight years ago, at Dad's funeral. She was only nine, and I was just fifteen. I miss him deeply. It feels as if there's a part of me that hasn't healed and probably never will.

I can see the disappointment on her face, and it breaks my heart. I would go to the ends of the earth to protect my little sister, even if it means facing anything or anyone who dared to hurt her.

"But you know what? I'll take you up on the cooking offer. We'll have a blast," I say, hoping to lift her spirits.

She brightens immediately, "Perfect! And then we can have a karaoke session!"

"Agreed, moghel!" I laugh, and we both head to the kitchen to start the day.

After cooking and our impromptu karaoke, we call it a night early. Monday promises to be a busy day, and I'm ready to dive in. I dream of the day when my expenses will allow me to finally buy a car. For now, it's taxis and long queues, but I know this phase won't last forever.

Monday morning arrives, and I follow my usual routine, but today is special. My first stop is at Mogorosi Incorporated to hand in my signed contract. I'm thrilled to break the news to my team about our newest client.

When I arrive at Mogorosi's reception, the familiar receptionist isn't there. A pang of disappointment hits me, as I wanted her warm smile to calm my nerves. After about twenty minutes, my wish is granted as the elevator opens, and Tsebo steps out.

"Tlhalefo! What are you doing here so early, looking lost?" he says, a hint of humour in his voice.

"Good morning to you too, Tsebo," I reply. "I came to drop off my signed contract, but no one was at the reception, so I thought I'd wait."

"You have my number; you could've called me," he says, feigning irritation.

"Oops, completely slipped my mind. Silly me," I respond, chuckling.

He places a hand over his heart dramatically. "Breaking my heart, Tlhalefo, breaking my heart!"

We both laugh as he leads me to his office, its elegance still awe-inspiring every time I step inside. "Here you go—signed, sealed, and delivered!" I say proudly, handing him the contract.

"I thought you'd let your attorney look it over. You've got to be careful about those fine prints," he says, eyebrows raised.

A twinge of embarrassment hits. I don't have an attorney…yet. "I'll get one soon," I say, trying to keep my voice steady.

"And why didn't you reply to my SMS?" he asks, ever the unpredictable one.

"I had better things to do," I reply nonchalantly. The look on his face is priceless. Satisfied, I grab my bag and make my way to the door. He stares, open-mouthed, as I make my exit.

"Just like that?" he calls after me.

"Just like that. Thank you for your time, Mr. Mogorosi. We'll talk," I say, flashing a grin before heading out.

Back at N-AMI, Themba is in full swing as usual. "Cup of coffee for the boss lady?" he asks, grinning.

"Yes, a strong one! And please arrange a meeting with all department heads for 11:30a.m. No excuses," I say, taking the cup.

"What's the meeting about?" he asks, curious.

I take a deep breath, unable to contain my excitement. "Mogorosi Incorporated is our newest client—all thanks to yours truly!"

"Oh my word! We bagged Mogorosi? Thatha, girl!" Themba exclaims, practically bouncing. "This is going to be a milestone for N-AMI. Watch this space!"

We both share the excitement, knowing how big this is for us. While Themba organises the meeting, I dive into some research on Mogorosi Incorporated, and—out of pure curiosity—a little on Tsebo himself. Turns out he has businesses across South Africa, Zimbabwe, and even France, primarily in IT. He also owns two farms, in Rustenburg and the Eastern Cape. His full name is Tsebo Likhayalimile Mogorosi, which I find fascinating—there's a lot more to him than meets the eye.

I shake myself out of it as the clock approaches 11:30a.m, just in time for the meeting. In the boardroom, I break the news about Mogorosi Incorporated to my team, who can barely contain their excitement. We brainstorm on their mission, values, and expectations, and by the end, the room is buzzing with energy and ideas.

I couldn't be prouder of my team—they truly are a creative bunch. As I look around, I realise that this is the start of something great.

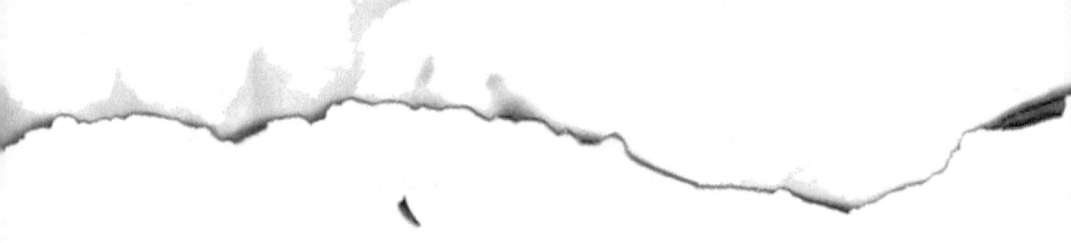

CHAPTER THREE

"We found our IT guy. I have a great feeling about him," says Gugu, our Head of HR, with a confident smile.

"I liked the Indian candidate more, but I trust your judgment," I reply thoughtfully.

"She was impressive, but Brian is more qualified and has a great personality. I think he's the right fit," Bongi, our HR assistant, chimes in.

"Alright then. You both know best—let's reach out to him," I say with a nod.

Bongi immediately gets to work contacting our new hire, and I turn my attention to today's big event: a meeting with Mogorosi Incorporated. This client is our special "baby," and today we'll be pitching a re-branding project that could redefine their brand image. I'm hopeful our ideas will resonate—there's a reason they chose us, after all. The only part I'm dreading is facing Ms. Khumalo. She has a way of making everything tenser than it needs to be. Lord, give me strength!

I head to the bathroom to do a final check on my appearance. My black dress hugs my curves, just a touch below the knee, paired with striking red stilettos. My afro is pulled back into a neat, curly ponytail. I look the part—confident and composed—but as I return to the boardroom, nerves flutter in my stomach. Why am I suddenly so nervous?

Moments later, they arrive. Themba, my team, and I are already seated as Mr. Mogorosi walks in with Ms. Khumalo and a few other representatives. Greetings are exchanged, professional and formal. I can't help but notice Ms. Khumalo casting strange glances my way, a mix of coolness and scrutiny that makes me wonder if I'm missing something. The meeting goes well; our ideas are received positively, and both parties seem satisfied.

As we're packing up, everyone begins to head out—everyone except Tsebo. He catches up to me just as I'm about to leave.

"Ms. Khama," he says with that trademark charm, "you're looking beautiful as always. You never disappoint."

I smile, though I'm slightly uncomfortable. I'd hoped we wouldn't talk after the meeting; throughout our presentation, I'd caught him watching me intently, his eyes sending unspoken messages that made my heart flutter unexpectedly. Why am I reacting like this? I'm usually calm and professional, but something about him makes me feel exposed, vulnerable.

"Well, thank you, sir," I respond, trying to sound unaffected. "Is there anything else?"

Without a word, he steps closer, his expression shifting to something deeper, almost hurt. He reaches for my hand, and the warmth of his touch sends a current through me. My heart races. I can't even meet his eyes.

"Please, stop doing this, Mme Khama," he says quietly. "I can't take it anymore."

Before I can react, we're interrupted. "Tsebo! Are we leaving, or what?" Linda's voice cuts in sharply, her irritation evident. She's standing by the door, arms crossed.

Tsebo sighs, visibly annoyed. "Linda, just go. I'll meet you at the office," he replies, his hand still holding mine. She throws me a furious look and stalks off. Did I just miss something?

He turns back to me, his face softening. "Sorry about that. Would you like to go to lunch with me?"

"Sure, let me grab my bag," I reply, still a bit dazed.

As we head to my office, I compliment him on his suit, hoping to lighten the mood. He relaxes a little, though I catch his gaze lingering on my lips and figure, an intensity that feels... complicated. Awkward, yet oddly flattering. We reach his car, and within minutes, we arrive at a high-end restaurant I'd always wanted to try but never had the budget for. The waiter leads us to our table, and Tsebo pulls out my chair before taking his seat across from me.

"Did I mention you look beautiful?" he says, smiling warmly.

"You did," I tease, "but you're welcome to say it again if you're enjoying it so much."

He laughs, a rich, genuine laugh that has an infectious effect on me.

"I could say it every day, you know—especially if it means waking up next to you," he says seriously. I'm momentarily stunned, not knowing what to say.

He seems to read my silence, chuckling softly. "You don't have to respond."

I gather my composure. "It was a great meeting today. I'm glad you're pleased with our work," I say, steering us back to safer ground.

"Tlhalefo, I didn't bring you here to discuss work," he replies, shaking his head. "I wanted to spend time with you and get to know you."

"Oh... I'm sorry." I feel myself relax, caught off guard by his straightforwardness. "So, what would you like to know, Likhayalimile?" I say, emphasising his full name.

He raises an eyebrow, surprised. "I see you've done your homework on me. Smart move, since we'll be spending a lot of time together."

"Nothing personal, just due diligence," I say, half-convincing myself as I try to brush it off. He laughs, that deep laugh that always seems to lighten my heart.

"Sure, if you say so, Tlhalefo. And how's Botlhale doing?" His question catches me off guard, my protective instincts flaring instantly.

"How do you know about her, Tsebo? And why are you even asking? I swear, if you try anything with her, you'll regret the day you were born," I say, my voice sharp.

His face is a picture of shock and hurt. "Tlhalefo, what's wrong with you? Why would you think I'd ever harm Botlhale? Do you really see me that way?"

"Answer my question, Tsebo. How do you know about her?" I demand, leaning forward, ready to leave if he doesn't give a good answer.

He exhales slowly, his expression sombre. "I did a little research, as you did with me. Her name came up, and when I saw you together at the mall, I assumed it was her. I was only asking out of care. Don't you ever raise your voice at me like that again. Do you understand?"

I feel my pulse quicken, anger bubbling up. "You're nothing to me, Tsebo. Stay away from her!" I say fiercely before standing up, determined to leave.

"Sit down, now," he says, his voice low and commanding.

"I'm not taking orders from you, Tsebo. Goodbye. And from now on, any communication between us will be strictly professional," I snap, already heading toward the exit.

"Tlhalefo!" he calls after me, but I don't look back.

Once outside, I catch a cab and try calling Botlhale, but there's no answer. Panic rises. When I arrive at work, still no response. I can barely contain my anxiety as I head to Themba's desk.

"Are you alright?" he asks, noticing my frantic expression.

"Do I look okay?" I retort. "Cancel the rest of my meetings. I'm leaving."

Themba: "Yoh aii sana! Whatever's eating you is bad. Fine. I'll do as you ordered, boss!"

"Don't you dare disrespect me like that Themba. I'm still your boss and I can fire you any second from now! Bye!" I say as I storm out of the office.

I take a taxi to Botlhale's school, anxious to see her safe. Finally, I reach the main office and ask them to call her. Relief floods over me when she walks out, confused but unharmed.

"My baby! Are you okay? I've been trying to call you," I say, hugging her tightly.

"Ausi, I was in class. What's going on?" she asks, puzzled.

"Nothing. Let's go home," I say, waving off her questions.

Back home, I start cooking something simple—mince and spaghetti. Botlhale watches me cautiously, sensing my unrest. I can't meet her eyes, focusing instead on the pots in front of me.

"Ausi, are you taking your pills? Do you need me to get them for you?" she asks gently.

"Botlhale, I don't need you to worry about my pills. Just go study," I say, forcing calm into my voice.

"You're doing it again. You're scaring me," she whispers, her voice breaking slightly.

Her words slice through me. Tears I didn't know I was holding back begin to flow. I pull her close, resting her head on my chest, and we hold each other as the weight of everything settles. "I'm so sorry, ngwana wa ko gae. I'm really sorry," I manage, my voice choked with emotion.

24

"Please take your pills. I'm begging you," she says softly.

"I will, I promise," I say, wiping my eyes and forcing a smile. "Now, go study. Dinner will be ready soon."

* * * * * *

The next day at work, the tension between Themba and me is thick. I regret my outburst, knowing I hurt him. Finally, I approach him.

"Themba, can we talk?" I ask hesitantly.

"Ms. Khama, whatever you need," he replies stiffly.

"Themba, please, I'm really sorry. Yesterday was rough, and I took it out on you. Forgive me?" I say softly.

Themba: "Ms. Khama, you are very much allowed to take your frustrations out on me. You are the boss lady after all and I just happen to be little Themba who helps you with your schedule. Yesterday you made that very clear and trust me, I got the message loud and clear!"

I don't know what to say or do anymore. I've lost all willpower. Themba is just being difficult for no reason at all.

Me: "Themba please. I'm trying here."

Themba: "You know, we all have problems or bad days, but you don't see us taking out all our frustrations on every little thing that stands in our way."

Me: "I understand all of that and I'm really sorry. Please stop with the formality now."

Themba: "It's okay, as long as you understand. I'm always here if you need to talk; you know that."

Me: "I know that. That's why I love you."

After a pause, he smiles. "Come here, you stubborn friend of mine!" He hugs me tightly, and I feel relief washing over me. We laugh, and everything feels right again.

Themba: "And you owe me lunch."

He's right; it's been a while since we spent time together out of the office.

Me: "If it's lunch you want, it's lunch you will get. Let's say. 3:00 p.m today at The Zone? I want to work from home today, so I'll meet you there. Please divert all calls to my personal phone."

Themba: "Consider it done. 3: 00 p.m it is! Can't wait!"

Botlhale. Check!

Themba. Check!

Tsebo. Well...

Later, I call Tsebo to apologise.

Tsebo: "Ms Khama. Are you your own PA now? And how's the project going?"

Me: "Tsebo..."

"Mr. Mogorosi to you." He interrupts me.

Me: "Okay. Mr. Mogorosi. To answer your question, No, I'm not my own PA and I didn't call you to talk about work."

Tsebo: "Oh. I thought that's the only communication that's supposed to take place between us from yesterday onwards. Why are you going against your word?" Shuuu! That was cold.

This is going to be one long phone call! Well, that's if he doesn't hang up.

Me: "I want to apologise for my behaviour yesterday. It was uncalled for."

Tsebo: "Is that how things are done these days? Apologies over the phone?"

Me: "Let me come to your office then. That's if you don't mind."

Tsebo: "Why would I mind? I'm working from home. Let me send a cab over to fetch you."

Me: "Okay. Thank you."

He just hangs up without saying anything. I really don't mind, though. I deserve it, after what happened yesterday. The last thing I need is to have a sour relationship with my biggest client.

The cab gets here and in about an hour or so, we've arrived at Tsebo's house, or should I say 'mansion'! The driver drives through the gate, and I can see Tsebo standing at the main door. I believe that door could pay for Botlhale's schooling fees until she graduates! How wealthy is this guy!?

"Mr. Mogorosi." I say as I'm approaching him.

"Tlhalefo. Let's go inside." Tsebo says as he holds my hand and leads me inside. This house cannot be real! Everything about it is just so perfect and looks expensive. He gives me a glass of red wine and sits next to me on the couch. A little too close to me, if you might ask.

Me: "Ntate Mogorosi. Please forgive me for what happened yesterday. I really feel stupid right now. I'm embarrassed by my actions."

Tsebo: "I didn't like the tone you used Tlhalefo. But don't sweat it; it's all in the past now. And stop with the formality please. Mind telling me why you reacted the way you did yesterday?"

I've never narrated this to anyone before. I'm ready to share. Even if it means I'll be judged. I want to get this out of my chest.

"It's strange, thinking back to a time when things were simpler, when my world was still whole. Our father, Goitsimang, was the anchor of our lives. He was a man of quiet strength, but his presence filled every space he entered. For Botlhale and me, he was everything—a father, a guide, a protector. Mom left when we were young. I was only seven; Botlhale barely a year old. We never really knew why she left or what happened to her. Ntate never spoke ill of her. He just... did his best to fill the gap.

For years, it was just the three of us. Ntate used to take us on little weekend adventures—trips to the park, drives to nearby towns, teaching us everything from how to ride a bike to how to make his famous Sunday stew. He was gentle, always patient, but he made sure we understood the value of independence and strength. I thought he would always be there to protect us.

But then, one night, he didn't come home. I was fifteen. I remember the worry, the pacing, my heart racing as the hours dragged by. When he finally returned in the early hours, his shirt stained, his face bruised; he didn't explain. He just held us close and told us he loved us.

Two days later, I witnessed his murder. It's a memory that refuses to fade, a nightmare that plays in my mind over and over, sharp and vivid. It was our uncle—Ntate's brother—who betrayed him. There was a dispute over family property, I would later learn. The details still blur, but the outcome was clear. That night, our father was gone, leaving us orphaned and alone.

Life after that was a blur of social workers, courtrooms, and the looming fear of separation. I fought hard to keep us together. The world felt cold, harsh, and I clung to every lesson Ntate had taught me, every scrap of strength he had instilled in me. But the trauma took its toll. At eighteen, I was diagnosed with severe depression. The weight of grief, of guilt, of helplessness was overwhelming. I lost myself, and for a time, I could barely take care of myself, let alone Botlhale.

For months, I sank into a darkness I couldn't escape. I neglected everything—Botlhale, school, friends. People began to talk, and social services stepped in. They were going to take her away, to put her with relatives or foster care. I was barely hanging on, terrified, and it was then

28

that I realised I had to fight. I sought treatment, attended counselling and took medication. Slowly, I began to stabilise, though I was never quite the same.

Things seemed to improve for a while. I managed to get a bursary for university, studying Marketing Communications, and I balanced school with weekend jobs, using the little inheritance Dad had left to keep us afloat. But two years later, the darkness returned. It was different this time, sharper, more erratic. I'd slip from moments of complete numbness to flashes of anger, outbursts I couldn't control. During one of those episodes, I almost set our home on fire after I forgot a pot on the stove. That was when the diagnosis shifted to bipolar disorder.

I told Botlhale everything, sitting her down and explaining as best as I could. She was still young, but even then, she had a wisdom beyond her years. She held my hand and told me she'd always be there for me, no matter what. She became my reason, my anchor. The medication helped me regain some balance, though it was a constant struggle. Over time, I started to build a career, and eventually, I saved enough to start my own agency, my dream of becoming self-employed finally within reach.

But I know I haven't healed, not completely. I'd stopped taking my medication recently, believing I could handle things on my own. Yesterday was a reminder of how fragile that balance is."

For the first time, I feel unburdened. He pulls me close, comforting me as I let my emotions flow freely.

Tsebo: "How do you cope Tlhalefo?"

I can feel the tears forming in my eyes. My throat is starting to hurt. I don't want to cry. I can't let him see me like this. My tears betray me...

Me: "Alcohol." I'm now crying on his chest.

"Ke kopa o intshwarele Mogorosi" The words are even struggling to come out.

29

Tsebo: "Sshhhh…. Let it all out. Don't hold anything back. Let it all out. Right here, right now." Still holding me to his chest. It feels so warm.

I do as he says. I cry, I scream, I curse. All on his beloved chest. I let it all out. I never realised how hurt I was. How angry I was at my mother for leaving us for another man. How angry I was at my father for passing on when we still needed him. How angry I was at my mind for not being normal. How angry I was at life. I cried and cried and cried, the peace that came with it…

* * * * * *

Waking up in Tsebo's bedroom, light filtering through the curtains, I feel oddly at peace, though a little out of place. I don't even know what time it is. Memories of the morning drift back, hazy but powerful—I'd let down my guard, revealed the parts of myself that I'd kept hidden for so long. My past, my struggles… it's like a dam wall had finally broken.

Tsebo is sitting quietly on the small couch next to the bed, watching me with a calm, steady gaze. There's no pity in his eyes, only understanding. A faint smile plays on his lips as I sit up. He leans forward, resting his elbows on his knees, and simply says, "Oh… she's alive."

I offer a small smile, feeling embarrassed. "Did I… did I really fall asleep on you?" I ask.

"You did," he says with a chuckle, his voice warm and gentle. "And you cried yourself to sleep. I had no intention of waking you. You needed it."

A wave of embarrassment sweeps over me, but Tsebo doesn't let me dwell on it. Instead, he pours me a glass of water and hands it over, his expression soft and patient.

"I didn't mean for any of this," I murmur, still feeling the vulnerability lingering.

He shifts closer, his hand reaching out to touch mine. "You shared something real with me, Tlhalefo. You trusted me with the truth, and that means a lot." He pauses, his gaze meeting mine. "So, don't regret it."

There's a moment of silence, the kind that seems to slow time. We sit in silence for a long time, the world outside feeling distant and quiet. Finally, I pull away, wiping the last of my tears and managing a small smile. "Thank you," I say, my voice barely a whisper.

"For what?" he asks, brushing a tear from my cheek.

"For... everything. For listening. For not judging. For just... being here."

His eyes soften, and he takes my hands in his. "You don't have to thank me for that. I'm here because I want to be. And I hope you'll let me be here for you—for both of you."

I don't know what the future holds. But in this moment, sitting in his home, I feel a glimmer of hope—a feeling that perhaps, after all this time, I don't have to carry this burden alone.

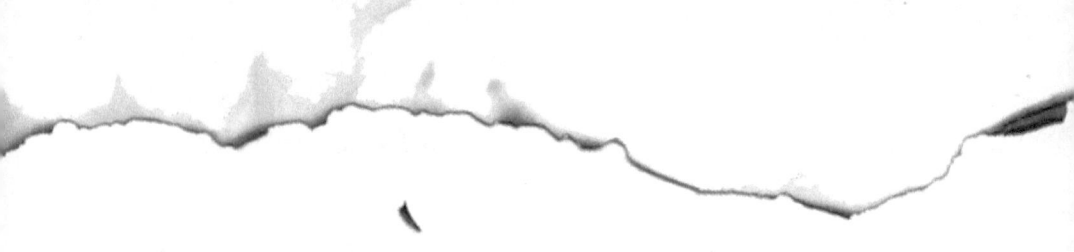

CHAPTER FOUR

Today feels like it's going to be one of those days that stretches endlessly. Our team is set to pitch an anorexia awareness campaign to MacroMedics—a project that's long overdue. We crafted the campaign with the goal of not only raising awareness but also positioning MacroMedics as a socially responsible company. I'm confident they'll love it, and it's high time we push this forward. Unfortunately, the client has been indecisive, delaying every step of the process. But as the strategist, I have to smile, keep generating solutions, and work my magic.

The day is packed. We also need to do some serious damage control for one of our most challenging clients, Mr. Derrick Linton. He's a public relations nightmare, and this time, he's under fire for drug use and reckless behaviour on social media. It's not his first scandal—in fact, just months ago, he was arrested for a hit-and-run incident. We managed to salvage his and his brand's image then, and after that, we pulled him through a domestic violence accusation. His brand is popular, and people adore his clothing line, but this behaviour could send his entire reputation spiralling. Crisis management is part of N-AMI's PR package, but this man seems determined to send us all to early graves.

To top it off, I'm also handling an ad campaign for a new energy drink, OnTheFly, with a client meeting scheduled later in the day. Oh, and our new IT specialist, Brian, starts today. A lot to juggle, and by the looks of it, I'll need two bottles of red wine by day's end.

Themba walks in, holding his usual tablet with my to-do list, and he starts running through today's agenda. He's giving me curious glances, and I can tell he has something to say.

"So, Tlhali," he begins, a mischievous glint in his eyes, "when were you planning on telling me?"

"Tell you about what?" I ask, feigning ignorance.

"Oh, please!" Themba rolls his eyes, grinning. "You and Mr. Mogorosi!"

My heart skips a beat. How does he know? It's barely been twenty-four hours since Tsebo and I made things official.

"I still don't know what you're talking about," I say, attempting to keep my composure.

"Uh-huh," he says with mock disbelief. "Well, yesterday, he answered your phone when I called you. He told me you were asleep and cancelled our lunch plans. That can only mean one thing."

I'd completely forgotten about that! Tsebo really did me in.

"Oh, that! I went to his house to discuss some project details, and I ended up falling asleep on the couch," I say, hoping it sounds believable.

Themba raises an eyebrow. "You must have been *really* tired, huh? And he just *let* you come over to his house? How generous!" He says, dripping with sarcasm.

Suddenly, a young delivery boy walks in, carrying a clipboard and a bunch of red roses. "Delivery for Ms. Khama," he says.

"That's me," I reply, signing for the flowers. The roses are beautiful, their fragrance filling the room. I open the attached note:

Red roses for a lady who hates red wine. Your love, T.M.

33

I can't help but blush, my heart fluttering as I read his words. Tsebo has a way of making even the darkest days feel a little brighter.

Themba lets out a laugh. "Wow, Mogorosi's got it bad! But wait—why does he think you hate red wine? That's your favourite, right? Or does he not know the difference between love and hate?"

I burst into laughter at his comment. "Wena! Stop insulting my man!" I say playfully.

Themba's eyes go wide. "YOUR man?!"

My cheeks flush red. "Between us," I whisper, leaning in, "we kissed. And he told me he loves me."

Themba's eyes light up, and he claps his hands in delight. "I knew it! I saw the way he looked at you the first time we met with them. Uyajola wena? The weather is making sense now, uyajola mntase!"

We both laugh, and I finally manage to usher him out of my office, insisting I need to work. Once he's gone, I dial Tsebo's number, and he picks up after just one ring.

"Beautiful," he says warmly. "How are you?"

"I'm great, thanks. I got the roses and the note. Mara wena!"

"I'm serious, Tlhalefo," he chuckles. "You're giving up red wine—you have me as your new punching bag now."

"Hee bathong! A punching bag?" I reply, laughing.

"If I could take away all the pain in you, I would," he says, his tone suddenly serious. "I meant it when I said I love you, Tlhalefo."

A warmth spreads through me. "That's sweet, Tsebo. I don't even know what to say."

"Well, you could start by telling me you love me too," he says playfully.

"But Tsebo, I don't like lying," I tease, barely able to hold back my laughter.

"Oh, so you're on a mission to break my heart, neh? But I won't surrender," he laughs.

We share a laugh before saying our goodbyes. I realise I'm running close to the time for our pitch to MacroMedics, so I dive into final preparations.

Soon, there's a knock at my door. I look up to see Brian, our new IT specialist. He's young—barely twenty—and his thick glasses, braces, and tucked-in shirt complete his nerdy look.

"Come in," I say, glancing at my watch. "I only have a few minutes. How can I help you?"

"Thank you for hiring me. I've always wanted to work with you," he says earnestly.

"Thank you, Brian. Welcome to New-Age Marketing Intellects."

He notices the roses on my desk. "Lovely flowers. Are they from your husband?"

"No, they're from my boyfriend. Anything else?" I ask, eager to wrap this up.

"No, that's all," he replies, his expression falling slightly. "See you around."

The interaction leaves me feeling a little uncomfortable. But I shake it off and focus on our pitch. We take one of our company minibuses and head to MacroMedics. The pitch goes off without a hitch, and I can tell from their expressions that they're pleased. Mission accomplished.

Next, we move on to the energy drink client, OrganicBev. When we arrive, a stunning woman with a chocolate complexion and impeccable posture greets us. Her presence is commanding yet graceful.

"You must be Ms. Khama, CEO of N-AMI?" she says with a warm smile.

"Yes, that's me. And these are my partners," I say, introducing my team.

"I'm Rose Mogorosi, CFO of OrganicBev. Nice to meet you."

My mind reels. *Mogorosi?* Is this a coincidence?

We settle in the boardroom, and as I start presenting, Rose keeps stealing glances at me, smiling as if she knows something I don't.

Me: "Good afternoon, ladies and gentlemen. I'm Tlhalefo Khama, CEO of New-Age Marketing Intellects. OrganicBev chose our agency to handle the marketing and sales of their new energy drink, OnTheFly. We are very honoured to work with such a huge beverage company and as always, we've done our magic. Ladies and gentlemen, please take your time to watch this forty-five-second advertisement we've compiled for OnTheFly. Enjoy."

I play the advertisement, judging by the body language, small whispers amongst themselves and facial expressions, positive feedback can be expected.

Jackie stands up and explains the whole advertisement to the clients. They are happy. They are happy with everything. The feedback we get is surely on a hundred. Mission accomplished! Meeting adjourned. And again, we are bringing this advertisement to life! Everyone starts exiting.

As everyone files out, Rose approaches me, her smile widening. "Great job! I knew you wouldn't disappoint."

"Thank you, Rose. I'm glad you're happy—it's what I do," I reply, maintaining a professional tone.

"And how did you know I was Ms. Khama?" I ask, trying to mask my curiosity.

"Well, I saw your picture on a certain someone's phone. That 'someone' couldn't stop talking about you."

"Does this 'someone' have a name?" I ask, feeling my heart skip a beat.

"No, I don't think he does," she teases, her eyes twinkling with mischief. "We should do lunch sometime. I think we'd have a lot to talk about regarding this 'someone.'"

We exchange numbers, and I tell her I'll reach out soon. She accompanies me to our minibus, cracking jokes the whole way. As we say goodbye, she laughs. "Tell *him* I said hi."

When I return to the office, I find lunch on my desk: a Rib and Avocado Foldover, Cheesy Chips, and Sprite from The Zone. There's a note beside it.

Here's your favourite, my sweetheart. Enjoy. I love you. Oh, and hi to you, too.

I dial Tsebo's number again, barely containing my smile.

"Lorato la me," he answers.

"Thanks for the lunch, stalker," I laugh.

"I got your message. Hi to you, too," he replies smoothly.

"Yeah, yeah. So, who is she?" I ask, pressing him.

"Ask her," he chuckles. "I love you."

"Bye, Tsebo," I say, trying to sound annoyed.

"One day, those three words will come out of your mouth," he says confidently. "Bye, sweet lips."

I laugh and hang up. The butterflies in my stomach won't seem to settle, and I savour my lunch, appreciating the thoughtful gesture. Themba returns from his lunch date, visibly cheerful, carrying a bag of leftovers.

"Sthandwa sam, I brought you lunch! Umntu wam spoiled me rotten today," he announces with a grin.

"In case you haven't noticed, I also have a boyfriend who spoils me," I reply, pointing to my lunch.

He laughs, and we both bask in each other's joy. Moments like this remind me of how precious friendships are.

But then, his office phone rings. When he returns, his face darkens. "Linton is here."

I sigh, bracing myself. "Take him to Morris' office and tell Jackie to meet us there."

Morris is our Social Media Analyst and Jackie is the Head Strategic Communicator.

Themba: "Good luck. You'll need it. People on Twitter are fuming about that man's scandals"

Me: "You are not making me feel any better."

He shakes his head and goes out to do as I instructed.

This is the part where I really need that red wine, or a shot of vodka, just to give me strength and inspiration. That man can be difficult. I make my way to Morris' office, and I find all three of them. Mr. Linton smells like a brewery!

Me: "Mr. Linton. I see you are back; we've missed you" in a sarcastic tone.

Jackie is trying so hard not to laugh, Morris, like me, cannot wait to get this over and done with.

Mr. Linton: "Haha. I am back, you can't blame me for living my life and having some nice time."

Having some nice time? This man is sixty-two years old for crying out loud!

Jackie: "Well, not if 'having some fun time' will tarnish your reputation and be the downfall for your clothing line. You must be careful of these things."

Morris: "Good people, let's get started. Every second counts." I can see some irritation on his face. I feel you, guy!

Linton tells us the whole story, Jackie and I come up with damage control strategies and Morris uses his skills.

Finally, we are done. We've been here for the last two hours and a few minutes.

Morris: "Just don't get yourself in the public eye for all the wrong reasons again, please Mr. Linton."

Linton: "Haha I'll try, but you don't know what tomorrow holds." He laughs and winks and he's out, just like that.

Some client we have! I really hope all our hard work was not in vain. I hope the public respond well to the statement released. We'll see the effect in a few days.

Finally, the day winds down, and as I call Botlhale to let her know I'm on my way. She informs me that dinner is already in progress.

"You are such an angel, Botlhale. Did you lock the door?" I ask.

"Yebo."

"Alright, I'm heading to the taxi rank now. See you soon."

She hangs up, and I smile, feeling a rush of gratitude for the stability she brings to my life. Despite the chaos of the day, I know I have a home waiting for me, a place where love, laughter, and my sister's steady presence can calm the storm.

* * * * * *

I've decided to work from home today—no meetings, just a bit of work to finish. Since I have the house to myself, I've invited Rose Mogorosi over for lunch. I also have a parents' meeting later at Botlhale's school and plan to pay for her Gold Reef City trip while I'm there. It's only 11:30 a.m., but I've already had two glasses of wine. No breakfast yet—just wine. Bad habits die hard, I suppose.

My phone rings. It's Tsebo.

"Motho waka," I answer, a smile tugging at my lips.

"Whoo, calling me motho wa gage now, are we? We're inching closer to those three words, slowly but surely," he says without even greeting.

I laugh, shaking my head. "We'll see about that. How are you?"

"I'm not good. I miss you. I'm coming to fetch you later. We're going out for lunch," he declares.

"I'm not at work," I reply, curious as to how he plans to "fetch" me.

"I know." His tone is casual but laced with mystery.

I laugh, rolling my eyes. "I won't even ask how you know that. Anyway, I already have plans with someone."

There's a pause. "Who?" he asks, his tone shifting to something cautious.

"Someone," I tease.

"Who the hell is 'someone'?" he asks, his voice low but unmistakably tense.

"Baby, relax! It's just Rose," I say, trying to hold back laughter.

"You could've just said that from the beginning," he mutters, a bit of irritation creeping into his voice.

"I love you, Mogorosi," I say suddenly, enjoying the way the words feel.

He goes silent, and I can picture his reaction on the other end of the line.

"Are my ears deceiving me? Please, say that again," he whispers, his voice full of awe.

I can barely contain my amusement. "I said, I love you, Ntate Mogorosi."

"Shit! I told you we'd get here! I love you too, baby! I love you, rato laka!" he shouts, his laughter echoing over the line.

I'm laughing so hard I have tears in my eyes. This man! "Alright, alright! You're going to deafen me! Slow down!"

"Okay, okay," he says, calming himself. "Say it one last time, my love."

"Aii, Tsebo, kganthe keng?" I ask, laughing.

"Please?" he pleads, his tone softening.

Rolling my eyes playfully, I relent. "Kea go rata," I say with a smile.

"O rata ke nna!" he exclaims, then laughs loudly. *Lord intervene,* I think to myself, shaking my head.

"Goodbye, Tsebo. We'll talk later," I say, grinning.

"No 'I love you' one last time?" he protests.

With that, I hang up, chuckling to myself. Moments later, my phone pings with a message:

I LOVE YOU MME KHAMA.

I feel my cheeks heating up, and I smile at the screen, savouring the moment.

I decide to start cooking. Spaghetti bolognese will do. In about an hour and a half, I'm finished. I take a shower and slip into a floral maxi dress with a touch of cleavage, some simple white sandals, and fluff out my afro.

Rose arrives right on time at 2:00p.m. Talk about punctuality—it must be a family trait!

"Hey, girl! I hope I'm not late," she says as I open the door.

"Right on time!" I reply, giving her a big hug. She's dressed in tight jeans and a crisp white shirt, her weave on point. This girl is effortlessly stunning.

"I brought a chakalaka salad," she says, holding up the container. "I thought about bringing wine, but my brother specifically instructed me not to give you any alcohol, no matter what." She laughs, but I can feel a flicker of irritation at Tsebo's overprotectiveness. He should know I'm not a child.

"Oh, I see," I say, trying to keep my tone light. "The chakalaka smells amazing. Come on, let's dish up."

She drops her bag on the couch and follows me to the kitchen, taking in my apartment as she goes. "Nice apartment, mo'ghel! I see you're doing really well for yourself."

"Ah, just trying," I say with a shrug. "I'm hoping to upgrade to something bigger soon—and maybe even get a car. But all in due time."

She laughs, a full-bodied laugh that reminds me so much of Tsebo's. "You sound just like my brother described—ambitious, driven, and a total hard worker. He said you remind him of me. Apparently, we're both like that."

I can't help but smile. "Seems like he's told you a lot about me. Hopefully, it's all good things?"

"Oh, trust me, he never shuts up about you," Rose replies. "He's never talked about any of his girlfriends, but with you, it's different. Believe me, abuti really loves you." She pauses and smiles warmly. "Well, I love you, too."

I feel a lump in my throat. I'm not the type to get emotional, but her words hit me hard. "You're going to make me cry," I say, laughing to mask the tears pricking at my eyes.

"I'm just happy to see my brother this happy. It's a rare sight," she says, her tone suddenly serious. I wonder what she means by that, but I let it pass.

"Let's eat—I'm starving. I haven't eaten anything all day!" I say, leading her to the sitting room.

Over lunch, we chat, gossip, and laugh, exchanging stories and advice. She tells me she's twenty-three, just like me, a qualified chartered accountant who designs clothes as a hobby. My phone rings in the middle of our laughter—it's Tsebo. I ignore it, still nursing a grudge over the "no wine" rule. Rose's phone rings next.

"Abuti," she says, answering. I can already guess the conversation. "Yes, I'm with her at her place. We're having lunch together." She pauses, giving me a mischievous look. "Juice," she says, rolling her eyes. Clearly, he's asked what we're drinking.

"Okay, I'll give her the phone," she says, handing it to me.

"Hi," I say, trying to sound indifferent.

"My love. Why aren't you taking my calls? Are you upset with me?" he asks, his voice tinged with concern.

"What do you want, Mogorosi? Just say whatever you want. I'd like to get back to my Oros," I reply, pretending to be irritated.

He laughs softly. "Ah, so that's what this is about. Look, you can be as angry as you like, but I'm not letting you touch alcohol. It's for your own good."

"Goodbye, Tsebo," I say, sighing.

"I love you. Oh, and my favourite is cranberry juice—you should try it," he adds, ever the tease.

I hand the phone back to Rose, who's chuckling and enjoying her pasta. "Alright, abuti, we'll talk later. And no, I'm not bringing you a lunchbox. Goodbye," she says, hanging up.

"Nare, what's with this alcohol issue he's so obsessed with?" Rose asks, raising an eyebrow.

"Uhm… I get sick when I drink alcohol," I lie quickly, hoping she doesn't press the issue.

"Oh, got it," she says, nodding. "By the way, he asked me to bring him some of your spaghetti. I told him no." She laughs.

"Good!" I reply, laughing with her. This girl is amazing company.

After a couple of hours, Rose glances at her watch and sighs. "Girl, I should get going. I have a meeting with my fashion tutor. Thanks for the delicious meal and the awesome time!"

"You're welcome! We should definitely do this again," I say, giving her a hug as I walk her to her car—an X3, no less. Thatha girl!

She hugs me back tightly. "We will. Bye, mo'ghel!"

After she drives off, I tidy up the kitchen and check the time. It's 4:30p.m, just enough time to make it to Botlhale's school for the parent meeting. Tsebo's probably not coming to get me, and honestly, that's for the best. After that call, he must know that he'd risk being strangled if he showed up today.

I lock up, grab my side bag, and head out, leaving the leftover spaghetti bolognese for dinner tonight. Back to the world of taxis, queues, and all the joys of public transport.

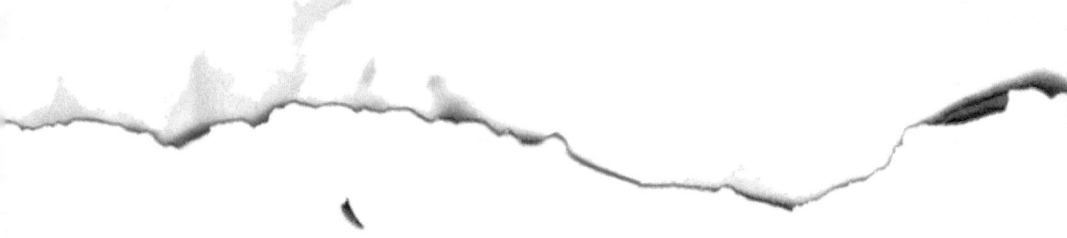

CHAPTER FIVE

It's Saturday, and while Botlhale is off on her school trip to Gold Reef City, Tsebo is on his way to pick me up. We're set to spend the day together, and I can't help but hope that wherever we go isn't too crowded. It's month-end, after all, and you know how that can get.

"My baby, Daddy has arrived!" Tsebo announces, barging through the door without so much as a knock. Whatever happened to knocking?

"Can't you knock anymore?" I retort, feigning indignation.

"Nope," he replies, a playful smirk dancing on his lips.

Before I can respond, he wraps his arms around my waist and kisses me, sending butterflies fluttering in my stomach. "How's the love of my life doing?" he asks, his voice warm and teasing.

"Ke siame, motho waka. How are you?" I smile up at him, feeling small in his tall embrace.

"Looking beautiful as always. Those jeans suit you," he compliments.

Honestly, I'm not a huge fan of jeans; I own just three pairs because they always feel so uncomfortable. Today, I'm in my tight skinny jeans paired with a white lace top, red heels, a silver watch, and a red bag. My long braids cascade over my shoulders—I'd grown tired of combing my hair every morning. I've opted for a touch of nude lipstick, and I'm feeling myself. Thatha girl!

"Well, thank you, my love. You don't look too bad yourself. O snack!" I grin back at him.

He's rocking black fitted jeans, a white polo, white sneakers, and a black cap topped off with a Rolex watch. My man is a snack—no, he's a whole meal! I just hope no one else has their eyes on him; otherwise, there'll be hell to pay.

"Your snack," he says, leaning in for another kiss.

"Yeah, yeah. So, where are we headed?" I ask, eager to know our destination.

"Off to Zuri, and then we'll spend the rest of the day at my place," he says, casting me a lustful glance. I hope he doesn't get any ideas.

"Oh, okay. I can't wait to chill with you," I emphasise the word "chill" to make my intentions clear.

We both burst into laughter for reasons I can't quite pin down. After locking up, we hit the road.

When we arrive at Zuri, a young white lady greets us with a smile.

"Good day, table for two?" she asks.

"Yes, please," I reply.

She leads us to a cozy corner table, perfect for our intimate outing.

"My name is Gladwyn, and I'll be your waitress. Here are your menus; just call me when you're ready to order," she says before disappearing.

I scan the menu, feeling a cocktail or some wine in my future. I refuse to let this handsome bully next to me let me die of thirst.

"Ready to order?" Tsebo asks, looking expectantly at me.

"Yep!" I respond.

He waves Gladwyn over. "I'll have the steak, ribs, and chips combo, with a Castle Light."

"And ma'am, what would you like?" Gladwyn asks me.

"Um... I'll have a rib burger with cheesy chips and a Piña Colada cocktail," I reply.

"She'll have her meal with a Sprite, Gladwyn," Tsebo interjects.

"Pina Colada, Gladwyn!" I assert, determined to stand my ground today.

I can see Gladwyn struggling to keep up with our back-and-forth.

"Tlhalefo. I'm not in the mood. Gladwyn, she'll have a virgin non-alcoholic Piña Colada then," Tsebo declares, shooting Gladwyn a dismissive look.

"Coming right up," she replies, scurrying away.

"Tsebo, you're embarrassing me right now. I can make my own decisions; I'm not a kid," I retort, exasperated.

"Have I ever told you how beautiful you are?" He leans closer, licking his lips and caressing his perfectly groomed beard. I can feel my resolve weaken.

"You have. A million times," I reply, blushing under his gaze.

"And you want a phuza face? Psshh. Don't bore me," he teases, his tone dismissive.

Ouch! That one stings. I silence myself, pulling out my phone and scrolling through social media. I can feel him watching me, but I'm not about to look back. Thankfully, our food arrives, and I can't wait to dig in!

"How's your cocktail?" Tsebo asks, laughter in his voice as he leans back, clearly enjoying my discomfort.

"I don't know," I reply, trying to keep my tone flat.

He laughs again, downing a large jug of beer as if it were water. How selfish!

"It's really no use being mad at me, baby. I'm just trying to do what's best for you here," he insists, his tone shifting.

Suddenly, it strikes me that I don't really know much about this man. I mean the real him, beyond the success and surface. "Where are you from?" I ask, curious.

He goes serious in an instant. "Rustenburg, Tlhabane."

Really? Is that all he's going to share? I feel he's reluctant to discuss anything deeper, so I decide to push a little further.

"Tsebo, who are you? You know almost everything about me. I'd really appreciate it if you shared a bit more about yourself."

"Tsebo Likhayalimile Mogorosi. Thirty years old. I have a younger sister, Rose. My father was Moeti Mogorosi, a Tswana man, and my mother was Nomandla Buswayo, a Xhosa woman. Like I said, I'm from Rustenburg, ko Tlhabane. I'm a qualified IT specialist, a qualified agriculturalist, and a businessman." He shares, but I'm still not satisfied.

"So, you're a Tswana-Xhosa man. I always thought you were purely Tswana," I respond.

"I am Tswana, and that's it," he snaps.

That felt weird. I notice he's uncomfortable talking about himself, but why? I decide to lighten the mood.

"You forgot something," I say playfully.

"What's that?" he asks, suddenly looking alarmed, though he's trying to hide it.

"You forgot to mention that you're taken by a beautiful Tswana woman, Tlhalefo Khama," I tease.

He sighs, then laughs. "I was going to add that, but you interrupted me while I was still talking, wabona baby?"

I roll my eyes, but we share a moment of laughter, and I can't help but feel lucky to have fallen for such a delightful lunatic.

After we finish eating, we take a stroll around the mall, hand in hand, stealing kisses here and there. It's safe to say I'm in love.

"We're in a mall, babe, for crying out loud! And you're empty-handed. O jwang mara?" Tsebo chides.

"Helang. What are you talking about, Rra?" I ask, genuinely confused.

"Your hands should be full of shopping bags—clothes, jewellery, the works! I mean, your man is Mogorosi, by the way," he says with an air of arrogance.

I can't help but laugh, but the truth is, I'm not keen on spending anyone's money but my own. It makes me uncomfortable.

"But, baby, I don't want anything. Having you by my side is all I need right now," I tell him sincerely.

"Here. You'll find me in the car. Buy the whole mall if you need to. 2690. I love you," he says, handing me his BLACK CARD as casually as if he were tossing me a stick.

My heart skips a beat. I can't believe this! He walks away, leaving me standing there in shock.

With no choice, I decide to buy a few dresses and some nice things for Botlhale. As I enter a fancy boutique, I receive a text notification:

> *Don't forget to buy some lingerie. Can't wait! I love you!*

Mxm. I refuse to reply to this nonsense. I have serious shopping to do!

I dive into shopping and can't stop! I snag beautiful dresses, tops, skirts, two suits, and four pairs of heels. I even grab a few clothes for Botlhale and two pairs of Nike sneakers. For Tsebo, I find killer cufflinks and a Louis Vuitton belt.

As I head back to the car, I pray he won't be mad about my splurge. Just as I approach, he comes out to help me with the bags. *Fingers crossed!*

"Jeez, Mme Khama! You really cleaned out the whole mall!" he exclaims, laughter bubbling from him.

"I got something for you," I say, unable to hold back my excitement.

"Mmh. I see you got my SMS. Can't wait! You'll show it to me when we get home, don't ruin the surprise," he says, his eyes sparkling with mischief.

Poor guy; if only he knows it is nothing close to what he's thinking. "It's nothing big, though," I tease.

"Ssshh. Don't ruin it," he insists.

I can't wait to see the disappointment etched on his face!

Once we're in the car, he drives us to his place.

We arrive and collapse onto the couch.

"Should I go fetch the shopping bags?" he asks after a moment, a look of mischief in his eyes.

Me: "Oh yeah sure. I almost forgot."

"How can you forget something like this baby?" He still has that smile. He goes back to the car and comes back with all the bags.

Tsebo: "Here baby. I'm ready. Or should we go to the bedroom?"

Me: "Nah. I'll do it right here."

Tsebo: "Okay then. Let me just sit back and relax."

Poor guy. I take one of the bags, take out the box that has the cufflinks, and I also take out the belt.

Me: "Here you go baby. This is what I got you."

Tsebo: "Put them on the table, I'll check them out later, after the real surprise."

Me: "What real surprise janong?"

Tsebo: "Hau moratiwa. The lingerie."

Me: "I didn't buy that nonsense."

The look on his face! He pops his eyes out, stands up and sits down again. He looks so disappointed.

Tsebo: "But why baby? I was looking forward to seeing you in it..."

Me: "I didn't want to get your hopes high for nothing baby. I know you are a man and you have needs but I'm not ready to have sex, yet."

Tsebo: "What do you mean 'you are not ready to have sex'?"

I sit down next to him. I'm looking down; I can't look him in the eye.

Me: "Tsebo. I... I..."

"Wetsang?" He interrupts me. I think he's getting impatient with me right now.

I stand up and go stand by the stairs; I fold my arms. He also stands up and stands opposite me, with his hands in his pockets.

Me: "Tsebo. I've never had sex. What I'm trying to say is... I am a virgin"

I'm still looking down. I'm sure what I've just told him irritated him even more.

He comes closer. He takes my hands and wraps them around his waist. He kisses my forehead and puts my head on his chest, the beloved chest. He's holding me tight.

Tsebo: "Go siame moratiwa wa me. You don't have to feel bad nor embarrassed about anything. I'm sorry for putting you under pressure. I'll wait for you. I promise you."

I feel so safe right now. I could reside in his arms till forever comes. There's so much peace in his arms.

Me: "You promise?"

Tsebo: "I promise my love. I love you so much, Tlhalefo. I really love you."

Me: "I love you more, Mogorosi"

He takes my head so I can face him. He has that stupid smile on his face.

Tsebo: "Say that again."

Me: "Wa simolla akere?"

Tsebo: "Baby waka hle."

"I love you Mogorosi. I love you; I love you; I love you" I say while kissing him all over the face.

He's dying of laughter. He has tears in his eyes and he's even out of breath, still laughing. He really looks like a little boy right now. I can't help but laugh at the sight of all of this. He pulls me up and starts spinning me around.

"I love you more MmeKhama. Moratiwa wa pelo yame!!!" He's shouting.

We laugh together from all the craziness. We are now sitting on the stairs. He's sitting behind me; I'm sitting in between his legs and my head is resting on his beloved chest. He has his arms wrapped around me. I could live like this until forever comes. After about an hour, I get an SMS notification. I stand up to go and check.

> *Ausi. The bus is about to arrive at school. Please come and fetch me.*

I had told Botlhale to text me when she got back from her trip because I know they always come back late. It's 7:38p.m.

Me: "Babe. I have to fetch Botlhale; she's arrived at school from her trip. It was great spending time with you."

Tsebo: "Okay, let's fetch her then."

Me: "No babe. That's not necessary; I'll take a cab."

Tsebo: "When are you really going to acknowledge my presence in your life as your man, Tlhalefo?"

Honestly, it's going to take me some time to adjust to having a man who loves and cares for me this much. I'm used to handling stuff on my own.

Me: "I'm sorry, my love. Let's fetch her together then."

Tsebo: "Nxa aii man Tlhalefo, you like being difficult for no reason at all."

He takes all the bags and puts them in his car again. Poor guy. We are off to fetch my baby girl. In less than an hour, we are at the school. I get in to fetch her then take her to the car. I'm quite nervous about what she'll think about Tsebo. Will she even like him? I know my little sister; she's one person who can't pretend at all. She's way too hardcore than me. I'm a softie compared to her. I find her waiting for me by the buses and we go to Tsebo's car.

Me: "Botlhale. This is Abuti Tsebo. He's my friend."
Tsebo looks at me then rolls his eyes.

Botlhale: "Dumela Abuti Tsebo."

Tsebo: "Dumela Botlhale. Your sister and I are VERY good friends. So you'll see me a lot. How was your trip?"

I can see Botlhale trying to hold her laughter. I think by now, she has figured out that Tsebo is my boyfriend.

Botlhale suddenly lights up and tells us about her trip, even some unnecessary stuff. I actually feel like a third wheel here because Tsebo and Botlhale are on fire. I don't even think they remember that I'm in the car. These two get on like a house on fire.

We arrive at my apartment, I take Botlhale inside and Tsebo takes all the bags inside.

Botlhale: "Good night Abuti Tsebo, I hope to see you soon!"

Tsebo: "I'll be sure to come here often. Good night angel"

They high five each other and Botlhale goes to her bedroom. No goodnight for me? Okay! I'll show her the stuff I bought for her tomorrow, I guess.

"Thank you for today my love. I really had a great time." I say as I put my hands on his shoulders and he puts his on my waist.

Tsebo: "I had a great day myself. And found myself a new friend."

Me: "Mxm thanks Mogorosi for stealing my little sister from me."

Tsebo: "It's only a pleasure, my love."

Me: "I love you."

Tsebo: "I love you too. You mean the world to me."

Me: "Oh, before I forget, here's your card."

Tsebo: "Keep it. It's yours"

We share a very long, passionate kiss. I walk him out, and he kisses me again.

Me: "Goodbye, my love"

Tsebo: "Goodnight, beautiful"

Off he goes.

Gosh! I'm in love!

I'm running down a dark street. I see a silhouette of a tall man. I run towards him. I run. I run as fast as I can. The nearer I get to him, the further he gets away from me, but he is not even moving.

I give up; I'm out of breath, and I just drop to the floor. I lift my head up to look at him. He laughs.

* * * * * * *

I was at work, sipping my coffee and minding my own business—just the way I liked it—when a voice broke my concentration.

"Delivery for Ms. T. Khama," said the delivery guy, standing there with a bunch of sunflowers.

I frowned. Sunflowers? I hated those things with a passion.

"That's me," I replied, trying to mask my distaste.

"Please sign here for me, ma'am," he said, handing me a clipboard. I signed, and he handed over the flowers with a small, professional smile.

As I glanced at the note attached, my heart sank.

"You really look beautiful in that pink suit. My heart beats for you and only you."

That was a little awkward, especially because it wasn't the tone Tsebo would typically use. Besides, I hadn't even seen him that day. How did he know what I was wearing? I decided to give him a call. The phone rang once before he picked up.

"Missing my sexy voice already, beautiful? We just talked about an hour ago," he teased.

"Who lied to you and told you that you have a sexy voice?" I shot back.

"You did. You always do," he replied with a chuckle. He wasn't wrong—I always told him that.

"Whatever, handsome. I got the flowers you sent me. You know very well I hate sunflowers. Why did you buy me those?" I asked, trying to sound annoyed but secretly still flattered.

"I didn't send you any flowers..." he said, and my heart dropped.

"What do you mean you didn't send me any flowers?" I repeated, confused.

"What's going on, Tlhalefo?" His voice was suddenly serious.

"I got sunflowers and a note telling me how beautiful I look today. I thought it was you," I explained, feeling a knot tightening in my stomach.

"WHAT?! I'm coming over there. Right now!" he declared, urgency rising in his tone.

"Okay, baby," I replied, not wanting to argue with him when he was like this. I knew it wouldn't end well.

Thirty minutes later, he arrived, his face taut with concern. "Baby. Are you okay? Where are those stupid flowers?"

"Geez, Tsebo. It's only flowers," I said, trying to keep the situation light.

He grabbed the flowers off my desk, scanning the note quickly.

"Shit. Who's this idiot? What the hell does he even want from my woman?!" he growled, fists clenched, his voice a low rumble.

Even in his calmness, there was something unsettling about his demeanour.

"Babe, we aren't even sure it's a man. It could be a woman for all we know. Please relax, you are scaring me," I urged, my own anxiety bubbling to the surface.

"Nxa, aii maan Tlhalefo! How can you tell me to relax? Some little idiot has his eyes on my woman. My woman!" His shout filled the small office, echoing off the walls.

"Oh please, Tsebo! Stop overreacting! I shouldn't have told you!" I snapped back, frustration surging through me.

"Why are you raising your voice at me? Who the hell do you think you are talking to, Tlhalefo?" he retorted, his tone shifting back to low and threatening as he stepped closer.

"I... I didn't mean to..." I stammered, fear creeping into my voice.

He simply looked at me, silence hanging heavily in the air. Then, without another word, he turned on his heel and walked out. I was left standing there, heart pounding. He had never treated me like this before. I closed the door behind him and sank into my chair, tears streaming down my cheeks, though I couldn't quite understand why I was crying. I hated feeling this way.

The hours dragged on, and by the end of the day, I was exhausted. I checked my phone and saw six missed calls and four messages from Tsebo. I didn't even bother to open them. Meetings came and went, and finally, it was time to go home.

As I stepped outside, I spotted a silver-grey Audi Q5 parked nearby. I knew that car. Just as I turned to head back inside, I heard him call out.

"Tlhalefo. Baby. Please talk to me." Tsebo was running towards me, his expression softening.

"Tsebo. Please. I don't feel like talking to you right now. Just... just go," I pleaded.

"Not until we sort this out. Let me take you home so we can talk about this. Please," he insisted.

I knew I wasn't going to win this one, so I relented and climbed into the car, silence settling between us. He leaned in to kiss me, but I turned my gaze out the window, not ready for any intimacy just yet. The drive home was tense, both of us lost in our thoughts.

Once inside my apartment, Botlhale greeted Tsebo with enthusiasm. "Abuti Tsebo! How are you?" she chirped, rushing over to hug him.

"Botlhale wame! I'm good thanks, my angel. How are you?" he replied warmly.

"Ke siame. I've missed you!" she beamed.

"I've missed you too. Just that I've been busy, a lot. Don't worry, I'm here now," he reassured her.

"Great. I'd love to sit and chat, but I have a lot of studying to do," she said before disappearing into her room.

I felt a twinge of irritation—she hadn't even greeted me. "Okay," I said in a low tone, feeling overlooked. Tsebo shot me a glance and laughed, "Mini you right there!"

I flopped down onto the couch, flicking the TV to the fashion channel. "Can I have a drink?" Tsebo asked, but I didn't look at him.

He opened the cupboard, and suddenly, I heard him exclaim, "Shit!"

I glanced over to see him rummaging through the fridge. "Shit!" he repeated, irritation threading through his voice.

I cursed under my breath, realising I had forgotten to hide the wine bottles.

"Keng mara ye? I thought we talked about this shit of yours!" he exclaimed, frustration boiling over.

"Those are not mine," I insisted defensively.

"Hehe, badimo ba Mogorosi! Who do they belong to? Botlhale?"

"Look, that's my coping mechanism! I admit; I'm addicted and unfortunately, there's nothing I can do about it! Deal with it or get out of my life!" I shot back, my voice rising.

"Ke masepa nthweo! Rubbish at its highest grade! I told you I'm willing to help you through this and be with you EVERY STEP OF THE WAY! Go na janong o mpolella masepa fela!" he yelled, his anger palpable.

"Please! Just please! Don't shout at me!" I begged, tears welling up in my eyes, my voice breaking.

Botlhale was still in her room, blissfully unaware of the storm brewing in the living room. Tsebo moved away from the kitchen, his shoulders slumped as he sat down on the couch, looking defeated with his hands covering his face.

"Come and sit with me, Tlhalefo," he said softly. I did as he asked, inching closer to him.

"My love, forgive me for scaring you earlier and for shouting at you. I'm trying really hard not to be like this. Trust me, I'm trying! I won't have an alcoholic wife; having alcoholic parents was enough for me. It's something I won't tolerate, come rain or shine. I'm trying to do what's best for us here. I want you to run to me when you feel any kind of pain, anger, or irritation. Tlhalefo, I see a future with you. I see you as the mother of my kids, my wife, my whole life! Please, allow me to help you. Allow me to be there for you, to love you wholeheartedly, to protect and care for you with my whole being. Allow me to be your peace. I'm begging you," he poured out his heart.

I couldn't help the tears streaming down my face. His words hit a sacred space in my heart, making me realise how much he truly cared. I leaned against him, wrapping my arms around his waist, wanting to be close.

"The love and care you have shown me is overwhelming. Thank you for that. I'm so sorry for being difficult. I promise I'll trust you, I'll stop with the alcohol. I love you so much, Mogorosi. I can't even put it into words," I murmured, my heart swelling.

"Ke go rata ka pelo yame yotlhe, Mme Khama. I see a future with you," he said, looking deeply into my eyes.

"And please throw away those bottles. Our children can't have a drunkard for a mother," he added gently.

I laughed, a mix of surprise and disbelief. "Children?!"

"Hee bathong! Yes, children! We are going to have a netball and soccer team!" he exclaimed, grinning widely.

"We'll see about that," I replied, shaking my head, but smiling nonetheless.

He burst into laughter, standing up. "We sure will see about that."

"I love you so much," I said, feeling lighter.

"You are loved by me," he replied, his eyes sparkling.

And for the first time in a long time, I felt like everything was going to be okay.

****

The Mogorosi Incorporated rebranding project is progressing remarkably well. With a generous budget at our disposal, we were granted the creative freedom to execute our vision. The truth is, rebranding is an expensive endeavour—millions are often at stake—and it demands extensive work and strategic planning.

As for the OnTheFly energy drink from OrganicBev, the response from the public has exceeded our expectations. Within just a week of launching the advertising and distribution to wholesalers, consumers across the country purchased sixty thousand cans. Our efforts to elevate OrganicBev's visibility have paid off; the brand is now more beloved and recognised than ever, largely due to our introduction of social responsibility initiatives and enhanced customer engagement.

OrganicBev now donates school shoes, uniforms, sanitary pads, and energy drinks to primary and secondary schools throughout South Africa. They've also launched monthly quizzes on social media, offering fans a chance to win various prizes. Trust me, these initiatives have not only attracted a large customer base but have also fostered a loyal following, paving the way for enduring relationships—all thanks to N-AMI!

Tomorrow marks the launch of the anorexia campaign for MacroMedics, which will occur semi-annually. I genuinely hope everything goes smoothly.

On a less positive note, Mr. Linton's recent statement has not resonated well with the public, and his company sales have taken a hit as a result. Our feedback percentage was only 47% positive regarding his scandal. We've organised a press conference for him at the end of the month, allowing him to share his side of the story with the public. In the meantime, we're hard at work on comeback advertisements and promotions for his clothing line. We've proposed that Mind-To-Soul, one of our clients specialising in depression, anxiety, narcotics, and alcohol addiction, partner with him on his journey to recovery. This collaboration would not only aid him but also serve as a strategic marketing move for them, increasing their exposure. They will also be present at Linton's press conference.

Most of my other clients are satisfied with our work, requiring mainly advertising and promotions, along with a bit of damage control here and there. Overall, everyone is happy, and I can't help but feel proud of how far I've come with N-AMI. What was once a dream has become a reality.

Life is treating me well. Botlhale is excelling in school; my company is thriving; my bank account is looking great; I'm back on my medication; and I have a man who loves me to bits! What more could a girl ask for?

Jackie and I are heading to Mogorosi Incorporated to go over a few things. We're taking her car, but I'm the one driving.

Upon our arrival, the receptionist leads us to the boardroom, where Tsebo, Linda, and two other guys are already seated. Tsebo winks at me, and I can't help but blush.

We discuss everything on the agenda, and everyone contributes their thoughts—except Linda. She merely sits there, nodding at everyone's points except mine. It's infuriating; I don't even know what position she holds here.

During the meeting, Tsebo sends me a text.

> *My love. Not even a kiss when you arrived? But it's cool. I'll see you in my office after we're done here.*

> *Haha. My other boyfriend is here, so I couldn't kiss you. I'll see you in your office.*

> *Don't play like that, Mme Khama. End this meeting already.*

> *No. You end it.*

> *Mxm!*

We continue with the meeting, and thirty minutes later, we wrap up. Everyone disperses.

Me: "Jackie, you'll have to go back alone. I have something I need to take care of."

Jackie: "Oh no. That means I'll have to drive? I was enjoying your driving so much."

Me: "Sorry, girl."

Tsebo stands at the end of the office corridor, leaning against the wall, one leg crossed over the other, hands in his pockets.

"I wonder how long you've been standing there," I say, reaching out to hug him.

Tsebo: "Since you left the boardroom. Akere, you didn't even bother to wait for me."

Me: "Whatever. Let's go."

Tsebo: "Go ahead; I'll find you in my office. I have something to take care of in HR; it'll only take a few minutes."

Me: "You could have used the time you spent staring at me while I was talking to Jackie for that."

Tsebo: "Helang. I was just enjoying the view. Shoot me for that."

Me: "Just go already."

Tsebo: "Yes, ma'am!"

I step into the elevator, and guess who's inside? Yes, it's Linda Khumalo! She's wearing a tight, extremely short leather skirt paired with a green velvet bodysuit and red heels. Yikes! I keep my mouth shut and mind my business, but she keeps giving me nasty looks.

Linda: "Where are you going? The meeting is over, sweedy."

Me: "How is that any of your business?"

Linda: "Stay away from Mr. Mogorosi. He's mine and mine alone. I don't even know why he chose that stupid agency of yours!"

Wait, what?!

Me: "Who do you think you are? I'm not going to entertain you and stoop to your level. Stop meddling in my affairs; I'm warning you."

She looks at me, shocked. I guess she didn't expect that response from sweet little Ms. Khama. The elevator doors open, and I step out onto Tsebo's floor, glancing back at her.

Me: "Oh, and please fix that lipstick of yours; it's ruined. It must be all this nonsense you keep talking."

The doors close behind me as I head to Tsebo's office. I sink into the small couch and pull out my phone to scroll through social media, but Linda's words replay in my mind. What did she mean by that?

About fifteen minutes later, Tsebo arrives.

Tsebo: "Sorry to keep you waiting, beautiful."

Me: "What's going on between you and Linda?"

Tsebo: "And now?"

Me: "And now, answer my question!"

Tsebo: "She works here because of her rich father. We once had a one-night stand, and she wants me badly. That's it."

Me: "Oh. So you've never dated her?"

Tsebo: "Never! Keng? Is she still giving you an attitude?"

Me: "Nope. Just curious."

He pulls me in for a passionate kiss.

Me: "I have to go; I don't want to be late. I'm having lunch with Rose."

Tsebo: "Oh yeah, she told me. The Zone. Let me drop you off there; I have some errands to run." This guy is always busy with something!

Me: "Geez, Rose tells you everything, huh?"

Tsebo: "Yep. Everything."

We arrive at The Zone a few minutes later; it's conveniently close to his workplace.

Me: "Hey girl, sorry to keep you waiting."

Rose: "No problem! I just got here. I've missed you so much!"

Me: "Ke nna oo! Have you ordered?"

Rose: "Nope."

Tsebo: "Hee, bathong Rose, Dumela! I'm here too!"

Rose: "Oh, Abuti, dumela. Who invited you?"

Ouch! Serves him right! Now he knows how it feels when Botlhale does this to me. I can't help but laugh.

Tsebo: "Nxa. I know when I'm not wanted. Let me go to the kitchen."

Me: "Good riddance!"

Rose: "Aii! Abuti can be tiring at times."

The waitress arrives to take our orders.

Me: "I know, right? Anyway, what's he going to do in the kitchen?"

Rose: "I guess he's checking to see if everything is running smoothly."

Me: "Huh?" I'm confused.

Rose: "Uhm, in simple terms, he owns The Zone."

Me: "Eng? He never told me that!"

Rose: "There's a lot you're going to learn about him. This brother of mine!"

To say I am shocked would be an understatement.

We continue chatting and laughing when I receive an SMS notification. I pull out my phone to check the message.

Come back. I miss you already. I can't get you out of my mind. I'm in your office right now. It feels so empty without you here.

I nearly choke on my drink. Who the hell is this?!

Rose: "A o siame?"

Me: "Uhm, yes, yes. I just forgot I have to get back to work."

"Oh okay. Don't worry about the bill; it's already settled." She laughs and winks at me.

Me: "Cool. Let me call Tsebo."

Rose: "Okay girl. I have to get back to work too. We'll talk. Love you!"

She hugs me, and off she goes. I call Tsebo.

Me: "Baby, please take me back to work; I'm done."

Tsebo: "Okay, I'm coming."

He arrives within moments, and we get into the car, heading back to my office.

Tsebo: "Are you okay? You don't look too good."

"Yes, baby, I'm fine. I'm just tired. And you! Why didn't you tell me that The Zone is yours?" I say, playfully tapping his thigh.

He laughs. I don't even know what's so funny.

Tsebo: "I thought you knew."

Me: "No, I didn't."

Tsebo: "Well, now you know."

We arrive back at the office, and he drops me off. After our goodbyes and a kiss, I decide not to mention the SMS; I know he'll make a big deal out of it. I head straight to Themba's desk before going into my office.

Me: "Themba, did you see anyone enter my office while I was gone?"

Themba: "Nope. I didn't see anyone. Why?"

I step into my office, and everything is in order. Still, I can't shake the feeling of panic creeping in. I call Themba to come to my office so we can hang out and chat. The truth is, I'm scared to be alone. He arrives with two glasses of orange juice, and we chat like crazy.

Suddenly, another SMS comes through.

> *Good, you're back. Now I can work. Queen of my heart.*

This is really freaking me out now! Who is this person, and what do they want from me?!

Themba: "O right chomi?"

Me: "Yes, yes. Just a message from Botlhale. Another school trip, imagine!"

Themba: "Hehe. Lomntwana uyazi that her sister has money. She's smart. Ndiyam'thanda!"

I laugh, although I'm hardly paying attention to what he just said. This is really starting to freak me out. I'm scared.

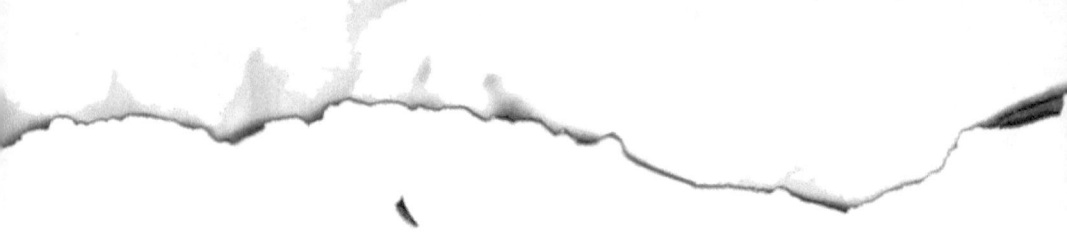

CHAPTER SIX

It's already late November, and Botlhale is just a week away from starting her final Grade 12 exams. It's amazing how quickly time flies.

Last week, I introduced Botlhale to Rose, and oh my, do I regret that decision! I thought Botlhale was Tsebo's best friend, but it turns out that Rose has gracefully taken that title. They've been having ice cream dates, going to amusement parks, watching movies together, and exchanging gifts—all without so much as a glance in my direction. Both Rose and Botlhale can be backstabbers, but at least I have Tsebo, and that's enough for me.

Speaking of which, I'm spending the entire weekend at Tsebo's place, while Rose has offered to keep Botlhale company. I'm not even going to ask what they'll be up to.

"Are you done packing? Rose will be here any minute," I say, trying to keep my tone light.

"Yebo yes! She just texted me on WhatsApp. I'm all packed," Botlhale replies. Oh great, so they're chatting on WhatsApp now? Wonderful.

"I can't wait! We're going to have so much fun!" Botlhale exclaims, her excitement palpable.

"Okay," I respond, shrugging my shoulders.

Botlhale catches my look and laughs at my jealousy. This girl! Just a few minutes later, Rose walks in.

"Hey girls! I'm here. Tlhali, are you ready?" Rose asks with a bright smile.

Botlhale and I exchange a knowing glance and burst out laughing.

"And then?" Rose prompts.

"The thing is, we're both 'Tlhali' when our names are shortened," I explain, still giggling.

"Ohhh, yeah! I'm only just realising that!" Rose says, clapping her hands.

"Yup, that's how it is!" I reply.

"Yoh, hebanna! Aii, Mini-Tlhali, let's go!" Rose announces.

"Let me grab my bag," Botlhale says before darting off to her room.

Just then, Tsebo walks in.

"My two favourite ladies in one room! Dumelang, le ntse yang?" he greets us, leaning in to kiss me.

"Re siame, abuti. How are you?" Rose replies cheerfully.

"My love," I say, returning his affection.

Moments later, Botlhale emerges from her room, bags in hand. I can't help but feel a twinge of sadness; I'm going to miss her so much. A whole weekend apart feels like an eternity!

"Botlhale! It's been a while," Tsebo says, a warm smile on his face.

"Abuti Tsebo! It really has been a while. I've been so busy, but I promise to make time for you," Botlhale replies with a cheeky grin.

Whose little sister is this? Tsebo and Rose burst into laughter at Botlhale's sassiness.

"Okay, we really have to get going now. Bye, guys! Have a great weekend!" Rose calls out.

"Bye, ausi waka! I'll miss you so much. Bye, abuti Tsebo," Botlhale says, wrapping her arms around me in a warm hug.

"Bye! Enjoy!" Tsebo and I say in unison.

With the two best friends gone, I'm left alone with Tsebo, who suddenly seems a bit serious, as if he's wrestling with something he wants to say.

"My love, a o siame?" I ask, joining him on the couch.

"Ke siame, rato lame. I've just been thinking hard about something..." he trails off, his expression earnest.

"What's that?" I prompt him gently.

"I'm worried about your safety," he finally admits.

"Okay, where is this coming from? What do you mean?" I ask, furrowing my brow.

"I'm talking about taxis, Tlhalefo. They limit you, and they aren't safe. I can't have my woman relying on them," he insists.

"Oh, that. I'm still working on it, my love. I'm sure I'll have a second-hand car in my name by early next year," I reassure him.

"What the hell, Tlhalefo? I gave you my card for a reason. I wanted you to buy yourself a brand-new, expensive car. To this day, I haven't seen a single notification of you using that money since we went to the mall together, and it frustrates me, maan," Tsebo says, his frustration evident.

"Tsebo, I want to buy a car with MY own money—the money I've worked hard for. I don't want to depend on anyone. Besides, I wouldn't want to deplete your finances," I respond, trying to stand my ground.

"What do you mean, 'deplete my finances'? Baby, I wouldn't mind spending my very last cent on you. Your happiness and safety come first to me. I thought about surprising you with a car, but then I remembered how stubborn and 'independent' you are. So, giving you my black card was the best solution. Mara, o slow Tlhalefo, waitsi," he argues.

"Tsebo, please try to understand…" I plead.

"Understand what, Tlhalefo?" he counters, crossing his arms.

Honestly, I do want to buy a car using my hard-earned money, but his words are starting to sway me. I just don't want it to feel this way. "And what if we break up? What happens then?" I ask cautiously.

He raises his eyebrows, clicking his tongue. "Who said we're going to break up?" he replies, his tone incredulous.

"Heee, bathong! I said 'IF,'" I clarify.

"There's no breaking up here. Lebala, ausi. Look, the first time I saw you at your previous job, I was visiting my friend, who happened to be your manager. You didn't even acknowledge my existence! You were wearing a navy-blue pencil skirt and a white shirt, your hair in long braids. From that moment, I knew I had found my wife, mme wa bana bame. I couldn't get you out of my mind. I did my homework on you, and here we are. I love you, MmeKhama, with all my heart. So, get that 'breaking up' nonsense out of your mind because that's not happening—ever," Tsebo declares.

"You've been stalking me all this time? You really have time and energy, Mogorosi. And I love you for that," I tease, placing a gentle kiss on his cheek. He blushes, and I can't help but smile.

"So, we're off to the dealership now, then home later, right?" Tsebo asks, his eyes lighting up.

"Yes, baby," I reply, still in disbelief.

What?! I can't believe I just agreed to this! An entire Tlhalefo Khama allowing a man to buy a car for her? What is this man doing to me?

"That's my baby! Now, which one do you want?" Tsebo asks enthusiastically.

"Well, I actually have four dream cars. I'm not sure which one to choose," I admit.

"Why choose? You can take all four of your dream cars!" he says with a grin.

"Uh-huh, Mogorosi. Don't push it," I reply playfully.

"Okay! Okay! We'll just take one then," he concedes, raising his arms in mock defeat.

"Good. And please stop with this 'wife' talk," I say, trying to maintain my composure.

"Haha! I've already told you what you need to know, MmeKhama. That is going to happen, one way or another," Tsebo declares confidently, causing my cheeks to flush.

"Whatever. Let's go," I say, laughter bubbling up inside me.

When we arrive at the dealership, we're greeted by a kind and professional Indian man who seems to know Tsebo very well. I can hardly contain my excitement—I'm about to get my very own wheels! No more taxis or cabs for me! Botlhale is going to be sooooo happy!

"Man T, it's been a while!" Greg exclaims, his face lighting up as he approaches.

"It has been a while, Greg. You've been good?" Tsebo replies, clasping his friend's hand warmly.

"I've been okay, just busy, you know how it goes. Argh! Where are my manners? Mrs. Mogorosi, how are you?" Greg adds, turning to me with a smile as he offers a handshake.

Whoa! Mrs. Mogorosi? Tsebo glances at me, suppressing a laugh with a shrug.

"I'm okay, Sir. How are you?" I manage to say, feeling a bit flustered.

"My love, this is Greg, a good friend of mine. He's also the owner of this car dealership. Greg, this is Tlhalefo, the love of my life," Tsebo introduces me proudly.

"You've found a beautiful one here! But not even an invitation to the wedding? You're a cruel one, Man T!" Greg teases.

"We've only done the traditional wedding, and it was just family. A small, intimate affair. But don't worry, my bro, the big one is on the way, and you know very well you're at the top of the guest list," Tsebo explains.

I'm doing my best not to laugh, and I can feel my cheeks heating up.

"Very well then. I'll be waiting for the invitation, big man. Ma'am, it's a pleasure to meet you," Greg says, nodding at me.

"Likewise, Sir," I reply, still feeling a bit shy.

"How can I help you today?" Greg asks, turning his attention back to Tsebo.

"We want to purchase a car," Tsebo states.

"I see. Do you have any idea of which one you want?" Greg inquires.

"I was thinking of a Range Rover, but I'm just not sure which model," I admit.

"I know just the perfect one for you. Please, follow me." Greg leads us through the showroom, stopping in front of a shiny red Range Rover Velar.

My heart skips a beat as I gaze at it, imagining myself behind the wheel. I'm in love with this beauty already!

"Perfect! Perfect, Greg. I love it! What do you think, my love?" I ask Tsebo, excitement bubbling inside me.

"I love it, baby. But I love you more," Tsebo replies, trying to lean in for a kiss, but I playfully dodge him.

"Oh, please, you two! Get a room. Or even better, get a car!" Greg jokes, and we burst into laughter, while Tsebo looks utterly confused.

"Sales jargon, baby. You wouldn't understand," I explain with a grin.

"Whatever. We'll take the Velar, Greg. Babe, are you happy with the colour?" Tsebo asks, looking at me.

"I'm happy with everything!" I say, my excitement palpable.

Greg goes on to explain all the features, showing us the interior and specifications. After a brief test drive, we're both thrilled.

We finish all the necessary paperwork, and Tsebo pays for the car in cash! I can't believe it—this is Tlhalefo Khama's very first car! I'm over the moon!

"Baby, thank you so much for this. I really appreciate it. I love you so much, Mogorosi!" I say, pulling him into a tight hug, fighting back tears of joy.

"Your happiness is my happiness. I love you more, my love," Tsebo responds.

"Nchooah," Greg interjects, and I can't help but laugh.

"Aii, fuck off, man Greg!" Tsebo says, shaking his head. Laughter fills the air once again.

"And I'm driving us home. In MY car, non-negotiable!" I declare.

"I knew it. I expected that from a bully like you. I'll have my car delivered at home. What choice do I have?" Tsebo retorts.

"None. You are a smart man, Mogorosi," I tease back.

"Mxm. Whatever, Mrs. Mogorosi," Tsebo replies with a playful eye roll.

"My bro, thanks for your services—top-notch as always!" Tsebo says, clapping Greg on the back.

"You know me. It's what I do, Man T," Greg replies with a smile.

"Bye Greg! We'll see you at the wedding!" I call out as we head out.

"Can't wait, ma'am!" Greg responds, waving.

"Sure thing, my bro!" Tsebo adds as we step outside.

The moment we get inside the car, we're both doubled over with laughter. I can't believe we had Greg convinced we're really married! And the respect he gave me? Hilarious! I could get used to this Mrs. Mogorosi life. Haha, just saying.

As I drive us to Tsebo's place, we share stories, laughter, and kisses. I'm in love—with Tsebo and my new car. Life feels so perfect.

After about two hours, we arrive, and I immediately start preparing supper. I know that once I sink into those comfortable couches, I won't want to get up again. Tsebo, however, disappears into some part of his mansion, and I don't care where he goes as long as I can keep my car keys in sight. I decide to make samp, beef stew, and creamy spinach for dinner, which we'll enjoy with cranberry juice. *Sigh.*

Just as I'm about to sit down and wait for the food to be ready, my phone buzzes with a new message.

I miss you. I love you. I want you to be mine. And you will be mine.

This is really starting to piss me off. Should I tell Tsebo? Ugh! I decide to ignore the craziness and switch to my favourite show, *The Real Housewives of Potomac*. Then, I video call Rose.

"Heyyyyyy!" Rose and Botlhale chime in together.

"Hi, girls! And what's that on your faces?" I ask, noticing their silly expressions.

"It's a face mask! We're having a movie night!" Botlhale exclaims.

"Oh, you guys are making me jealous," I say, feigning hurt.

"Oh, don't worry, lovie! We have all the time in the world. We'll have plenty more of these, all three of us!" Rose reassures me.

"Anyway, I have a surprise for you two. Botlhale, you are sooo going to love it!" I tease.

"Mmmh, sounds nice. What is it?" Botlhale asks eagerly.

"You'll both see it on Sunday," I reply, smirking.

"Ahhh, girl! O re bolaisa ka dipelo hle!" Rose exclaims.

"Patience, girls. Patience," I say playfully.

"We can't wait!" Botlhale chimes in.

"Let me get back to my pots. Enjoy! Love you two!" I say, smiling.

"Love you!" Rose and Botlhale respond in unison.

I head back to the kitchen to check on my pots, and just as I'm stirring the stew, Tsebo reappears out of nowhere. He hugs me from behind, and I revel in the warmth. Without his glasses, he looks even more handsome.

"You look so beautiful, Mme Mogorosi," Tsebo whispers.

"Don't start, I'm not Greg," I tease back.

"Haha! I'm just telling it like it is," he responds.

"Yeah, yeah. Where have you been?" I ask, curious.

"I was having a smoke by the pool," he replies nonchalantly.

"A smoke or smokes?" I question, arching an eyebrow.

"Okay, you got me. Smokes," he admits sheepishly.

"Mogorosi, I told you to limit it," I remind him.

"I only had two. See? I'm getting there," he counters.

"Mxm. I hope I won't have to repeat myself again. Dinner will be ready any minute now," I say, turning back to the stove.

"Okay," he replies.

He strolls over to the fridge, grabs a bottle of Castle lager, and plops down on the couch, changing the channel to watch rugby. The nerve!

"Mogorosi! I was still watching *The Housewives*! Why did you change?" I protest.

"I want to watch some rugby. I don't get that nonsense you love watching," he replies, not even glancing at me.

"Mxm, fine. I'll just sleep in the other room so I can watch my shows in peace," I huff.

He nearly chokes on his beer. Haha!

"Geez, woman! You're such a bully! You'll be responsible for my heart attack one of these days!" he says, placing a hand dramatically on his chest.

"Ke tla reng? I want to watch *The Housewives*, mos!" I say, sticking to my guns.

"I see. You're taking notes, preparing to be a Mogorosi housewife, huh?" Tsebo smirks, that naughty smile creeping across his face.

Before I can respond, he's up, sweeping me into his arms and kissing me passionately. I'm lost in the moment...

I manage to slip away, setting the table and dishing up dinner.

"My love, dinner is served," I announce, trying to keep the air light despite the heavy tension from my phone.

Tsebo looks excited as he sees the plates.

"I can't wait. You know I love your cooking!" he beams, and I can't help but blush at his compliment.

"Yeah, yeah. Just dig in, baby," I chuckle, and we start eating.

I'm not really one for praying. I've honestly lost all faith in God's existence since my father's death. Even Tsebo doesn't really pray, we just eat.

Tsebo: "Mmmh my love! I promise this is the best beef stew and samp I've ever had! I'm not even a fan of veggies but this spinach... damn!"

Me: "Haha. Told you I never disappoint when it comes to the kitchen."

Me: "Can you even cook, Tsebo?"

Tsebo: "I can cook the basics, nothing fancy."

Me: "Mm, a man who knows how to cook!"

Tsebo: "It's not like I had a choice. I had to cook for Rose and me while we were growing up. But that's a story for another day sweetheart." He suddenly looks a bit down and serious, but he's trying to hide it.

Me: "What do you mean 'you had no choice'?"

Tsebo: "Like I said, that's a story for another day. You look beautiful my love"

He's trying to change the subject. But I'll let it pass.

Me: "Thank you."

Now there's some awkward silence on the table, forced conversations and one-word answers given out. Honestly, I'm worried about Tsebo. I feel like there's more to him than meets the eye.

We are done eating. I stand up to clear the table. Tsebo just stands up and disappears to I don't know where again. I go to rest on the couch and go through my social media, nothing interesting, just the usual... celeb gossip.

It's already 9:00 p.m and I can feel myself becoming sleepy. Let me do the dishes before going to bed.

As I finish up by drying up the dishes, I can feel the warmth of his hands on my waist, the smell of cigarettes and his chest at the back of my head. He bends over and lowers his head so he can kiss me on the neck. I feel so warm.

"Thank you for dinner. It was great" He whispers, slightly breathing on my neck.

"Always a pleasure, my love" I say, trying to gather up the words. I'm becoming breathless.

Tsebo: "I love you. I want you. Now."

His hands caress my body. He goes on to touch my stomach... breasts. His warm breath is on my neck... the soothing kisses. I feel so hot right now. His whispers keep intoxicating me.

"I... I..." I have no strength.

"Sshhh. Don't say a word" He's now going down my lower body, lifting up my mini dress. He turns me around so that I can face him. I slowly reach out to his shoulders, and I kiss him on the lips.

He slowly unbuttons my dress.... It's on the floor. I'm left with only a bra and a lace panty. He slowly let's go of me and steps back to look at me lustfully.

He comes back to me, picks me up and places me on top of the counter... kissing my cleavage. I want him. I really do. I take off his golfer shirt and expose his dark, firm abs. He grabs me tighter, kisses me intensely and carries me to the bedroom. He throws me on top of the bed and gets on top of me, unhooks my bra and I have my big plumps exposed. He kisses my nipples slowly; I've never felt like this before... my nipples harden second by second... he goes on to kiss my stomach until he reaches my inner thighs. He takes off my lace panty and now I'm fully naked, he's lying in between my legs... still kissing my inner thighs slowly till he stops and looks at my womanhood.

"Damn!" He says and starts kissing me down there. I can't even describe what I'm feeling right now.

"Mmmhhhh. Yes baby" I moan.

He comes up to kiss my breasts and finally, my lips. I unbuckle his belt... he takes off his pants.

Tsebo: "I'll be gentle."

Slowly but surely, he's in... I've never experienced this feeling before... I'm lost in his world...

****

I woke up to a warm kiss on my forehead. "Good morning, beautiful. Slept well?" Tsebo's voice was soft, pulling me from my dreams.

"Morning, handsome. I slept well. Did you?" I smiled back.

"Come on, let's take a shower together," he said, his eyes glinting with mischief.

We stepped into the shower, the warm water cascading over us. Lost in each other's arms, we made love until I thought I might dissolve from happiness. I was head over heels in love.

After we dried off, I slipped into my black leggings, a red shirt, and sandals. I let my braids fall freely, opting for a touch of shiny gloss on my lips instead of makeup. Tsebo dressed in denim shorts, a black golf shirt, and black-and-white Puma sneakers, completing his look with a black watch, a cap, and his spectacles.

"Hebanna, you look smart. Going somewhere?" I asked.

"Yeah, I have a meeting. It'll only take a few hours," he replied, his tone casual.

"I thought we were going to spend the day together..." My heart sank a little.

"Baby, I'll be back before twelve. I promise," he assured me.

"Aii... okay," I sighed, a hint of disappointment creeping in. I didn't want him to leave. He pulled me closer, kissing me gently.

"Don't miss me too much," he said, flashing that charming smile before heading out.

After he left, I made myself breakfast—just a cheese sandwich, orange juice, and a fruit salad—before plopping down on the couch to watch whatever was on TV. Midway through my meal, my phone rang. I glanced at the screen, and my stomach dropped. It was the same number that had been sending me creepy texts.

"Hello?" I answered, my voice shaky.

"Hello? Who is this?" came my own voice, echoing back through the line.

Silence filled the air, and all I could hear was the steady breathing of the unknown caller.

"Who the hell are you, and what do you want from me?!" I shouted, frustration boiling over. But before I could catch my breath, the line went dead. Almost immediately, I received a text.

> *I just needed to hear your voice. I'm so happy.*

> *"Who are you, and what do you want"*

I typed back, my fingers trembling.

> *"I want you."*

> *Who are you!?*

But there was no response. Panic gripped me. I thought about calling Tsebo but hesitated. He would definitely blow this out of proportion. I was still unsettled when I finished eating and drifted off to sleep on the couch.

A loud knock jolted me awake.

"You! What are you doing here?" Linda sneered, her arms crossed defiantly.

"This is my man's house! You can't just ask me that rubbish. What the hell do you want?" I shot back, anger flaring.

"I came to check up on him. Now, where is he?" she demanded.

"Check up on him for what? Nretse fa wena mosetsana wa mo Zulu, if you are not out of here in the next minute, you'll regret it, wautlwa?!" I yelled, feeling my blood boil.

"No need to get all kasi-chick on me. I'll go... and don't tell him I was here," she replied, her tone dripping with arrogance.

"How the hell did you get in?" I asked, bewildered.

82

"The security guy knows me. Bye, Miss Perfect!" she tossed over her shoulder as she strutted away, her red leather dress hugging her curves and her black heels clicking sharply against the floor.

I rolled my eyes, exasperated. This girl really needed some fashion advice.

The rest of the day dragged on, my mood sour from Linda's visit and the anxiety about my stalker. When Tsebo finally returned, I was still brooding.

"Baby, told you I'd be back before twelve. It's three minutes to twelve," he announced with a grin.

"Really now?" I shot back, my irritation bubbling to the surface.

"And nou? What's wrong?" he asked, noticing my expression.

"Your girlfriend was here," I said, refusing to meet his gaze. My eyes were glued to the magazine I was holding.

"My girlfriend?" he echoed, confusion furrowing his brow.

"Linda," I clarified, finally looking up at him.

"Shit! I swear that woman will regret the day she ever laid her eyes on me. Did she do anything to you?" He was instantly serious.

"Nna? She would never!" I assured him.

"Thatha girl!" he huffed, unable to suppress a laugh.

"Okay, okay, I'll sort this out, okay, baby?" he said, his tone softening.

"If you say so," I replied, feeling slightly better.

We went out for lunch at a shisanyama, and I had to admit, I had the time of my life. We were laughing, eating, and I got to meet some of his business associates. Like me, he didn't have many friends. We even brought home takeaways for dinner since I didn't feel like cooking.

By the time we got back, it was 8:00p.m, and I craved a glass of red wine.

"Baby, I really need wine. Even if it's just one glass," I said, trying to sound casual.

"Tlhalefo, please don't start," he replied, already anticipating my protest.

"Argh, man Tsebo! Just one glass!" I shouted, unsure why I was raising my voice.

He stormed up the stairs, disappearing into the bedroom. I followed him.

"You really need to stop acting like my dad! You're making me out to be some kind of alcoholic. I only need one glass!" I yelled, frustration seeping into my words.

"You don't understand, do you? One fucking glass is all it takes! One damn glass!" he snapped back, his eyes blazing.

I fell silent, taken aback. He sank onto the bed, burying his face in his hands, defeated.

"See, Tlhalefo. My parents were alcoholics. Both. They weren't even married, but they stayed together, and we had to witness it all. I didn't have a rosy upbringing. Each and every night, there were fights. Rose and I had to witness our mother being battered almost every fucking night! They weren't even there for us. My mother would go to 'work' and come back drunk. My father spent all his days at the tavern, drinking and gambling. I had to take care of Rose. I took on my father's role. I had to take her to school, buy her things, cook for her, wash for her, and most importantly, I had to protect her. Our mother's family was full of drunkards, and our father's family didn't want us, so we had nowhere to run to.

I got tired of seeing my mother being battered by that monster. One night, while they were fighting, I instructed Rose to go to the bedroom and stay there. I tried to protect my mother, but he wouldn't let me. He kept beating both of us. I crawled to the kitchen, grabbed a knife, and stabbed him to death. I killed that monster who was my father, Tlhalefo. I was so sick of his abuse. Two years later, my mother died from cancer. It broke Rose. I

worked so damn hard to get us out of that shitty life. I can't go back there!"
His eyes were full of tears, revealing a vulnerability I had never seen before.

I moved beside him, wrapping my arms around him, letting him rest his
head on my chest. He sobbed into me, and I whispered, "It's okay... it's
okay."

"It doesn't end there. I need you to know who I am. I need you to know
what you're getting into. I'm a thug. A criminal. I'm a murderer. I'm a man
who killed his own father, Tlhalefo. I'm in the diamond-trading business;
I'm in the weapon-smuggling business. See, if I have to kill to get what I
want, then so be it. If I have to kill to protect what I love, then so be it.
That's Tsebo Likhayalimile Mogorosi," he confessed, his voice trembling.

"And I love you with all of that, my love. I'm yours; I'm not going
anywhere," I replied, my heart swelling.

This was deeper than I had thought. Seeing him like this made me love him
even more. I wasn't going anywhere.

"I love you so damn much, Tlhalefo Khama!" He looked deeply into my
eyes, and I kissed him, feeling the intensity between us. We undressed each
other and made passionate love. I loved him; I really did. Knowing who he
truly was only made me love him more.

* * * * * * *

Sunday morning arrived too soon, and I had to go back to my apartment.
A wave of sadness washed over me as I woke to breakfast in bed prepared
by the love of my life. We showered together and took a walk in the park,
returning to his apartment. He seemed much better than the day before.

I grabbed my bag and headed to my car.

"You really don't have to go, baby," Tsebo said, his expression sorrowful.

"I would love to stay, but I can't. I've got work tomorrow, and Botlhale is coming back today," I explained.

"Thanks for an amazing weekend. I love you, Mme Khama," he said softly.

"I had a great time too. I love you, Ntate Mogorosi," I replied, feeling the weight of my departure.

We made our way to my car, and he insisted on driving me. He said he'd request a cab on his way back.

Arriving at my apartment, we saw Rose and Botlhale pulling up at the same time. These two were crazy about my wheels; Botlhale couldn't stop touching and talking about it.

We all went inside to have a few drinks. An hour later, Rose decided to leave, and Botlhale drifted off to sleep on the sofa. I wondered what had worn her out so much. Tsebo requested a cab, which arrived quickly.

I walked him outside. "Goodbye, my love. Call me when you get home," I said, my heart heavy.

"Goodbye, rato lame. I'll do that. And thanks for an amazing weekend," Tsebo replied, pulling me in for a kiss before climbing into the cab.

CHAPTER SEVEN

It's Tuesday morning, and the shrill ring of my phone jolts me awake. I squint at the clock—04:00a.m. What on earth could Rose want at this hour?

"Rose... ka nako ye?" I mumble, still half-asleep, the remnants of last night's drink fogging my mind.

"He was shot," Rose sobs through the line, her words tumbling out in a torrent of emotion that I can barely grasp.

"Who? Who's been shot?" Panic surges through me, snapping me to full alertness.

Rose's cries fill the silence, and I can't decipher anything beyond her heartbreak. It's terrifying.

"Rose! Bua hle! What's going on? What are you talking about?" My voice is rising, urgency clawing at my throat.

"A... Abuti. Please come to Carstenhof Hospital," she manages to gasp before a wail escapes her lips. My heart races—what is happening?

I scramble out of bed, throwing on a pair of tracksuits and slippers, and bolt to Botlhale's room.

"Botlhale! Botlhale! I need to sort something out at work. Come and lock the door. Don't open for anyone," I urge.

"Hebanna! Ausi, what's going on?" Botlhale blinks, confusion etching her features.

"I really don't have time to explain. Just come and lock," I insist, urgency tinging my voice.

She follows me into my room as I snatch my phone and car keys. I speed towards Carstenhof Hospital, my mind a chaotic whirlwind of dread.

Arriving at the hospital, I dash inside, weaving through the sterile hallways until I spot Rose huddled on a bench near the wards, curled into a foetal position.

"Rose!" I call out, rushing toward her.

"Tlhali!" She leaps into my arms, and her sobs resonate through me, filling the air with despair.

"Please, talk to me. What happened?!" My heart pounds in my chest, panic rising anew.

"They shot Abuti. I don't know the full details. The doctors are still working on him. They won't let me see him. It's bad, Tlhali. Really bad."

Her words whirl around me, and I feel light-headed, cold fear gripping me.

"Wh… what do you mean it's bad?" I stammer, heart racing.

"Internal bleeding," she replies, tears streaming down her face. I wrap my arms around her tighter, unable to suppress my own tears any longer.

"Ssshhhhh…" I murmur, trying to soothe her, though I'm just as frightened.

"He will be fine. Don't worry," I whisper, attempting to convince both of us.

After a few moments, Rose succumbs to sleep on my chest. I sit up, carefully laying her head on my lap. Just then, a doctor steps out of the room and approaches us.

"Sawubona. I understand you are here for uLikhaya?" he asks.

"Yes. Yes. How is he? What's the problem?" My voice is strained; I can't stand while Rose rests on me.

"Dr. Radebe here. Calm down, ma'am. He was shot four times. Luckily, the bullets didn't hit any vital organs, but he has experienced severe internal bleeding and lost a lot of blood in a very short space of time. He's still unconscious, but we managed to stabilise him."

"Is he going to be fine? Is there anything I can do?" I plead, desperation clawing at me.

"Ma'am, you can help us by calming down. He's not that bad; he was lucky, even."

"Can we see him?"

"I'm afraid you can't, not now. You'll only be able to see him after a few hours. Please, go home and get some rest," the doctor says gently.

"We're not going anywhere," I retort sharply, frustration spilling over.

"Ma'am..."

"I said we are not going anywhere!" I snap back, my heart racing with emotion.

"Very well then. I'll let you know when you can go in," Dr. Radebe concedes.

"You do that," I reply curtly, feeling a swell of anger and helplessness.

With Rose still asleep, I can't close my eyes. My eyelids feel heavy and swollen from crying, and all I can think about is Tsebo—his warmth, his laughter.

* * * * * * *

"Tlhalefo! Tlhalefo! They said we can go in and see him. Tlaya!" Rose exclaims, startling me awake.

I must have dozed off. Rose looks more alert, though her eyes are still puffy from tears. I follow her and Dr. Radebe to the room.

"He's fine. Don't be scared. Tlaya," I reassure her, though I'm trembling inside.

As we step inside, a wave of dread washes over me. Tsebo lies there, surrounded by a mass of machines, and my heart aches at the sight. It's too familiar; I can't shake the memory of my father in a similar state.

"His head is safe, right?" I ask, my voice barely a whisper.

"His head is alright. I did say he was a lucky one," Dr. Radebe replies.

"Thank God," Rose breathes, relief mingling with grief.

"My love. It's me. Please wake up. Tsebo, you are a fighter. You know this. Please, my love," I whisper, tears streaming down my cheeks.

"Abuti wame. I still need you. Tsoga hle, Tau entle," Rose pleads, her own tears falling freely.

"He can hear you," Dr. Radebe assures us.

I reach out to touch Tsebo's hand, pressing a kiss to his forehead, while Rose kisses his cheek. After a moment, Dr. Radebe tells us he needs to rest, so we step back outside.

I leave Rose on the bench, promising to fetch us something to eat. When I return with muffins and coffee, I check my phone. It's nearly 11:00 a.m, and I know Botlhale must be worried sick.

"Ausi. A o siame? Where are you?" Botlhale asks as soon as I pick up.

"Ke siame nnake. I'm just sorting something out here at work. What time is your exam?" I lie, trying to shield her from the chaos.

"12:30. What time will you be here?"

"I don't know. Good luck, ngwana ko gae. Write well," I say, forcing a lightness I don't feel.

"Thanks. Bye," she replies, relief washing over her voice.

"Bye," I echo, though my heart feels heavy.

I send a quick text to Themba, telling him I'm sick and won't be coming to work. Rose is busy on her phone, calling in sick as well. We settle into a routine of waiting at the hospital, resigned to the unfolding tragedy of the day.

The hours stretch on, and by 7:00p.m, Dr. Radebe approaches us with concern etched on her face.

"Ladies, sitting here won't change anything. You need to get some rest. We'll call you if there are any changes," she urges.

I glance at Rose, who nods in agreement. Dr. Radebe is right.

"Please do call us if there's any change," Rose insists.

"Ndizaw'enza njalo, sisi," Dr. Radebe replies with a reassuring smile.

Rose takes her car, and I drive back home, where I find Botlhale studying on the couch.

"How many papers are you left with?" I ask, though I don't have the energy to care.

91

"Three," she mutters, not even looking up.

I head to my bedroom and collapse onto the bed, silent tears spilling from my eyes. I feel empty, helpless, as if I've lost a part of myself.

****

Two full weeks have passed since Tsebo was hospitalised, and he remains in a coma. I finally told Botlhale after her last exam—her suspicion was growing, and she took the news hard. I invited Rose to stay with us; she didn't protest. We thought it would be easier to navigate this darkness together. Our lives feel frozen. Rose hasn't been to work; Botlhale hides in her room most days, and I go to work only occasionally, labelled a 'zombie' by Themba.

It's the first week of December, and we had so many plans for the festive season. Now, they feel like distant dreams. Every day, during visiting hours, we ensure we're at the hospital.

"Good day. How is he today?" I ask, heart heavy with dread.

"Good day, ladies. He still hasn't woken up. We managed to remove all the bullets, and his body seems to be responding well to the treatment," Dr. Radebe informs us.

"That's good. At least there's some improvement," Rose murmurs.

"Can we go in and see him?" Botlhale asks, her voice filled with hope.

"Yes. You can. You know the way. I'll be with you in a few," Dr. Radebe replies, leading us to the room.

Once inside, it's the same routine. We've grown accustomed to the grief; we don't even cry anymore. We sit beside Tsebo, talking about mundane things, staring into the abyss. Botlhale shares her exam stories, how excited she is to finish matric, while Rose reminisces about their childhood.

"Please wake up, Tsebo," I whisper, desperate for a response, anything.

As days pass into weeks, I can feel the light dimming in Rose's eyes. The endless waiting gnaws at us, an agonising cycle that makes the holidays seem insignificant.

"Hey, beautiful," I say softly, finally mustering the courage to break the silence.

"Hey, babe," she replies, voice wavering.

"Have you thought about going home for a bit?" I suggest, feeling the weight of her despair.

"I don't want to leave him. I can't," she replies, tears brimming in her eyes.

"I understand. But you need to take care of yourself too. You have a life, Rose. We all do," I encourage gently.

"I know, but I just can't," she admits, fear creeping into her voice.

I reach out, squeezing her hand. "You don't have to do this alone."

But she doesn't respond, lost in her thoughts as we sit in silence, the world outside spinning on while we remain trapped in our own limbo. The days blur into a montage of hospital visits, shared silences, and whispered hopes.

****

It's 11:00a.m and I've just woken up; I must have really slept late last night. After taking a shower, I go and join Rose and Botlhale in the sitting room.

Me: "Morning morning"

Rose: "Hey hey. So late?"

Me: "I slept in the early hours of the morning. I was working."

Rose: "Shame man"

Botlhale: "You still look tired"

Me: "Yhuuu! I know I'm ugly; don't sugarcoat it. You guys don't have to rub it in,"

Botlhale: "Trust me, we all look horrible right now!" We all burst out in laughter.

Me: "Why don't you two go out, have some fresh air, go to the spa and maybe spoil yourselves a bit?"

Rose: "I really wouldn't mind. Wena ga o tsamaye?"

Me: "Nope. I have a lot of work to do"

The two besties go out, I don't even ask where they chose to go. I'm left lazying around the house and frequently getting on my laptop to do some work. I've given up on watching TV because it has all those festive and Christmas advertisements all day long! I never liked them anyway.

I decide to take an afternoon nap and I'm woken up by a phone call. I check the time; it's 2:37p.m.

Me: "Hello"

Caller: "Hello. Is this Ms. Khama?"

Me: "Yes it is. To whom am I speaking?"

Caller: "My name is Layla. I'm calling from Casternhof Hospital, with regards to Tsebo Likhayalimile Mogorosi"

My heart skips a beat.

Me: "Is he okay? What's happening?"

Caller: "Ma'am please calm down. Please come to the hospital. He has woken up."

I cannot believe my ears! I'm not even thinking straight. "Oh My! Thank you so much! I'm on my way!"

I go straight to the hospital. I arrive in less than half an hour. I find Dr. Radebe coming out of Tsebo's ward.

Me: "Dr. I heard he woke up. Can I see him?"

Dr. Radebe: "We've also tried calling Rose Mogorosi's phone, but it was off. And yes. He is awake, finally. You may go in." She says all of this with a huge smile on her face. I go inside. He's even sitting up straight; he looks a little pale. He still has an oxygen mask on, but he looks so much better.

Me: "My love!"

He removes the oxygen mask and gives me a weak smile. I think he's still a little drowsy from all the medication.

Tsebo: "Rato la me. Missed me?"

"I'm so happy you are back my love. I've missed you so much" I say as I give him a hug.

Tsebo: "I've woken up... just as you were busy nagging me with that."

Me: "Huh? You were hearing us all this time?"

Tsebo: "How could I not? Akere you were busy disturbing my sleep every single day"

I can't help but laugh. My Tsebo is back!

Oh! I nearly forgot. Let me call Rose. Her phone goes straight to voicemail. I call Botlhale; she picks up. I was starting to get worried.

Me: "Botlhale. Are you with Rose?"

Botlhale: "Yes. We are on our way to the restaurant. Why?"

Me: "Tsebo has woken up. Tell Rose and come to the hospital"

Botlhale: "That's great news! I'll tell her! We'll be there in a few!"

I honestly can't believe my Tsebo is back! He keeps looking at me and laughing. I can't help but worry though.

Me: "Are you in pain my love? How do you feel?"

Tsebo: "Tlhalefo my love, I was shot, so pain is expected. But it's not that bad. I'll be well soon. Stop worrying."

Rose and Botlhale arrive with lots of fruits and food. Good thinking, girls!

Rose: "Abuti! O tsogile ka nnete!" She goes on to give him a hug.

Botlhale: "Abuti Tsebo! How are you feeling?" She also goes on to give him a tight hug.

Tsebo: "Hebathong! Calm down girls. Do you want to send me back to my deep sleep?!"

Rose: "I'm so happy you are getting better Abuti. We were so worried about you!"

Tsebo: "Don't worry. I'm back. I'm not going anywhere, not anytime soon. Ke Mogorosi nna!" The arrogance!

Botlhale: "We've brought you a whole lot of goodies!"

Tsebo: "Can't wait to chow on them!"

Dr. Radebe comes in, all smiles.

Dr. Radebe: "Forgive me for being a party pooper, but our patient here needs some rest. I think he's had enough for today"

Tsebo: "Tell them, Doctor. I was even scared to say."

I can see that he needs to sleep now; he can barely keep his eyes open.

Rose: "Bye Abuti. Keep well. We'll see you tomorrow"

Me: "My love. O tla sala sentle. I'll see you tomorrow"

As we are going out, he grabs my hand and pulls me closer to his bed. Rose and Botlhale are now outside, I can hear them laughing about God-knows-what. Dr. Radebe also goes out; she catched on that we need some privacy.

Tsebo: "You know that I still love you, right?"

Me: "I know. And I love you too"

Tsebo: "Thank you for taking care of Rose

Me: "We were taking good care of each other"

Tsebo: "Haha. Rose may be the same age as you but we both know you are the responsible and matured one here." What he's saying is true. Rose acts more like Botlhale's age; I think that's why the two are so close. I guess I've always been the uptight one.

Me: "Don't let her hear you say that!"

He laughs out loud. I've missed that laughter of his.

Tsebo: "Come here and give me a kiss! I've missed those sweet lips." I lean in to give him a kiss. It feels so great to have him back!

Me: "Goodbye, my love."

Tsebo: "I'll see you tomorrow. I love you"

I come out of his ward and go straight to Dr. Radebe's office. I knock softly.

Dr: "Come in"

I get in. She gives me a warm smile. There's something special about her. She's got that motherly welcoming. I know it's awkward, but her presence is one that can fill up a room with warmth. She's got smooth chocolate skin, tall, and full-bodied. She's got long dreadlocks, and I picked up that she's Xhosa.

Dr: "I was expecting you"

Me: "Oh really?"

Dr: "I knew you'd come straight here. You really love that man in there"

Me: "I do. I really do"

Dr: "You two remind me of my husband and me. But that's a story for another day."

Me: "When do you think he'll be out?"

Dr: "He's responding very well to the treatment. He's a fighter. Always has been."

She's now staring into blank space as she says this. Okay. She has lost me now.

Me: "Always has been?" I'm confused.

She snaps out of it.

Dr: "Uhm. Yes! He's been a fighter since we admitted him to this hospital. Anyway, I'm planning on discharging him two days from now, on Sunday. He's fit for home-care now."

Me: "That's great to know. Thank you so much Doctor. For everything"

Dr: "It's my job"

"Kudos. I'll see you tomorrow. Keep well." I say as I head to the door.

Dr: "Ms. Khama. Please take care of them. Goodbye."

I'm kinda lost right now. I just nod, go out and close the door. That was rather... awkward.

I go to the parking lot, only to find that Rose and Botlhale left me. They went in Rose's car. Mxm. Good thing I came with my own car.

* * * * * *

We arrived at Tsebo's place, eager to prepare for his return. After everything he'd been through, we wanted to ensure he felt comfortable. Rose and I hopped into the car and drove to the hospital to fetch him.

As we pulled up, Rose squeezed my hand. "Tlhali, you're going to stay with him until he gets better, right?"

"Of course. That was my plan all along. Don't worry," I reassured her.

"Whew. Great," she sighed in relief.

Inside the hospital room, we found Tsebo already dressed, looking like we'd interrupted a serious conversation. Both he and the doctor paused, staring at us.

"Are we interrupting something?" I asked, eyeing them curiously.

"No, I was just advising him to take it easy and not be too hard on himself," the doctor replied.

"Ready to go, Abuti?" Botlhale asked with a bright smile.

"Ohh, I can't wait to get out of this place," Tsebo responded, his face lighting up.

Dr. Radebe handed me a list of prescribed medications along with instructions on how to care for him. "Bye, Doc," Rose said, waving.

"Saleka'khle, Noluntu. Sizawubonana," Tsebo said to the doctor with a nod.

That was the first time I've ever heard him speak IsiXhosa'

"Hambe ka'khle nyana. Uphole," Dr. Radebe replied, a hint of warmth in her voice. The air felt charged, and I couldn't shake the sense that something was off between the doctor and Tsebo.

As we exited the hospital, I couldn't contain my curiosity. "You guys know each other?" I asked, glancing at him.

"Yeah," Tsebo shrugged nonchalantly, brushing off the question.

We drove to Tsebo's place in Rose's car, with Rose at the wheel, Botlhale riding shotgun, and me in the back, holding Tsebo's hand. I asked Rose to stop by the pharmacy so I could pick up the pills Dr. Radebe had recommended. I also needed to buy some contraceptives; getting pregnant right now was simply not an option. Botlhale suggested we swing by the shops for vegetables because we were cooking up a storm tonight.

"A person should get shot more often. The special treatment I'm getting here is way out of this world," Tsebo joked.

We exchanged glances, and I felt a flash of irritation at his insensitivity. "Not funny. Not funny at all," Botlhale retorted.

"Geez, I'm just joking, ladies. Relax," Tsebo chuckled, but the light mood didn't settle well with me.

While Botlhale scrolled through her phone, Rose shook her head, choosing silence. I pulled my hand away from Tsebo's. "Hau?" he exclaimed, clearly puzzled.

"Mxm," I replied curtly.

"Yoh," he said, sensing the shift in my mood.

"Finally. Re fitlhile," Rose announced as we arrived home.

"I've missed my place so much! Whoo!" Tsebo exclaimed as we unloaded the car.

Inside, we carried in all the grocery bags, relieved we had prepared the place for him the previous day. The last thing I wanted was for him to come home after being shot and wake up in an uncomfortable environment.

"I'll be in my bedroom. I want to take a nap," Tsebo announced, and I couldn't help but notice how easily he slipped into that role.

"Seems like you're enjoying this sleeping thing lately," Botlhale teased, and we all laughed. Tsebo pulled me close, wrapping his arms around my waist as we headed toward the bedroom.

"My love, how are you feeling?" I asked gently as we entered.

"Just fine, baby. You know your man!" he said with a grin, kissing me softly.

"Tsebo, stop acting strong. Are you in pain?" I pressed, concern etching my features.

He let go, opened the blinds, and sat on the bed, motioning for me to join him. "To be honest with you, I am. I'm in so much pain, baby. My stomach and right arm hurt so bad; it must be from the operation. This hot bandage isn't helping, either. I have a constant migraine, feel dizzy when I stand too long, and I want to sleep most of the time. There, you have it," he admitted, his eyes drifting to the bandage wrapped around his stomach, anger simmering beneath his pain.

"But you've been taking painkillers, and you're lucky because you're left-handed," I pointed out, trying to remain hopeful.

"Pills don't work for me. They never have," he sighed, looking defeated.

"Don't worry. I'll take care of you, and you'll be back to a hundred in no time!" I promised, hoping to lift his spirits.

But he looked so sleepy; it was as if I were speaking to a statue. I stood up to take off his shoes, and as I turned to leave, he said drowsily, "Tlaya o tlo robala le nne."

"A ke batle," I replied firmly.

"Nx!" he shot back, then succumbed to sleep.

I joined Rose and Botlhale downstairs, curious about their activities. Rose was busy preparing dessert and salads while Botlhale cooked rice and chicken stew.

"What can I help with?" I asked.

"Nnyaa hle, ausi. You've done so much already... and you need to relax," Botlhale replied.

"She's right. We've got everything under control. Just save the dishwashing for later," Rose added.

"Haha, ke tsebile. Thank you, ladies," I said, feeling a mix of gratitude and guilt. I should have taken Tsebo up on his offer to rest with him. Instead, I decided to take a bath, hoping it would help me unwind. My body was sore, my back ached, and I could see bags forming under my eyes.

* * * * * * *

Dinner was a delightful affair. The ladies had gone all out, and the food tasted fantastic. I noticed Tsebo enjoying every bite.

"Tlhali, it's getting late. We have to get going," Rose said, glancing at the clock.

"Yeah, let me grab my bag," Botlhale added.

"Abuti, o tla sala sentle. Please make sure to get enough rest," Rose instructed.

"Get well soon, Abuti Tsebo. I'm so glad you're back home. Ausi, o tla sala sentle. I love you!" Botlhale added warmly.

"Thanks, ladies. I'll take it easy," Tsebo replied, a soft smile playing on his lips.

"Nchoah, I love you too, ngwanako gae. Le tla tsamaya sentle," I chimed in.

"Bye, guys! See you!" Rose called as they left.

"Bye. Drive safe," Tsebo and I said in unison, our voices mingling in the air. I could hear them laughing as they walked away, and it struck me that those two always seemed to gossip about Tsebo and me. I wondered what they were saying.

"Are they heading to your place or Rose's?" Tsebo asked, leaning back on the couch.

"I'm not sure. I didn't ask, but I think they're going to my place," I replied.

"Those two should just move in together. Plus, you'll be moving in here with me soon anyway," he remarked casually.

"Hehe! Who said I'll be moving in with you?" I teased, raising an eyebrow.

"I did. It's going to happen, sooner or later. Trust me, Mme Khama," he said confidently, his attention focused on the television.

I fell silent, clearing the table before heading to the sink. As I was about to start washing the dishes, I heard him call out, "Tlogela dijana tseo and come here."

"I'm busy," I shot back, keeping my gaze averted. I felt him approach, and before I knew it, he had wrapped his arms around me from behind, kissing my neck slowly and passionately. It took me back to our first time together; it was intoxicating.

"Tsebo..." I breathed.

"I've missed you so much," he murmured, his hands exploring my body. I could feel his warmth against me, and my heart raced.

"I don't want to hurt you. You said you're in pain," I cautioned, my voice barely above a whisper.

"It's nothing I can't handle," he insisted, determination flickering in his eyes.

Before I could respond, he lifted me effortlessly, carrying me to the bedroom. He tossed me onto the bed and, in a flurry of movement, tore off my dress, unhooked my bra, and pulled off my panties. Then he stood before me, eyes wide with desire, as I lay exposed before him.

"Damn! I must be the luckiest man alive!" he exclaimed before diving back in, his tongue exploring my body. My breath caught, leaving me lost in waves of pleasure.

"I'm... I'm all yours, baby," I managed to say, my heart racing.

As he slowly entered me, the world faded away, leaving only ecstasy in its wake.

* * * * * *

The night passed in a haze of sleep and restless dreams, and I was jolted awake by Tsebo's unsettling movements. He tossed and turned, letting out heavy sighs. I glanced at the clock; it was 3:00 a.m.

"Baby, are you okay?" I whispered, my voice thick with concern.

"Ke siame. Go back to sleep, Tlhalefo," he said, releasing another heavy sigh.

"You don't look okay to me, Tsebo," I replied, my concern evident in my voice.

"Tlhalefo, ke itse ke siame. Robala!" he insisted, his breathing growing heavier. Despite his reassurances, I couldn't shake the worry settling in my chest as I reluctantly drifted back to sleep.

Suddenly, I was jolted awake by his voice. "Shit!"

I shot up, alarmed. I couldn't let this continue any longer. "Tsebo! What the hell is wrong? You are scaring me!"

"G... Get me some water!" he gasped, beads of sweat forming on his brow.

I dashed to the kitchen, grabbed a glass, and rushed back to him. "Better? Should I call an ambulance?"

"Much better. Thank you," he said, gulping down the water.

"Are you okay, Tsebo?" I pressed on, still worried.

"I have this shooting pain in my stomach and my arm. It must be from the operation," he explained, his voice strained but steady. "But I'll be fine. Don't worry. Sleep."

"What happened?" I asked, the curiosity gnawing at me.

"Kae?" he shot back, irritation creeping into his tone.

"What happened when you got shot? Who shot you?" I pressed further.

"Zikhali and his dogs. We've been rivals since forever began," he replied, dismissing the question with a wave of his hand.

"Why? Tell me everything," I urged, determined to understand.

"He's in the mining business. I told you I'm in the diamond-smuggling hustle. That's why he's always been after me, claiming I've been stealing and trading his resources," he elaborated, a hint of amusement creeping into his voice.

"Well, have you?" I asked, raising an eyebrow.

"Yes. And I'm not about to stop. Not anytime soon," he chuckled lightly, his bravado seemingly unfazed by the gravity of our conversation.

"So... I arranged for us to meet to talk about all this nonsense. I wanted to put an end to this rubbish. I told him I wanted peace," Tsebo continued, his expression shifting slightly.

"Did you really want peace? Were you really going to talk?" I questioned, skeptical.

"No. I went there to kill. Na ke ile go kgalemela lenyatso," he confessed candidly.

"Well, they messed you up pretty good. Look at you. Ba go sunne!" I exclaimed, shaking my head in disbelief.

"Hahaha. You should see all of them," he replied, a dark satisfaction in his tone.

"Are they also in the hospital?" I inquired, my heart racing at the implications.

"Their families have already buried them. All of them," he said, matter-of-factly.

"Tsebo!" I gasped, horrified.

"Keng? It was either me or them. Except they managed to take out two of my men," he shrugged, his casual demeanour unnerving.

"Aii no, this is too much for me," I murmured, grappling with the reality of his world.

"You said you wanted to know everything mos. I told you everything," he stated, as if it were a simple fact.

"And who exactly is Dr. Radebe? You looked like you know each other very well," I probed, sensing a shift in his mood.

Suddenly, he seemed frustrated and downcast. "Mam'ncane Noluntu Radebe. She's my mother's younger sister. She ran away from home because of all the alcoholism that was taking place. She went on to be a doctor. She wasn't even there on the day of my mother's funeral."

"But… her surname is Radebe…" I trailed off, connecting the dots.

"Duh, Tlhalefo! She's married. She's in a polygamous marriage," he replied, rolling his eyes.

"Ohhh… do you have a good relationship with her? Does Rose know her?" I asked, curiosity piqued.

"She's the only person I talk to from my mother's family. I have a good relationship with her. Rose doesn't know her, but MaRadebe knows her, obviously. It's best that way," he explained, a note of finality in his tone.

"This is too much. I find out something new about you every single day," I confessed, feeling overwhelmed.

"Akere o rata dikgang. I've told you everything," he said, a hint of pride in his voice.

"How are you feeling now?" I asked, wanting to shift the focus back to him.

"Much better. Akere I have you," he replied softly, his eyes warming.

"Haha, whatever Mr. Mogorosi. Let me change your bandage dressing," I said, ready to tend to him.

"Please do. I'd love to have you touching me now," he grinned, a cheeky smile spreading across his face.

"Tsebo!" I exclaimed, playfully punching his uninjured arm.

"Ouch! You are a cruel lady, Mme Khama!" he laughed, wincing slightly.

"I know," I replied with a smirk as I walked to the wardrobe to fetch the first aid kit.

"That's why I love you!" he shouted after me.

"Love you too!" I called back, grinning as I prepared to change his dressing.

As I tended to his wounds, I couldn't help but notice how he was still trying his luck with me.

"I'm hungry," Tsebo said, interrupting my thoughts.

I shot him an irritated look, to which he merely raised an eyebrow in challenge.

"I'll prepare something for you," I said, my tone languid.

"That's my lady!" he cheered, a gleam of mischief in his eyes.

In that moment, I reflected on what he had just revealed: his plans for murder, his ruthless past, and how he'd killed a group of men without remorse. Yet, instead of fear or anger, all I felt was relief that he was safe, alive. I knew it was selfish of me, but this was who I had become.

I honestly couldn't imagine my life without Tsebo. I'd never loved like this before. I'd never been loved like this before. Is this what love's supposed to be like?

CHAPTER EIGHT

It was finally Christmas Day, the 25th of December. Botlhale had been longing for this day all year long; she loved Christmas, or rather, she adored the festive season in general. I had never really understood the fuss about December or the festive fever, whatever they called it.

Tsebo had been getting a lot better, and I was still staying at his place. Rose suggested that we all spend Christmas at Tsebo's, and it was a great idea. I didn't feel like going anywhere, and quite frankly, I didn't even like my own place that much anymore. Tsebo had made it crystal clear that I wasn't going anywhere, even suggesting I sell my apartment since Botlhale had moved to Rose's, and they barely spent time at my place. Most of my things were at his place anyway. Selling my apartment was not something I planned to do anytime soon, so he could just drop that silly idea of his.

In the kitchen, Rose, Botlhale, and I busied ourselves preparing Christmas lunch. Instead of being helpful, Tsebo wandered off, disappearing into who-knows-where in the mansion. Just as I thought he might have gotten lost; he appeared out of nowhere.

"My lovely ladies! Please prepare a lot of food; I invited some people over." Tsebo declared with a grin.

"People? Who are they?" I asked, raising an eyebrow.

"Noluntu and her husband," he replied.

I frowned. Why would he do that? I thought he said things were better when they were distant from each other. He never ceased to surprise me. Aii!

"Who is Noluntu?" Rose inquired.

"Dr. Radebe," Tsebo said.

"Hau, why?" Botlhale exclaimed, her confusion palpable.

Tsebo looked at us with his wandering eyes, clearly at a loss for words. I decided to save him. "Uhm... he just wants to thank her for taking care of him while he was in the hospital," I lied, my gaze fixed on the potato salad I was busy with.

"Mmmh, okay. How thoughtful of you, Abuti," Rose replied, nodding approvingly.

"Haha! It's the least I could do," Tsebo chuckled.

"What time will they be here?" Botlhale asked.

"In an hour's time," he answered.

"Perfect! We are almost done here," Rose chimed in.

"Cool." Tsebo's eyes flickered with worry, but he was trying to hide it, as usual. He winked at me, and I rolled my eyes, trying to suppress a smile. He laughed out loud and gave me a playful spank.

"Tsebo!" I shouted, smacking his hand away.

"Ehh. Yoh," Botlhale exclaimed, clearly amused.

"Keng? I'm not allowed to touch my woman now?" Tsebo defended himself, feigning innocence.

Rose couldn't help but laugh, and I was honestly trying hard not to join her.

"Tsebo, just go back to wherever you disappeared to! You're disturbing us, eish!" I said, waving him away.

"Okay, okay, kea tsamaya. But tonight, ke nna le wena," he replied, giving me another playful spank.

"Hebanna!" Botlhale gasped.

I swore, if laughter could kill, Rose would have been dead by now! Tears streamed down her cheeks as she doubled over with laughter. Tsebo raised his arms in mock surrender, then walked away with that annoyingly naughty smile on his face. What was wrong with this man today?!

Once he was gone, Botlhale and I exchanged glances with Rose, who was still giggling, and we burst into laughter ourselves.

"Ausi, see that 'VERY GOOD FRIEND' of yours?" Botlhale said, struggling to get the words out.

"I didn't know my brother was capable of that!" Rose replied, wiping tears from her eyes.

"Believe it or not, that is what I have to deal with every single day of my life!" I admitted, shaking my head.

"Whoo aii!" Rose gasped.

We continued preparing lunch and desserts. Within an hour, we were already setting the table when Tsebo appeared once more, this time holding a stress ball.

"You ladies are done? Perfect timing! Our guests are here," he announced.

I felt a wave of anxiety wash over me. I didn't know why, but I had a bad feeling about this lunch we were about to have with Dr. Radebe and her husband. But then again, I might just be overthinking everything, as always. We could see them walking towards the main house through the glass doors.

"San'bonani ekhaya! Merry Christmas, everyone!" Dr. Radebe greeted, her tone betraying a hint of anxiety. It was as if she, too, was unsure how all of this would unfold.

"Noluntu. Tat' Radebe. Welcome," Tsebo said, shaking hands with both of them.

"Merry Christmas to you too, Doctor. It's nice to see you again," Botlhale added warmly.

Mr. Radebe kept stealing glances at me. At first, he looked shocked to see me, then he glanced at Botlhale, his eyes flickering with confusion. I couldn't fathom why he was acting this way; he appeared to be a respectable Xhosa man—tall, caramel-skinned, and handsome for his age.

"Siyabulela. Ndodana, it's been a while," Mr. Radebe finally spoke.

"It has," Tsebo replied, sounding rather uninterested.

"Uhm... good people, lunch is ready. Let's make our way to the table," I said, eager to change the subject.

"Very well then. Let us," Rose agreed.

We all settled down at the table. Tsebo and Mr. Radebe sat opposite each other at the rear ends of the table. I was next to Rose, and Botlhale was next to Dr. Radebe.

"You ladies really put your best foot forward! Nilishayile ibhodwe, mantombazane!" Dr. Radebe exclaimed as she dug in.

"Well... we tried. But thanks," Tsebo replied, his mouth full.

We all shared a laugh, and Mr. Radebe chuckled, "Aii, ndoda, uyalishaya ibhodo!"

"Abuti, stop lying, hle," Rose teased.

Tsebo shrugged his shoulders and continued eating, but Mr. Radebe's awkward glances toward Botlhale and me lingered, and I could sense he wanted to get something off his chest.

"Ntokazi, my wife did mention that you really look like someone; she just couldn't make out who exactly. I can also see for myself. Ngiyakufanisa. Actually, the two of you," Mr. Radebe said, his eyes darting between us.

This was awkward. I didn't know how to respond, and Botlhale seemed oblivious to the whole conversation.

"Haha! My lady and her kid sis are beautiful like that. I'm sure you might have seen them in a modelling show or something like that," Tsebo chimed in, trying to ease the tension.

"Oh, I see! Beauty at its best," Mr. Radebe said, nodding appreciatively.

Tsebo was trying so hard to act relaxed, but I could see the tension radiating off him.

"I understand that you have a second wife, Mr. Radebe?" Rose interjected, shifting the focus.

"Oh yes, Neoentle Radebe. She couldn't make it; we apologise on her behalf," Mr. Radebe replied.

"No problem. We hope to see her soon," I added politely.

"Noluntu, Radebe, there's a reason I invited the two of you over for lunch today. There's something important we need to discuss," Tsebo stated, his tone growing serious.

"Likhaya, I don't think now is the time for that..." Dr. Radebe protested.

"MaRadebe, it is about time. The truth must come out," Mr. Radebe interrupted her.

"What are you talking about? What truth? I'm lost here," Rose said, visibly confused.

Tsebo let out a heavy sigh.

"Rose, Dr. Radebe's maternal name is Noluntu Buswayo, the youngest sister of Nomandla Buswayo, who happened to be our late mother," Tsebo explained.

"What are you trying to tell me?" Rose shot back, rising from her seat.

"Ntokazi, ndiku mam'ncane wakho. That is what your brother is trying to say," Dr. Radebe said gently.

"What the...?" Rose exclaimed, her face a mixture of confusion and anger. Botlhale looked beyond shocked.

"Rose, nna hatse," Tsebo said, trying to calm her down.

I knew this wouldn't go as planned, but it's deeper and worse than I thought. I think this is a family matter.

Me: "Botlhale, let's go to the bedroom."

Tsebo: "I said everybody sit down!"

Botlhale: "Abuti, this is a family matter." I can see she is scared.

Tsebo: "What are you? Aren't you family? Now, I'm going to say this for the very last time. Sit down!"

We both sit down. I dread to see how this one will end.

"Wait! Uthetha uk'thini uk'ba ungu mam'ncane wethu?! Where the hell have you been all this time? When we were on our own? When umawethu eshona? Ubuphi na?!" Rose's voice rose in fury. I had never seen her this angry before.

"Sisi weh. I too, like yourself, was trapped in a life full of alcohol and violence. I am the last born; I was the youngest. I had no power. All I wanted to do was escape from that life. Why the hell do you think I escaped from ezilalini and came to Jo'burg? I wanted a better life for myself!" Dr. Radebe replied, her voice matching Rose's intensity.

"Oh! Oh! So your sister's children didn't matter to you, huh? You could have at least checked on us!" Rose screamed; her eyes ablaze.

"Noluntu, please! Not here, not today," Mr. Radebe said, his voice stern, but his wife wasn't backing down.

Dr. Radebe: "I did what I could to survive. Look. I had to get away from that toxic place called home. I had to run away. I was tired. I was tired of the abuse. My father, your grandfather, used to rape me, over and over again. I had nowhere to run to. It didn't help that ubab'omkhulu wam,' my father's brother, used to do the same to me. I was the youngest. He used to tell me how fresh and tantalising I am. My father didn't even do anything about it, instead, sometimes they would even take turns raping me, in the presence of my own mother. She also didn't do anything to protect me; she'd only tell me that such is life. See, my mother was a good woman; she was a firm Christian woman… years later, she changed. She became a higher-grade drunkard. I guess she couldn't take the abuse she was experiencing from my drunkard father anymore, so she used alcohol and drugs as her escapism. Home was hell. Even our brothers turned into gambling, crime, and alcohol. They were twins, Solomzi and Ntsikayomzi. Solomzi was killed when he was trying to hijack a car and Ntsikayomzi was killed by our father. Up to this day, I don't know the reason. So, it was only Nomandla and I who were still alive. Your mother has always been a rebellious child; she used to date older men for money, sleep at taverns and just disappear for months. She too, was into alcohol, but not drugs. When she found uTat' Mogorosi, Likhaya's father, she told me that she had found her true love and was moving permanently to Rusternburg. Right there and then, I knew that I was alone. I wanted to run away, but for my mother's sake, I stayed. Five months down the line, my mother committed suicide. My father did not even have a care in the world; we had no money. I went to the back of our yard and dug a big hole; it took me four whole days. On the fifth day, I buried my mother in there, all alone.

No questions were asked about my mother's whereabouts. I was dead inside; I had no will to live. The rape by the two men continued. I couldn't take it anymore. I had just finished my matric. It was on the 5th of January when I ran away from home; I was only nineteen years old. I don't even know how I made it to Johannesburg, but I made it. I slept on the street for the first week, until one day, Tat' Radebe, my husband, came to me, and I told him my whole story. He moved me to one of his apartments and took me to school to study medicine. He did not even expect anything in return. I asked him to track down my sister for me, Nomandla Buswayo, only to find that she had passed away. Instead, he found Tsebo. I contacted him and the rest as they say, was history..."

She says all of this looking down, with tears in her eyes. Rose and Botlhale are also crying. It's only a matter of time before I realise that I also have tears running down my cheeks. Mr. Radebe is tightly holding his wife's hand and Tsebo is looking at all of this, not even a single trace of emotion on his face. I did say this was deeper than I thought.

Dr. Radebe: "I'm so so sorry sana lwam'. I should have known better than to run away. I'm sorry Rose. Ndixolele sana lwam'"

Rose: "No. I'm sorry 'ncane. I had no idea things were so rough. You had no choice. I'm sorry you had to go through all of that alone." She looks so apologetic.

Tsebo: "Bantu bam', let us leave the past in the past. We all know the whole story now. What matters is that we are all here now, together. There's no going back from here."

Dr. Radebe: "I'm here now. And I promise, I'm not going anywhere."

Rose: "Ohh 'ncane. I'm really sorry for my little tantrum. All of those things I said were uncalled for."

Dr. Radebe: "Stop apologising sana lwam'. Come here." The two share a long hug, all of this is quite emotional.

Dr. Radebe: "I love you so much"

Rose: "I love you too 'ncane."

I can see that Mr. Radebe and Tsebo are starting to get bored. Tsebo goes to the fridge and takes out two bottles of Castle Light. He comes to give Mr. Radebe one and opens the other with his teeth. I'm honestly being tested here!

Me: "And then? Beer?"

Tsebo: "Hau baby. It's Christmas."

Me: "So? We now drink beers ka di Christmas?"

Tsebo: "Just one. It won't do any harm."

Me: "Tsebo, you have not even fully recovered but you are already back to your tank tendencies. Please put that away now!" I'm already irritated now.

Dr. Radebe: "She's right. Put that bottle away."

Tsebo: "Hee bathong! Can I just have one bottle of my beer in peace?"

Me: "No! You can't have it, Tsebo!"

I swear I can see everybody trying to suppress their laughter. I don't even know what's funny here.

He puts the bottle on the table, goes upstairs to the bedroom, comes back to the table and kneels beside me on one knee. What the hell is happening here?!

Me: "Tsebo! Emoga."

Botlhale is already taking a video; I don't know what for.

Tsebo: "Well, if I can't have a bottle of beer, can I have you as my wife?"

117

Are my eyes and ears deceiving me? Did I hear well?

Tsebo: "Tlhalefo Khama. Will you make me the happiest man alive and be my wife?"

"Yes! Yes! I'll marry you!" Did I really just say that?!

He inserts the ring on my finger, picks me up, and kisses me. I honestly don't care who is in the room right now; I just kiss him back. I'm even crying; he can't stop laughing. Everyone stands up and congratulates us.

Mr. Radebe: "Ndodana! Usebenzile! Well done!"

Rose: "Tlhali! Congrats! Congrats! Wow!"

Botlhale: "Ausi! Come here and show the camera your ring!" She's still taking videos.

Dr. Radebe: "Ohh Likhaya! Tlhalefo! Congratulations! All the best!"

Tsebo: "A man's gotta do what a man's gotta do! I love you so much Mme Khama! Thank you my love!"

Me: "I love you too Mogorosi"

Tsebo: "What a Christmas it has been! Merry Christmas everyone!"

"Merry Christmas!" We all say as we exchange hugs.

I've never been this content in my life! This has to be the best Christmas I've ever had!

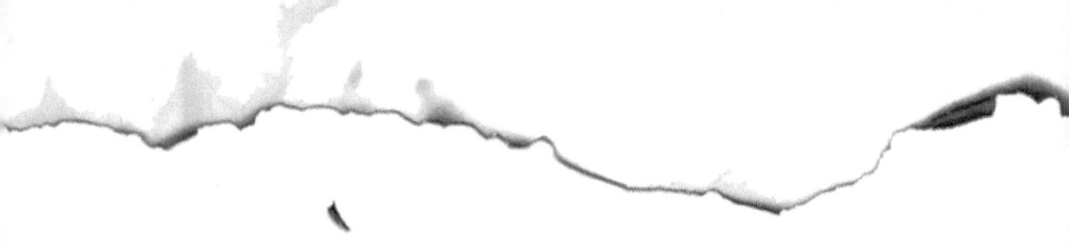

CHAPTER NINE

I awoke in a world so stark it felt unreal—a white bed in a purely white room, walls stretching into nothingness, empty of anything except that single bed. I was dressed entirely in black, the only dark thing in sight, a shadow in a sea of pale light. But that wasn't what made me tremble.

A scream echoed, faint and chilling. It was my father's voice, calling my name over and over. Desperate to respond, I opened my mouth, but no sound came out. I tried again and again, only to feel the suffocating silence pressing down on me. I searched, frantic, but saw nothing. Then a hand gripped my shoulder.

I turned to see him—my uncle. His clothes were as black as mine, but his hands were stained red with blood. He laughed, the sound rising, sickening, as his hands tightened around my throat. He kept laughing, harder and harder, while I struggled, screaming, but no one heard…

"Tlhalefo! Baby, wake up!" Tsebo's voice broke through the nightmare, and I snapped awake, gasping. My chest heaved and sweat drenched my skin as I clung to him, seeking to escape from the horror that lingered in my mind.

"What's wrong?" he asked, his face lined with worry.

"One of those dreams... They're getting worse, Tsebo. I don't know how much longer I can keep going." Tears pricked my eyes, my voice barely holding as I felt the weariness settle in my bones.

He pulled me closer. "You know what they mean, don't you? You know what you must do?"

"Yes, I know. But I'm scared, Tsebo. I'm so scared..." I couldn't keep back the tears any longer.

"Shhh, it's okay. You have nothing to be afraid of. I'm right here. We'll figure this out together, trust me." He held me tighter, the steadiness of his heartbeat against me grounding me back to reality.

After a few moments, he pulled away with a soft smile. "How about I make you breakfast?"

"Breakfast, huh?"

"Yes, wifey." His grin turned sly.

I rolled my eyes. "Wifey?"

"I told you—it's happening sooner or later. What did you say back then?" He gave me that cocky look of his.

"Just go make breakfast already."

With a chuckle, he sauntered off, leaving me to breathe through the remnants of my nightmare. I glanced at the glittering diamond on my finger, the ring that felt almost surreal. I checked the time—8:00 a.m. Time to call Themba about our lunch date.

I dialled him up. "Hey hey," I greeted.

"Heyyy stranger!" Themba's voice came through, warm and familiar.

"We're still on for lunch, right?" I asked.

"Of course. Ayijiki!"

"Perfect! I have some big news to share with you!" I couldn't wait to tell him.

"What's it? Don't tell me you're no longer pure?" Themba teased, laughing. If only he knew.

"Whatever, Themba. See you at 2:00 p.m at The Zone."

"Sharp, Mrs. Purity."

I laughed and hung up, feeling lighter. But a message notification snapped me back to reality. It was from a familiar, anonymous number. My stomach sank.

> *"I miss you. You haven't been in your apartment for a while. Where are you? I'm going crazy!"*

The message read.

I stared at my phone, hands trembling. This person knew where I lived. This was getting out of hand.

Just then, Tsebo entered with breakfast on a tray. "Delicious breakfast for a delicious lady!" He was beaming.

My hands shook as I handed him my phone, fear clouding my eyes. "Tsebo, this person knows where I live. This has gone too far."

His face darkened as he looked at the message. "Is this the same guy who sent the sunflowers?"

"Yes... he's been messaging me for months."

"And you didn't think to tell me?" His voice was calm, too calm; his eyes unreadable.

I stammered, "It's been quiet for a while… I thought it was over. I didn't want to worry you."

"Someone's been stalking you, Tlhalefo. That's not 'nothing.'" His voice was calm, but the edge was unmistakable.

"Tsebo…" I whispered.

"Who is this bastard?"

"I… I don't know." My voice faltered.

He clenched his jaw, the fire in his eyes searing through me. "Give me his number. Actually, give me the phone. And cancel your lunch with Themba."

"Why do I have to cancel lunch?" I protested.

"Damn it, Tlhalefo! He could be following you. This isn't a game." His words hit me hard.

"There's no need to insult me, Tsebo."

"What am I supposed to do, apologise? Cancel the lunch and give me the phone. I'll handle it."

I shot a message to Themba, then tossed the phone onto the bed, feeling the weight of everything pressing down on me. I needed a shower, to wash off the tension. When I returned, Tsebo was gone, and the breakfast he'd made was untouched.

I headed to the kitchen, preferring to make my own food. I chose pancakes and fruit, then settled in front of the TV, hoping for a moment of calm. As I ate, Tsebo came down the stairs, his face set in grim determination.

"I found the bastard's location," he said.

"Where were you? I thought you left," I muttered, picking at my food.

"Is that why you didn't touch my breakfast?" he asked, looking me over.

"I don't want your food."

"Fine. Suit yourself." He walked away, grabbing a jacket. I caught a glimpse of his gun tucked in at his side as he came down the stairs.

"Where are you going? Don't do anything stupid," I warned, a cold fear gripping me.

He paused, eyes blazing. "I'm going to handle this, like I would've done sooner if you'd told me."

"I'm coming with you," I insisted.

"No."

I stepped forward. "Tsebo, I need to know who this is. Please." I wasn't taking no for an answer.

He hesitated, visibly irritated. "Fine. Let's go. Five minutes." I changed quickly, then we drove off, silence filling the car as he tracked the message's location.

The minutes crawled by, but finally, we pulled into a quiet neighbourhood lined with trees and a worn white caravan house. Tsebo took my hand, sensing my unease.

"It's okay," he murmured.

He knocked sharply, but there was no answer. I knocked, softer this time. The door creaked open, and there he was.

Tsebo yanked him by the collar, his voice a dangerous growl. "You messed with the wrong woman."

I stared, disbelief coursing through me. "You? Brian?" He wouldn't even look at me.

"Wait. You know this man?" Tsebo's eyes shot to me, incredulous.

"He works for me. In IT..." My voice trailed off.

Tsebo's fury reignited. He turned on Brian, landing blow after blow, his rage spilling out as I stood there, my heart breaking at the betrayal.

Brian's words trembled as he forced them out. "I... I... I love you, Ms. Khama. And I don't regret anything. You're the love of my life... my reason for living... my heart." His voice was faint, punctuated by gasps, his face battered and swollen, with blood trickling from his mouth and nose. He clutched his stomach as if holding himself together.

"Bathong! Brian! I'm your boss, and I'm somebody's woman!" I protested, my voice trembling with a mixture of shock and frustration.

Behind me, I heard Tsebo chuckle, a strange and almost derisive sound. "Tlhalefo. Go to the car. I'll handle this," he said, his voice too calm, too composed.

"No. I'm not leaving you two alone!" I argued, panic flaring in my chest. I knew my fiancé's temper, his ruthlessness when he felt betrayed. But Tsebo's eyes flashed, the calm in them unnerving.

"Tlhalefo. I won't say it again." His voice dropped to a deadly whisper, and that steely tone sent me back to the car, my stomach twisting.

I sat in the car, a million questions spiralling through my mind. Why would Brian do this? Stalking me? Confessing his love? I was his boss, for heaven's sake! And yet... I'd always felt something unsettling about him, the strange way he looked at me. But this?

Moments later, the distant sound of sirens pulled me from my thoughts. Police and ambulance lights flickered in the rearview mirror, flashing ominously. My heart pounded. I threw open the car door, running back to where Brian lay motionless on the ground. His chest barely moved.

"Tsebo! What did you do?! Is he... is he dead?!" I gasped, unable to comprehend what lay before me.

Tsebo stared back at me, emotionless, his hands slick with blood. "The police are here," I murmured, my voice barely a whisper. Panic tightened my chest as the officers approached, weapons drawn.

"Sir, hands up. You're under arrest for assault and attempted murder," one officer ordered, gun aimed squarely at Tsebo.

As the officers moved closer, a neighbour, an older white man, smirked from his porch. "I called the cops. Knew something was up when I saw *them* get out of the car," he said, pride dripping from his words.

Tsebo glanced at him, almost amused. "You'll regret this," he muttered.

"Sir, enough," the policeman snapped, turning his attention back to Tsebo.

The paramedics leaned over Brian. "He's alive but barely. We need to get him to the hospital now."

"Damn it," Tsebo muttered, barely hiding his frustration.

"Will you just shut up?!" I snapped, anger boiling over.

A policeman's gaze shifted to me. "And who are you?"

Tsebo cut in, his voice chillingly calm. "She's my wife. Don't touch her." He held my hand tightly, his grip a warning.

The officer didn't waver. "Sir, you're under arrest for assault. Anything you say can be used against you in court." Tsebo barely resisted, but I saw the flicker of defiance as the officer snapped the cuffs onto his wrists.

"I can walk myself," he muttered, dismissing the cop's hold on him. After loading Brian into the ambulance, the officers escorted Tsebo to the police car.

"My love, take the car and go home. I'll see you later," Tsebo said. I bit back my anger and fear, turned on my heel, and left. The drive was silent, my thoughts storming within me.

At home, I paced the living room, my frustration mounting. Just days ago, we'd been happy, even celebrating our engagement. Now, this. A door creaked, and Rose entered, wearing a fitted yellow dress and heels, her eyes wide with excitement. .

"Hey girl!" she greeted, her voice bright.

"Hey," I mumbled, lost in thought.

She tilted her head, studying me. "Everything alright?"

Before I could answer, my phone rang, an unknown number lighting up the screen. "Hello?" I answered cautiously.

"My love, listen carefully," Tsebo's voice came through, low and hurried. "Go to my study, take my red laptop. The password is 97210RMgSI. Log in, access my banking app—you know my pins. Find the blue notepad in the drawer under the table. Prosecutor Grootboom's details are on page seven. Transfer R200,000 to him. Make it immediate."

I hesitated, fear gripping my heart. "Won't they trace it back?"

"They won't." he replied, then hung up.

"Rose, I've got work to do," I said briskly. I made my way to the study, following Tsebo's instructions meticulously, the weight of his request settling heavily on my shoulders.

Once done, I joined Rose in the game room. I could see that Rose suspected that something was wrong... I am that much of a bad liar. I honestly wanted to get rid of her because Tsebo could pop up any minute from now and I didn't want her seeing her brother like that, we were so not in the mood to explain what happened.

Me: "Rose, why is Botlhale so stressed? I mean, the results are only coming out on the 5th of next month."

Rose: "Since the beginning of the week. In case you haven't noticed, tomorrow is New Year's Eve, so practically, the 5th has arrived..."

Me: "Oh yeah! I forgot. I have an idea."

Rose: "Yeah?" At least she looks interested.

Me: "Remember when the two of you suggested that we go away as a family for Christmas and Tsebo and I turned you down? Well, I think that New Year's Eve and the first few days of the new year would be the perfect time for us to go somewhere as a family. So, why don't you go to Botlhale and make plans with her about tomorrow's trip so you can cheer her mood up a bit?" I hope she buys it.

Rose: "Great! Her mood will be so much elevated! We should have thought of that a long time ago!"

"Yeah. You guys have the freewill to choose anything, plus le batho ba style!" I say as I wink at her.

"You know what? Let me get going! There's no time to waste!" Rose says as she stands up.

Me: "Great! Please tell her I love her!"

Rose: "Will do. Cheers."

Rose goes out and I'm left alone in the lounge. I'm just wishing Tsebo can just appear out of nowhere and tell me everything is okay. As for Brian, I hope he is still breathing at whatever hospital he is in. The last thing I want is for my fiancé to be charged with murder while he was only trying to protect his loved one. Sitting here won't help me with anything; I need something to get my mind off things. I can't really hang out with Themba because today's lunch was the only opportunity I had to meet up with him before he flies to Paris with his other half tonight. I can't do any work because there isn't anything to do. I can't go to Rose and Botlhale because they'll obviously detect that something's wrong. Only one option left, Bake!

It always helps me take my mind off things and I also bake when I'm in a happy mood, bored or just when I feel like it. A banana cake and vanilla scones with a touch of orange essence will do!

I go to the bedroom to change back into my short yellow jumpsuit and slippers so I can be comfortable. I hate jeans with all my heart. I pace to the kitchen to start preparing for my masterchef baking and luckily, all the ingredients I need are here; I won't need to go to the shops for anything. I'll just start with the banana cake because it's the easiest. All the ingredients are already out and I start mixing all that needs to be mixed and in less than thirty minutes, the banana dough is already in the oven. I clean up and start with my scones mixture, exactly the way my father taught us. See that man, he was a man of many talents. He could cook and bake up a storm. He could sing and dance like nobody's business (I guess Botlhale inherited that from him). He always knew his way with our hair, and he was in construction. Although he was not educated at all, he treasured education the most and always wanted the best for us. I cannot even begin to put the love and care he gave us into words. He was a great man indeed.

"Something smells nice." Tsebo says as he's leaning against the door frame, leg crossed and hands in pockets. His shirt still has some blood on it; I don't even know what happened to the black jacket he was wearing.

"My love! Come here!" I say as I run to give him a hug.

"Woah... I thought I was going to be poured with boiling water when I came back. I thought you were angry rato la me." He says as he gives me the tightest hug ever.

Me: "I am angry at you. But we'll deal with that later."

Tsebo: "All I need right now is some cold beer, a few cigarettes and my woman's company."

Me: "Forget about all of that. I'm going to run you a bath right now and prepare some food for you after that, then you can have that disgusting stuff of yours."

"Oh Lord! Look who just called alcohol "disgusting." Hallelujah!" He says as he raises his arms in praise.

"Why did you even come back?" I say as I give him an annoyed look.

Before he can even answer, I wash my hands in the sink and make my way up the stairs to go run him that bath.

"I still love you!" He shouts. I guess we all know by now that I'm in a relationship with a mentally unstable idiot. So yeah, it's cool. I chose this life; I have to live it up.

"Love you too!" I shout back.

I run him that bubble bath and take out his brown cargo shorts and a black vest and put them on the bed. I meet him on the stairs as I'm going down.

Me: "Your bath is ready."

"Don't you want to join me?" He says with that annoying naughty smile on his face. I really am tempted to join him but nah.

"No. I'm still baking." I don't even want to look at him because I know I'll be in his game in a matter of seconds.

"Come on..." He says as he grabs me by my waist.

Before I can say anything, he has his lips on my lips and for a moment, I manage to pull away from his arms and make my way to the kitchen without saying anything and leave him standing there.

My banana cake is ready, and I take it out of the oven. Golden, just the way I like it! I divide the scone dough into balls and put them into three baking pans and in the oven, they go!

While I'm waiting for the scones to get ready, I make eggs, bacon, cheese, bread and avocado for that Tsebo and put them into the microwave.

I go and watch my favourite, *The Housewives of Potomac* while I wait for my scones to be ready, sipping on my champagne. Tsebo comes down the stairs looking all sorts of sexy.

Tsebo: "My love. How do I look?"

Me: "You are still ugly and that's never going to change, my love. Your food is in the microwave."

Tsebo: "Thank you for loving me with my ugliness, my love."

Me: "Who said I love you?"

"Come on. I can see the way you're looking at me right now. You've got love written all over your face. You want me so bad." Tsebo says as he comes to sit next to me with his plate.

Me: "Stop lying to yourself. I hate you." I can honestly feel my face becoming hot.

Tsebo: "My love, those chubby cheeks of yours are betraying you as we speak right now."

I'm a hundred percent sure my nose and cheeks are fire red right now. I hate this! I don't even have the strength to respond to this man's craziness, so I just keep my eyes glued to the TV. He bursts out in laughter.

Tsebo: "Damn! You should see yourself right now!" He's still laughing. I can't help but end up laughing too; I did say his laughter was one to make a dark day seem bright.

"Come here" He says as he pulls me by my neck. We kiss passionately and honestly; I could stay in his arms until forever comes. The stove alarm rings. Flip! I was having a moment here with my man!

I go and take out the three pans, refill them with the leftover dough and put them back into the stove then go back to join my man on the couch.

Me: "It's the 31st tomorrow. We are going away."

Tsebo: "Kae?"

Me: "I don't know. Rose and Botlhale said they are going to plan everything. I'm still waiting for their call with all the details."

Tsebo: "Oh ok. But why?"

Me: "Botlhale o tshwere ke stress sa di results. We hope this will help."

Tsebo: "Hee bathong! But she knows she passed mos. Drama keya eng?"

Me: "I know right? But don't let her hear you say that."

Tsebo: "When are we coming back? Is it too far?"

Me: "Hee bathong! Tsebo I said I don't know anything; I'm waiting for Rose to confirm!"

Tsebo: "Oh. Askies geh."

Me: "You can be really slow at times."

Tsebo: "I know."

Me: "You know, I'm still angry at you for what you did to Brian. You could have killed him!"

His mood suddenly changes.

Tsebo: "Tlhalefo, if you are expecting an apology from me, forget it. I'm not going to apologise for protecting what's mine."

Me: "Mogorosi, I'm just saying there's a better way we could have approached the situation."

Tsebo: "What better way? We should have sat down with the bastard and asked him if everything is okay at home? I don't have time for that nonsense."

Me: "Is he still in hospital?"

Tsebo: "Yes. And I still want to pay him a *visit*."

Me: "Me too. When is your trial beginning?"

Tsebo: "My trial? What did I do?"

Before I even find a chance to respond to this madness, I get a call from Botlhale.

Me: "Hey sis."

Botlhale: "Hey sis.

Me: "What's good?"

She bursts out in laughter from my question. At least she can still laugh.

Botlhale: "Yoh nnyaa ausi. Slang doesn't suit you. Anyway, I called you about the holiday outing. We are leaving for the Maldives tomorrow at 11:00 a.m. I booked three hotel rooms, one for Rose and me, one for Abuti Tsebo and you and one for Dr. Radebe. We are coming back on the 3rd."

Me: "Oh. She's coming?" I didn't expect this.

Botlhale: "Yeahp. Unfortunately, Mr. Radebe and the other Mrs. Radebe couldn't come because she is sick, and he is taking care of her."

Me: "Oh. That's a shame. Cool. I'll inform Tsebo."

Botlhale: "Coolies. Love you!"

Me: "Love you more! See you tomorrow!"

I hang up and tell Tsebo, who is not even paying attention to me, he even changed to the rugby channel.

Me: "Maldives tomorrow. 11:00 a.m"

"Ok." His eyes are still glued on the match.

"And… we are going to be sleeping in separate rooms." I say as I go to sit on the furthest couch from him.

Suddenly, his attention is back to me. Kudos Tlhali!

Tsebo: "Not possible at all. That's not going to happen. How will I survive a night without you?"

Me: "The arrangements are already done."

Tsebo: "Nxa aai maan Tlhalefo! I'll make the re-arrangements myself once!"

I'm really trying so hard not to laugh.

Me: "Eish. I'm kidding, Mogorosi. Now calm down"

"My love. Ke gore you are still on your mission to give me a heart attack neh? Don't play like that." Tsebo says as he places his hand on his chest.

The drama!

Me: "Haha. I'm sorry. Dr. Radebe is also coming."

Tsebo: "Really? I didn't think Rose would invite her."

Me: "Same here. But it is what it is."

******

It's the 31st, and as always on this day, I feel a heavy gloom. But I'm determined not to show it as I pack our things. Inside, I'm praying for the day to be over.

"So many clothes? Are they going to fit in all these bags?" Tsebo stands by the bedroom door, sipping coffee. "And do you have to pack all my clothes?"

"Mogorosi, we're going away for five days, and the weather there is unpredictable…"

"Then we'll shop over there. Each and every day if you want," he says with a shrug.

"Cool. I'll take only a few clothes, then," I reply, feeling the weight of the day more than ever.

Tsebo puts his coffee down, comes over, and wraps me in a tight hug. "I love you, okay? I love you."

Something about the way he says it feels different, like he's feeling sorry for me.

"I love you too. Let's go. We don't want to keep those two waiting."

We head downstairs to find Rose and Botlhale waiting impatiently, bags already packed in Tsebo's car. As we drive to the airport, I zone out, staring out the window. Rose's voice breaks my thoughts.

"A o siame?"

"Huh?" I turn back, trying to sound upbeat. "Yes, I'm okay, thanks. Can't wait."

Tsebo reaches over, squeezing my hand tightly. I glance at him, grateful, though the silence feels heavy.

"I can't wait. We're going to have so much fun!" Botlhale chirps, attempting to break the tension.

"I just can't wait to come back. I hate vacations," Tsebo grumbles.

"Abuti, you should have just stayed behind to avoid being a party pooper," Rose teases, and we all laugh, easing the mood.

At the airport, we meet up with Dr. Radebe, who's already waiting.

"Finally. You're here. Kade nda linda," she says, towering over for a hug.

"Blame these three. I had nothing to do with it," Tsebo says, throwing us under the bus, as usual.

"You know us girls. Sorry to keep you waiting, Doctor," Botlhale says with a smile.

"How's your sister-wife?" I ask.

"She keeps getting better, then it's back to square one. It's been over six years now. It's just…heartbreaking."

I can see the pain in her eyes. "I'm so sorry to hear that. I really hope she gets well."

"Ladies, time, please. Shall we?" Tsebo calls impatiently, and we head toward the gate.

* * * * * * *

The Maldives are breathtaking. The moment I step into our hotel room, I'm enchanted—it feels like paradise. I look around, soaking it all in, while Tsebo just lies on the bed, unimpressed.

"I honestly don't understand your fascination with this place. It's just basic."

I roll my eyes. "Just because you don't have style, don't assume the rest of us are like that."

"So, I must lie and say I'm fascinated?" he quips.

"Mogorosi, if you don't have anything nice to say, just keep quiet."

He grins. "Can't wait for the New Year. New year, new beginnings. Is that better?"

I don't respond, curling up beside him instead. He wraps his arm around me, pulling me close.

"I know you're not okay, my love."

"I'm okay. Can I sleep now?"

"I love you," he says, his voice soft.

I pull the duvet over my head, fighting back the emotions swelling inside me. Everything feels overwhelming, but I can't shed a tear. Exhausted, I clutch the duvet, letting sleep take over.

****

"Tlhali!" Rose's voice pulls me out of sleep. "Wake up, girl."

"Rose, you're disturbing my peace. What do you want?" I grumble, still half-asleep.

"We're on vacation, motho o robetse? Wake up and get ready."

"Get ready? For what?"

"We're about to have dinner. It's a formal occasion." She glances at me, amused.

"Hee bathong! Dinner?" I sit up, shocked. I must've slept longer than I realised.

"Yes, mo'ghel! And your outfit is ready, courtesy of your beloved fiancé. You'll find us by the pool."

She leaves, singing cheerfully. I shake myself awake, heading to the shower. After a refreshing wash, I step out to find a navy-blue mermaid dress on the bed, its glittering fabric catching the light. My heart skips a beat. There's also a matching pair of heels and a note on the bed:

"My love. Here's your outfit for tonight. I hope you find it appealing. After you're dressed, go to the next room; people are waiting for you. Then, meet me at the pool. I can't wait to see you. I love you. —Your Love, T."

I slip into the dress, amazed at the way it hugs my body, and make my way to the next room. Inside, two women greet me.

"Ma'am, I'm Priska, your makeup artist," a Korean lady says, smiling.

"I'm Charlize, your hairdresser," adds a white woman beside her.

I'm taken aback but grateful. "Uhm, thank you. Nice to meet you both."

They guide me to a plush chair, and Priska begins her work. "What kind of makeup do you want?"

"Uh... I'm not really a fan of makeup. Maybe something natural?"

She chuckles. "Too late—I'm going for a smoky look. It'll complement your dress. Trust me." She smiles, adding, "You're one lucky lady to have a man who cares like this."

Me: "Yeah?"

Priska: "You should have seen him when he gave us instructions. He didn't even want any mistakes."

Me: "Haha. He's like that. With everyone."

Me: "So, what about you? Any special somebody in your life?"

the luckiest man alive!" His voice was filled with awe, and he pulled me close by the waist, then let go just to take another long look. Such drama!

I laughed, brushing my hand across his suit jacket. "Well, you look ravishing yourself. And thank you for all of this."

We shared a kiss and settled at the table. Tsebo pulled out a chair for me, and as I took in the setting, I felt a wave of warmth. "The food looks amazing, and I love the romantic setup. But where's Botlhale, Rose, and Dr. Radebe?"

"They went clubbing, can you believe it?" Tsebo smirked. "And Dr. Radebe is at some fashion show across town."

My eyes widened. "Tsebo! Clubbing?"

He chuckled. "Relax, they're safe with security on hand. Tonight is about you, my love. Just you."

"About me? What's going on?"

Just then, a chef approached with a towering red velvet cake, placing it at the centre of the table before stepping back. My heart skipped a beat as I stared at the cake, feeling a mix of surprise and unease.

Tsebo leaned in with a gentle smile. "Happy birthday, my love."

I froze, the words catching me off guard. "H–how did you know?"

His gaze softened. "Tlhalefo, by now you should know there's nothing I don't know about you."

I felt a wave of emotion, my voice trembling as I looked down. "Tsebo... no. My birthday is my father's death day, and you know I don't celebrate it."

He took my hand in his, lifting my chin so I met his gaze. "I know, sweetheart; I know. But you can't keep carrying this burden. I'm not saying to forget—it's impossible to forget. But my love, don't let this day haunt you. I know he wouldn't want that for you. We all want you to find peace."

As he held me close, I felt the weight in my heart lift, like a heavy stone melting away. I looked up at him, teary-eyed but finally lighter. "Thank you," I whispered. "Thank you, Tsebo. And... I love you."

"Happy birthday, my love. I love you, with all my heart."

Suddenly, a familiar voice broke the moment. "Hey hey!" Botlhale was approaching, looking a little tipsy, and Rose was right behind her.

"Happy birthday, girl! You look like a million dollars," Rose grinned, leaning in to give me a hug.

Botlhale hesitated, her eyes a bit glassy. "Uhm... happy birthday, ausi."

I pulled her into a tight embrace, feeling tears well up in my own eyes. "Sshhh... it's okay, ngwana wa ko gae. He's here, with us. He has never left us. I love you so much, Botlhale."

She clung to me, nodding. "I know. He's always with us. I love you too, ausi wame. More than anything."

I glanced at Tsebo, who was visibly holding back his own emotions, quickly looking away when our eyes met. Rose, of course, was already tearing up, her face like a fountain.

I wiped my face, lifting the mood with a cheer. "Happy birthday to myself! Twenty-four unlocked!"

"Happy birthday!" they all echoed, breaking into wide smiles as we gathered into a group hug.

The countdown began as we saw people gathering by the pool, glancing out their windows and onto the balcony to join in the celebration.

"Five... four... three... two... one... *Happy New Year!*" the crowd cheered as firecrackers exploded into colourful lights above us. The night felt electric with excitement, laughter, and an overwhelming sense of joy.

Botlhale, true to form, was busy taking pictures and videos as Tsebo gathered us all into a hug. "I love you so much, my ladies. Happy New Year!"

Just then, Dr. Radebe arrived, just in time to join the group hug. "I hope I'm not late. Happy New Year, family!"

"Happy New Year, Doctor!" we all chimed in, grinning as Rose lifted her glass. "New year, new beginnings!"

"And lots of love!" I added, catching Tsebo's eye as he winked.

We burst out laughing, and the night unfolded in a blur of happy faces, warm embraces, and even a few dances with strangers who'd become friends in just a few hours. Who would have thought Dr. Radebe, of all people, would become the life of the party?

Life truly has a way of surprising you.

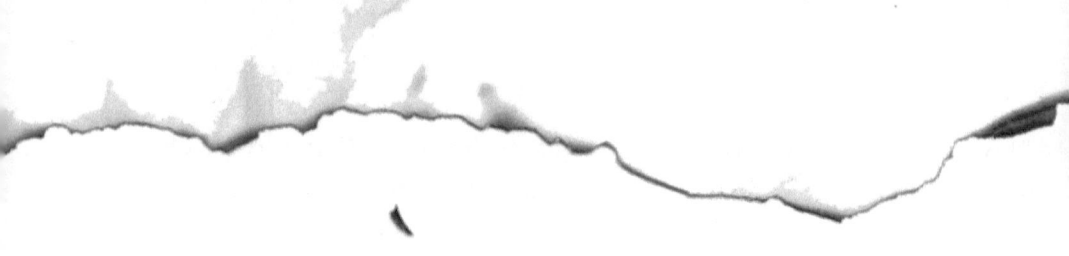

CHAPTER TEN

Two months into the new year, everything was going smoothly. Life finally felt like it was on my side. Botlhale had graduated high school with five distinctions and was now studying law at the University of Cape Town.

While I was proud of her achievements, her absence left an emptiness in my life that I couldn't quite fill. We'd been inseparable since, well, forever. Letting go of her on the day she moved into her dorm was one of the hardest things I'd ever done. It felt like she grew up too quickly, and part of me wasn't ready for that.

On the bright side, Rose had met someone—a charming Indian man named Pranav. However, Tsebo was blissfully unaware of Pranav's existence. Rose had asked me to keep her secret, though I wasn't sure for how long. She was doing well at work and even working on starting her own clothing line. Life seemed to be going well for everyone around me.

Tsebo, ever the go-getter, was busy "securing the bag," as he liked to say, healthier and more focused than ever. The last time I saw Dr. Radebe was on January 5th when we accompanied Botlhale to see her exam results, but we'd kept in touch over the phone. The Radebes seemed to be thriving as well, though I couldn't help but wonder how long that would last. As for me, I had no complaints. Everyone was thrilled about my engagement to Mogorosi. Work at N-AMI was flourishing; we'd landed new clients, and I had even been nominated for Young Businesswoman of the Year by the

Golden Awards. I finally hired an attorney, a dynamic young woman named Keabetswe Sekatane. At this moment, life was indeed golden.

That night, while I was lying in bed, lost in thought, Tsebo slipped into his pyjamas and joined me.

"Moratiwa," he murmured, teasingly. "Are you reading that book, or is the book reading you?"

I looked down at *Stay With Me* by Ayobami Adebayo, the book I'd been holding. In truth, I hadn't read a single page. My mind was too busy reflecting on life—mine and everyone else's.

"Oh, my love," I sighed. "I was just thinking."

"Hopefully about what we discussed. It has to be done sooner or later," he replied.

My mood shifted instantly. I wasn't even sure if I could go through with it. The truth was, I knew what those dreams about my father meant—I had to avenge his death. I could no longer deny that his spirit was not at rest. Facing my uncle, after all these years, was the only way forward. He had to pay for what he did to my family. The Tswana idiom, Molato ga o bole— a debt never decays—echoed in my mind.

And then there was Mogorosi, who wanted to pay lobola for me. But I didn't even have a family to speak of, and I doubted my father's relatives would want anything to do with us. The thought weighed heavily on me.

"Uhm...yeah," I finally replied to Tsebo, "but you know this isn't an easy task, right?"

"I know," he said, his tone firm but gentle. "But trust me, you'll be glad you did it. We can't avoid this; proper procedure must be followed. I want to make you my wife."

"Yeah, I guess," I murmured, defeated. "Let me sleep. I have an early morning tomorrow."

"Sleep well, my love," he whispered as I switched off my bedside lamp, resting my head on his chest.

Just as I was drifting off, Tsebo asked, "How would you feel if your mother showed up now?"

"Argh, Mogorosi, stop asking nonsense," I snapped, feeling a surge of anger. "You know I hate that woman, wherever she is. I would probably strangle her to death."

"Okay…" He paused. "I was just curious. Ga enne boroko," he replied.

His question lingered long after he fell asleep. I hadn't given much thought to the idea of my mother returning. She'd left a long time ago, and I'd made my peace with that. *Or so I thought.*

The next morning, my phone buzzed. It was Themba.

"Molo, Mrs. Mogorosi-to-be!" he greeted.

"Dumela, chomi. How are you?"

"Aii, sana, I'm not okay. What you're doing is risky. One day, that kind heart of yours will be the death of you."

Themba had a knack for speaking in riddles. "What are you talking about now?" I asked, exasperated.

"The stalker," he clarified. "I saw him at work today. Why didn't you fire him?"

"Oh, Brian? Don't worry, chomi. I'm not threatened by him. I'm sure he learnt his lesson."

"Tlhale! You can never be too sure. He's a psychopath!"

Themba had a point, but I'd kept Brian around because I wanted to keep a close eye on him. After our last encounter, I doubted he'd cause trouble.

As the workday passed, a text message from Dr. Radebe popped up:

Priska: "Argh. I can't really say he's special. But, we are married. It was an arranged marriage. We got married four years ago, blessed with two-year-old twin boys. The love of my life is my boys. Not that man."

Me: "How is he?"

Priska: "He doesn't care about me or our marriage for heaven's sake."

Me: "Shuu woman. I don't even know what to say." I really don't know what to say. This is too sad. I've recently turned into a firm believer in companionship.

Priska: "I think 'sorry' would do" She even looks stressless. I look at her and we both burst out in laughter.

Priska: "There. Done! You are so beautiful!"

After she's done, I catch a glimpse of myself in the mirror. My smoky eyes, cat-eye liner, and maroon lipstick make me look... like a goddess. Priska's work is flawless.

I thank Priska, and Charlize takes over, styling my hair into a sleek, long, curly ponytail with elegant edges. She then shows me the final look in a full-body mirror. "Beauty at its best!" she exclaims, admiring my engagement ring.

I smile, feeling like royalty. "Thank you both."

Leaving the room, I make my way to the pool. Tsebo is waiting, looking more handsome than ever in his navy double-breasted suit and fresh haircut. As I approach him, he stands, eyes shining as he takes in my appearance.

He walks toward me, his gaze soft but intense. "You look...beyond beautiful, Tlhali."

As we approached each other, Tsebo took a deep breath, his eyes lighting up. "My love! You look like a goddess—no, you *are* a goddess. I must be

138

Ntokazi. Dinner at my place tonight, 7:00 p.m. I've already told Likhaya. Hope to see you there. Love, Noluntu.

When I called Tsebo to ask if he knew anything about the dinner, he stammered and brushed it off, saying, "Baby, it's just dinner. Nothing hectic."

I felt a pang of unease, but I dismissed it. Later, when I got home, I found Tsebo sitting on the couch, lost in thought.

"Baby," I called softly. No response. "Mogorosi!"

He snapped out of his trance. "Tlhalefo! You're here. Are you ready?"

I blinked, momentarily confused. "Ready? For what?"

"He banna! Dinner with the Radebes," he reminded me, chuckling. "Let's go. We don't want to be late."

After a quick shower, I dressed in a grey jumpsuit, slipped on my sandals, and let my afro loose.

"You're really beautiful, motho waka," Tsebo said, grinning as he gave me a playful smack on the back.

When we arrived at the Radebes' house, Tsebo squeezed my hand. "Baby, I love you, okay?"

"Mogorosi…are you sure everything's okay?" I asked, feeling the nerves tighten in my chest.

He didn't respond, ringing the doorbell instead. Mr. Radebe opened the door, greeting us warmly.

As we settled in, I couldn't help but notice the tension between Tsebo, Mr. Radebe, and Doc as they exchanged loaded glances. Just then, a beautiful woman in a long, silky red dress descended the staircase, her blonde afro shining. My heart skipped a beat.

"Sthandwa sam', looking beautiful as always," Mr. Radebe said, casting a loving look at her, though Doc kept her eyes downcast.

"Mogorosi, Ntokazi," he said, turning to us, "this is my second wife, Neoentle Radebe."

Neoentle's gaze locked onto mine, her eyes filled with something I couldn't decipher. She smiled—a wide, unsettling smile. She slowly but proudly walked towards me.

"It's so good to finally meet you," she said. "You've grown up so much!"

The familiar voice made my stomach knot. I couldn't shake the sinking feeling that I knew her from somewhere.

"W-Who are you?" I stammered.

With a dazzling smile, she replied, "Like my lovely husband said, I'm Neoentle. Your mother."

My vision blurred. This couldn't be real. My heart pounded as I staggered to my feet, muttering, "I...I feel sick." I rushed down the hall and barely made it to the bathroom before I vomited, my head spinning.

Tsebo came running after me, his face a mask of worry. But by the time he reached me, everything had faded to black.

* * * * * * *

When I opened my eyes, he was holding a glass of water, his eyes filled with concern.

"Babe, wake up. Here's some water," he whispered.

I looked around, dazed. "Where...where are we?"

"We're still at the Radebes' house," Tsebo's voice murmured gently beside me. "But it's time to go home now."

I tried to shake off the fog in my head, but the pounding migraine made it nearly impossible. I was drenched in sweat. "I feel... awful," I whispered, closing my eyes against the nausea. "And I had the strangest dream. How did we even get here?"

His face tightened with worry. "I'm taking you to the doctor tomorrow, no arguments. And that wasn't a dream, my love."

"What do you mean it wasn't a dream?" I asked, barely holding back my frustration. "I dreamt about a woman... she called herself my mother. What kind of nonsense is that?"

Tsebo's hand reached for mine, his expression filled with a sympathy that unsettled me. "That actually happened," he said softly. "Right before you collapsed. I know it was overwhelming."

The words hung in the air, slowly sinking in as tears began to well in my eyes. I didn't trust myself to speak, not with this thick knot in my throat, so I let my head rest on his chest, and he held me, silent and firm.

My tears broke free. "I hate the Radebes!" I whispered bitterly. "If we'd known this dinner was going to unravel everything, we wouldn't have come."

He sighed, fingers smoothing my hair. "We had to come, baby. I couldn't keep this from you any longer."

My heart skipped a beat. A spark of anger ignited. "Wait... are you telling me you knew? All this time?" I pulled back to look him in the eyes, feeling my pulse quicken. "How long?"

"Tlhalefo..." he hesitated, searching for words.

"How long?" I demanded, every nerve on edge.

"Two months," he admitted quietly, the guilt plain on his face. "Please, don't be upset."

"Two months?" I recoiled. "I trusted you, Tsebo! How could you keep something this huge from me?"

Overcome, I snatched the car keys from his hand and stormed downstairs. I didn't care who saw my fury. There she was—Neoentle, sitting on the couch, sipping her wine with that same smug expression she'd had all evening. I wanted to scream, to break something.

"Tlhalefo, nna fatse re bueng!" Tsebo called after me.

"You keep your distance!" I shouted back, waving him away.

Dr. Radebe stood, trying to defuse the chaos. "Ntokazi, please calm down—"

"Calm down?" I snapped, turning my glare on her. "You think this is okay? You invite me here just to break me. How dare you!"

Neoentle scoffed from the couch. "So much drama from one person," she muttered, taking another sip of her wine.

The audacity! I rounded on her, my voice a crescendo of pain and anger. "You dare judge me? Where were you all these years? When Ntate was struggling to keep us afloat? When he died, and everyone abandoned us? I've fought every day to protect my sister and honour my father's memory. And now you waltz back into my life? For what? To rip everything apart?"

"Enough, Tlhalefo!" Tsebo's voice echoed, but I was past the point of caring.

Neoentle finally looked at me, her face twisted in anger. "I had my reasons for leaving—"

"Oh, spare me! Your 'reasons' don't excuse your betrayal. You left us for some married man, didn't you? How dare you show your face here, flaunting your selfishness!"

Neoentle's hand flew to her chest, and her face paled. She gasped, clinging to the arm of the couch. "My... my heart!" she choked out. "Noluntu, my pills!"

Mr. Radebe was at her side in seconds, panic in his eyes. "Stay with me, Neoentle. Noluntu! Get her pump and pills!" His voice shook, and I could feel Tsebo's hand reach out to steady me.

"Tlhalefo, get a glass of water for your mother!" Mr. Radebe called over his shoulder.

The word hit me like a slap. "My what?"

"There's no time for that! Just get her the water!" he ordered.

I froze, watching Neoentle, her face red and twisted in pain. A surge of anger welled up inside me, overshadowing any semblance of compassion. "No!" I spat. "Let her choke! For all she's done, she deserves it."

"Tlhalefo!" Tsebo shouted, but I was done.

I grabbed my phone from the table, turned on my heel, and marched out to the car. Tsebo chased after me, but I was already in, doors locked. He banged on the window, pleading for me to open up, but I ignored him. Soon, I was speeding away, leaving the Radebes and their poisoned secrets in the rearview mirror.

When I reached Tsebo's place, I grabbed my spare keys and car and drove straight to my own apartment. The place felt like a tomb, cold and lifeless. Once I closed the door, I sank to the floor, hugging my knees as the tears came, fierce and unrestrained. All I wanted was my father and my sister with me, to ground me, to tell me it would all be okay.

Hours passed. I don't know how long I stayed there, but eventually, a loud knock on the door jolted me awake. Tsebo. I didn't have the strength to face him again, so I silenced my phone and crawled under my blankets, shutting out the world.

When I finally got up the next day, it was nearly two in the afternoon. My face was a swollen, tear-streaked mess. Forty-two missed calls. Dozens of texts from Tsebo and a few missed calls from Dr. Radebe and Themba. Ignoring all of them, I realised I had nothing in the apartment—no clothes, no toiletries. I had left my purse at Tsebo's house. Rose was on vacation, so I was left with two options: return to Tsebo's or call him.

I sighed and dialled his number. He picked up immediately, desperation in his voice. "My love, are you okay? Please, come back home."

"Tsebo, I just need a favour. I need my things, and I need them now," I replied flatly.

He sounded relieved. "Of course. I'll be there in an hour."

He showed up exactly on time, a faint hope in his eyes as he handed me my bag. "You look so tired," he murmured, concern written on his face.

Me: "Wow! Thanks. Can I have my stuff now?"

"I didn't mean it like that. May I come in?" He says while still being adamant with my bag. This is so annoying, and I have no energy to entertain him, so I just stand there looking at him.

Without saying anything, he gently pushes me to the side and gets inside. The nerve. He even has some takeaway paper bag in his hand. Good.

"You must be hungry. I brought your favourite from The Zone." He looks so sincere. I kinda feel sorry for him.

"Thank you. O ka tsamaya yanong. I wanna bath."

"I'm not leaving without you. I'll wait for you until you finish whatever it is you wanna do. I have all the time in the world." He says as he goes to make himself comfortable on my couch and switches the TV on.

Like I said, I have no energy to entertain him so I just take my bag and go to the bathroom. I take the longest shower as the hot water feels so good on my skin. It is so well-deserved. I get out of the shower and go to my bedroom only to find this man busy with his phone on my bed. I'm only wrapped in a towel.

Me: "Please get out. I wanna get dressed."

Tsebo: "Hee banna! You can dress while I'm here moes?"

Me: "Just get out. Wa ntena maan!"

He says nothing and goes back to whatever he was busy with on his phone. I ignore him, apply my lotion and get dressed. I can feel his eyes on me. When I look at him, his eyes go back to his phone. This fool! I'm wearing my skinny jeans, white vest and white sandals. I tie my afro in a ponytail.

Tsebo: "You look beautiful."

I say nothing and go to dining room, he follows me. I open the food he brought me but I can't tolerate the smell. It's so bad!

Me: "Argh! Tsebo! Take this away! Di senyegile dijo tse!"

Tsebo: "Hee?! Why?" To say he is confused would be an understatement.

Me: "Can't you smell that? It's ruined!"

Tsebo: "What smell? This is how it smells moes, my love."

Me: "JUST TAKE IT AWAY!!!"

He looks at me like I'm crazy, takes the food and puts it into the fridge.

Me: "Tsamaya. I want to be alone."

Tsebo: "I told you that I'm not leaving here without you. Let's go."

I give him an annoyed look, but he couldn't care less.

Me: "Let me fetch my phone and keys."

Tsebo: "They are in my pocket. Ga re tsamaye."

We go outside and I don't even see his car. Where the hell did he park? I want him to go in his car, and I'll go in my car.

Me: "Where did you park?"

Tsebo: "I requested a cab. I didn't drive myself."

Me: "And why is that?!" I'm getting annoyed now.

Tsebo: "Stop acting stupid, my love. I knew you took your car; I didn't come with my car because we will use your car to go back home. Is that rocket science?"

He can be really arrogant at times.

Me: "Well, you better request that cab again. I'm going alone, in my car."

He takes out the key and unlocks the car.

Tsebo: "Get in, let's go"

I don't really have a choice; we all know by now that I live with a bully. I get in and look outside the window.

On the drive, he reached for my hand, his thumb brushing my knuckles.

"I'm sorry, Tlhalefo. I didn't mean to hurt you."

"You should have told me," I said quietly. "I don't know if I can trust you now."

He sighed, his voice filled with regret. "I know. I thought I was protecting you, but I realise now that I was wrong."

We drove in silence, the weight of everything lingering between us. "I love you, Tsebo," I finally whispered.

His face softened, and he glanced over, smirking. "Of course you do. Who wouldn't?"

"Oh, stop it," I muttered, shoving him playfully. We shared a small, bittersweet laugh, our fingers still intertwined.

Tsebo: "Come here. I want my kiss."

Me: "No. Oh and please stop at the market. I want to buy something?"

Tsebo: "Hee banna? Market? What do you wanna buy?"

Me: "I noticed that my peanut butter is almost finished. I wanna buy a few bottles. I'm also craving a pumpkin. Oh.. and lemon-flavoured water. Please remind me."

He looks so confused right now! Haha!

Tsebo: "Babe. The last time I checked, you didn't eat pumpkin le lemon, at all. You don't even like those. And what's with this new-found obsession with peanut butter? Keng Tlhalefo?"

Me: "Bathong? Is there anything wrong with change? Haai maan ska ntena!"

Tsebo: "Eh. I was just asking. Don't shoot me."

Me: "Au. Just drive. And don't look at me, don't talk to me, don't touch me, don't think about me. In fact, don't even breathe near me!" I'm so irritated right now. A few spoons of peanut butter would calm me down.

Tsebo: "Eh!"

I give him the deadliest look ever and he just raises his arm in defence and shrugs his shoulders then moves his annoying eyes away from me. Good.

We arrive at the market, he finds a parking space then looks outside the window.

Me: "You can go."

Tsebo: "Nna?"

Me: "No. The person next to you. Argh, just go, Mogorosi. I've told you what I want."

He reluctantly goes out. I can hear him mumbling something before closing the door and I just don't care. My mood has just dropped; I don't even know why. I call Botlhale, since she never calls me.

Me: "Ngwana ko gae."

Botlhale: "Ausi."

Me: "I miss you. When are you coming home?"

"Aii I'll see you. Talk to you later." She hangs up, just like that.

I feel like this girl wants me out of her life. It's like she's building a wall to keep me out, a wall I can never climb. I feel like I'm losing her, bit by bit. It's a defeating feeling. This man comes back after a good twenty minutes, with a trolley! It has a box of peanut butters, a sack of pumpkins and a twelve-pack of flavoured water! I've never been this excited my whole life!

I step out of the car with a smile, arms open. "Baby! Baby!" I call out as I approach him for a hug.

Tsebo chuckles, glancing at the bags. "Hope it's everything you wanted!"

"It is, and that's why I love you, munchy! Now, put all my precious cargo in the trunk, will you?" I say, giving his nose a playful stroke.

He rolls his eyes, grinning. "Geez. Are we opening a mini-mart here or what?" But he's already pushing the loaded trolley to the back of the car, arranging all my goodies neatly in the trunk.

Back at home, it takes us less than fifteen minutes to get everything inside. Tsebo lugs my bags into the kitchen, and I waste no time digging in. I start prepping my pumpkin, savouring the idea of the cozy meal to come. My phone buzzes mid-peel, and I glance at it: Dr. Radebe. I press decline, shaking my head. Not today.

Tsebo raises a brow from the living room. "Aren't you going to answer that?"

"Nope. Busy." I keep my eyes fixed on the pumpkin.

He lets out a sigh. "Babe, you can't keep ignoring her."

"Watch me," I mutter, not even looking up. He knows better than to argue when I'm like this. Good man. The phone rings again from the coffee table, and I ignore it, my irritation building.

Tsebo leans back, glancing at the screen. "It's not Noluntu this time. It's your...friend."

"He has a name," I say with a pointed look. Tsebo's casual homophobia is something I've warned him about before.

"Hau, I was just saying."

"Was there really a need?" I ask, not expecting an answer.

I get back to cooking, and once the pumpkin is simmering, I pick up the phone and return Themba's call. He answers immediately, his familiar voice a comfort.

"Chomi, you're not at work today?" Themba teases.

"Nope. Working from home," I reply, a slight smirk forming.

"Why?" he presses, always playful but nosy.

"I'm your boss, remember?" I reply, feigning authority.

"Yoh! Don't forget the rest of us!" he laughs, tossing in a few jabs, which I fire right back at him. By the end, we're both laughing so hard I can barely catch my breath. Tsebo, meanwhile, is watching the rugby, casting annoyed glances my way.

As I settle in beside Tsebo on the couch, the laughter fades, and something heavier takes over. My mind drifts back to the call I ignored, and a wave of anxiety crashes over me. Tsebo notices the change, his hand resting gently on mine.

"Baby?" he asks, his tone soft.

"How is she?" I ask quietly, eyes fixed on my lap.

"Who?" I don't answer, but he understands.

"She's okay. Just an asthma attack last night, nothing serious. They didn't need to hospitalise her," he says, squeezing my hand.

"I... I didn't know she was asthmatic..." I can feel the familiar prick of tears.

"Neither did I. We only knew about the cancer and diabetes," he admits. "There's a lot we don't know."

"And we don't care, right?" I say, almost to convince myself.

He looks at me, his gaze steady. "She's still your mother, Tlhalefo. The one who gave birth to you and Botlhale. No matter how much you want to run from it."

"I know." I swallow hard, bitterness coating my words. "She could've just left without messing up my life. But...fine."

"You have to see her, Tlhalefo. Talk to her. At least hear her out. Before it's too late."

"With that attitude of hers?"

He shrugs. "She's still your mother."

I'm so relieved you never turned out to be like me, keep it that way. I'm proud of you. Tlhalefo ngwanake, I'm sorry. I'm so sorry." She's now weeping and biting her nails. She looks like a little kid. I hate the fact that I see a lot of myself in her! She's like the older and more beautiful version of me. I say nothing; I don't know what to say. As much as I hate to say this, I appreciate and admire her honesty. I can't stop the tears from flowing.

Silence settles between us, heavy and unbreakable.

"And now?" I ask softly.

"I'm dying, Tlhalefo. The cancer, diabetes, asthma... they're winning. I don't have long. I refused to leave this world without seeing my daughters. I want to see Botlhale before..." Her voice breaks, but she steels herself, her face a mask of determination.

"I'm sure we can fight this. You have to be there for Botlhale's graduation, for my wedding, for..."

She cuts me off gently. "My girl, it is what it is. Tell your sister I need to see her."

I nod, tears slipping down my cheeks.

"Do you go to church? What are your plans for tomorrow?" Neo asks.

It's a bit embarrassing to admit that I don't go to church at all. I remember how she used to drag us there every Wednesday and Sunday; her love for church was unwavering.

"No, we don't go to church. The thing is, I'm always busy. Running a company requires more than twenty-four hours a day. Sundays are my resting days," I replied.

"Bathong lena! I always told you the importance of church. A le tla bolokwa ke mang?!" Neo exclaimed.

"Aow, Neo. I take it you still go to church?" I tried to redirect the conversation.

"How could I not? You know I love church with all my being. And on top of that, I'm a pastor's wife," Neo responded.

"What? Mr. Radebe is a pastor?!" I was shocked; that was an understatement.

"Bathong! You didn't know? Anyway, we're going to church tomorrow. You and your man are coming with us. Give me your numbers so I can send you the location and details," Neo said, leaving me no choice. I surrendered with a resigned, "Okay then."

Just then, Dr. Radebe walked in. I had been wondering where she was; I expected to find her sitting with Neo. She looked exhausted.

"Babys, I thought I was going to miss you. An emergency came up at the hospital," Dr. Radebe explained.

"No problem. Did you manage to sort it out?" I asked.

"Yeah, it was nothing big. Has she been treating you well? Neo, you didn't even make her tea?" Dr. Radebe chided.

"We had important issues to discuss. We didn't have time for that, and besides, we drink champagne, right, Tlhalefo?" Neo replied, lost in her own world.

"Uhm... Yes. I guess," I mumbled.

I agree to avoid an argument. Dr. Radebe shook her head and went upstairs, leaving Neo and me alone again.

"So, how are you feeling today?" I asked.

"I'm okay, but I've seen better days," Neo admitted.

"Mmh. Let me leave you so you can rest then," I suggested, feeling a bit disappointed; I didn't want to go.

"Uh-huh. Stay. We still have a lot to talk about. Tell me about yourself. I can tell you're doing very well as a young woman," Neo encouraged.

"Haha. There's not much to know. I'm twenty-four, I have a Marketing Communications degree, and I own a marketing agency. That's all," I replied, feeling a bit serious. When someone asks me to talk about myself, I usually stick to the basics.

"Annnd... any children? Come on, there must be something worth sharing," Neo pressed.

"Haha. Me? A child? I'll think about that maybe after five years. I'm not ready for such a huge responsibility. Oh, I'm sure you know by now that Tsebo wants to pay lobola for me; we're engaged. And I've been nominated for the Golden Awards," I added.

"You lie! Those awards are such a big deal! In what category have you been nominated?" Neo exclaimed. I felt like I was in a talk-show interview.

"The Youngest Businesswoman of the Year, because of New-Age Marketing Intellects, my marketing agency," I explained.

"Wow. I'm proud of you. I really am. And you've found yourself a good man, although I can't even look him in the eye; he's scary. Does he ever laugh?" Neo asked.

I couldn't help but laugh; she wasn't the first person to ask that. If only they knew that an hour rarely goes by without him laughing and being silly.

"Haha. He does. He's actually a good person, though he sometimes acts like my father. But overall, he's great," I said.

Suddenly, Neo's mood shifted, and she looked a bit shattered. I hoped it wasn't anything I said or did. I remained quiet, staring at the glass wall.

"Do you... do you miss him?" she finally spoke.

"Mang? Tsebo? But he's right here, mos..." I replied, feeling exasperated by her question.

"Goitsimang," Neo pressed.

"Oh. Ntate. I miss him every second of the day. I can never get used to his absence. But life goes on; he's always in my thoughts," I confessed, trying to stay strong. I was teaching myself to talk about my father without feeling heartbroken.

"I miss him too. He was a good man. What happened? Natural death?" Neo asked, guilt and pain evident on her face.

"No. Ramokgolo Goitsione shot him in front of me. It was Sunday morning, and we were preparing Sunday lunch for my birthday when Ramokgolo came in. They got into a huge argument —I'm not sure what about. I decided to take Botlhale to the bedroom because I sensed things would get out of hand. I didn't want her to witness anything traumatic. When I came out, I saw a knife in Ntate's hand. He shouted at me to go back to the bedroom, losing focus on Ramokgolo. That's when Ramokgolo took the opportunity and shot.

The first bullet went straight into Ntate's chest, and he fell. I tried to run to him, but Ramokgolo pointed a gun at me and warned me to stay back. Then he shot eleven bullets in total. He looked at me and threatened that if I told anyone, he would come back and kill Botlhale; then he ran away.

Botlhale had been screaming in the bedroom. When I went to her, she was huddled in the corner, covering her ears. I took her to the bed, not wanting to let go. The door opened, and it was our neighbour, Mme Masango, followed by the police. I told them it was a robbery and said our mother died years ago. The paramedic lady just looked at me and nodded. I knew then that Ntate was gone. The very same Ntate we had been singing and dancing with just moments before—he was dead. That was the end of our beloved father. Botlhale couldn't even understand what was happening; she just kept holding me tight. I couldn't cry; I didn't know what to feel or what the next move was. I only knew one thing: from then on, it was just my sister and me. Mme Masango took us to her house, and from there, the funeral planning began. Ntate was gone," I recounted, my voice steady despite the turmoil inside. Neo was weeping, so I pulled her close and hugged her. It felt surreal.

"I'm so sorry you had to see all of that. I'm so sorry I wasn't there. I should have protected you from all of it," Neo said, her voice trembling.

"Shhh. What's done is done." I reassured her.

She couldn't say anything else; she just held me tighter and continued to cry. We shared a moment of connection.

Just then, Tsebo and Mr. Radebe walked in, laughing together.

"Nkosikazi, are you okay? Ukhalela ntoni?" Mr. Radebe asked.

"I'm fine, my love. Worry not," Neo replied, wiping her tears away.

"Uphi uNoluntu? I thought I heard her voice," Mr. Radebe said.

"She's back; she went upstairs to her bedroom. I think she's resting because she said she's tired," I explained.

"Oh, okay. I'll go check on her," Mr. Radebe said.

"Se si ya goduka vele thina ngoku, Radebe. Baby, o heditse?" Tsebo said.

"Yes, love. We can go. Neo, o tla sala sentle. It was great talking to you," I said.

"Ni za hamba kakuhle, ntokazi. Mogorosi, sizawubonana," Mr. Radebe replied.

"Sure. Bye, Neo," Tsebo added. There was something about Neo that made my man uncomfortable; it was as if he was disgusted by her very existence.

He couldn't even look her in the eye or stand too close to her, yet he was still trying to be civil for my sake. I didn't blame him.

"Goodbye," Neo said softly.

We said our goodbyes and made our way to the car.

"Lunch?" Tsebo asked, a mischievous glint in his eye.

"Yeah. Where?" I replied, amused.

"I don't know. You choose."

"Okay... Casabella," I said, but then I paused, eyeing both of us up and down. "But wait, we can't really go there looking like this."

"Bathong. Re jwang?" he replied, laughing. Tsebo was in ripped jeans and a tank top, while I wore a pink romper and slippers—hardly restaurant attire.

"We need to dress the part. You know what? Let's make it dinner. We still have to swing by the house and fix ourselves up."

"Actually...why don't we go big?" he suggested, leaning forward. "How about we go home, pack overnight bags, and spend a couple of nights at the hotel? A grand one."

"But why would we go to a hotel? Isn't that just a waste of money?" I was genuinely puzzled.

"Just nje," he replied, shrugging. "I feel like spoiling you."

"Ncoahh, okay, baby. I'm flattered," I said, my heart swelling. "Oh! We must not forget our second fittings—The Golden Awards are only three weeks away!"

"No worries, love. Let's go." He pulled me close, planting a kiss on my forehead.

* * * * * *

We stopped by McDonald's for a quick snack. Tsebo ordered his usual McFeast and Coke, while I went for my all-time favourite, the chicken foldover and McNuggets. My appetite had finally returned; I hadn't felt nauseous since I'd walked in. As we ate, the buzz of our impromptu getaway started settling in, and soon we were heading home to pack.

By six, we were ready, and the drive to the hotel filled me with butterflies— it had been a while since I'd been this excited. Two hours later, we arrived, and I could barely keep my eyes open.

"Whuu, I'm exhausted. My back is killing me," I groaned as we walked in. "I'm going to take a thirty-minute nap."

"You're not even thirty yet, and you're already complaining about your back?" Tsebo teased.

I slipped under the duvet without a word, ignoring his playful jabs. The bed felt so comfortable, and as I closed my eyes, he leaned over to say, "I'm going to the balcony for a smoke, then I'll shower. I'll wake you when I'm done."

"Alright, enjoy your four cigarettes," I muttered from beneath the covers. He chuckled, and I could hear him step outside.

I woke to the scent of his aftershave, crisp and intoxicating. "Oh, she's still alive!" he smirked, wrapped in only a towel. "I was about to wake you up. Go shower."

His bare torso glistened, and for a moment, I was captivated. He laughed, catching me staring. "When you're done admiring me, go shower."

I quickly pulled myself together and slipped into the bathroom. When I emerged, Tsebo was putting the final touches on his outfit, a perfectly tailored white shirt and black pants. On the bed lay a stunning red mermaid dress with sparkling lace, a pair of black Louis Vuitton stilettos, and a matching LV clutch. Beside them were diamond studs, a bracelet, and a bottle of BVLGARI perfume.

"Oh, baby..." I was overwhelmed, trying to keep my emotions in check.

Tsebo looked at me softly, pulling me into a warm embrace. "I love you, MmeKhama. Don't ever forget that."

"I won't," I whispered back, my voice choked with emotion. "Our love is forever."

He smiled, gently wiping my tears away. "Now, get rid of those tears and work your magic."

I quickly got ready, slipping on the dress and pairing it with the jewellery. After styling my afro into a sleek ponytail with curls, I did a smoky eye makeup look and finished with deep red lipstick. Tsebo's eyes never left me as I dressed, his gaze warm and adoring.

"Could you get any more perfect, my angel?" he said.

I took his hand and gave him a soft kiss. "I'm yours and yours alone, my love."

He smiled, his hand resting on the small of my back as we headed out. His occasional kisses sent a warmth through me that I hadn't felt so long.

* * * * * * *

The restaurant was grand, with soft lighting from burgundy chandeliers casting a warm glow. Couples filled the tables, each absorbed in each other's presence. After we ordered, we savoured our appetisers, a delicious brie and caramelised pear tart.

"For the main course, I'll have the roast chicken with prune and walnut stuffing," I said, glancing at the wine menu. "And some red wine, please."

"Make mine a buttered chicken with naan and a glass of scotch," Tsebo added, flashing me a playful grin.

"This food is to die for!" he said between bites.

"Agreed. The chefs here definitely know what they're doing."

He chuckled, taking my hand. "I see your appetite is back. You're no longer eating just 'nonsense.'"

"Haha, I told you it was just stress. I'm feeling better."

But I could sense a lingering question in his eyes. Finally, he asked, "How...how is she?"

I hesitated, knowing exactly whom he meant. "Dying," I murmured.

"And how does that make you feel?"

A long sigh escaped me. "Talking to her...it helped. For the first time, I felt a motherly love I'd missed. Knowing she has only a short time left...it hurts. But that's life."

"See? I told you talking to her would bring you closure." He kissed my hand, and the warmth of that small gesture filled my heart.

We both sat in silence for a moment, his gentle presence a comfort.

"Dessert?" I finally asked.

He smirked, giving me a look that sent shivers up my spine. "I'll have my dessert in a few hours," he said, eyeing me suggestively.

"Oh, just you wait," I replied in a sultry tone. He chuckled, clearly enjoying the game we were playing.

After dessert, we made our way back to the hotel. The second we walked through the door, he was all over me, his kisses passionate. I laughed, pushing him back.

"Not yet! You'll ruin the surprise," I said, slipping away to the bedroom, where I'd made special arrangements with the hotel staff. The lights were dimmed, roses scattered across the room, and soft music played in the background. I changed into a black lace set, slipped on red stilettos, and adjusted the lighting near the pole I'd requested.

When I called him in, his eyes widened as he took me in, his jaw dropping. "Damn."

I took his tie, led him to a chair, and gave him the show of his life, moving with confidence and teasing every bit of his self-control. His breaths grew ragged, and he looked ready to explode.

After what felt like an eternity of bliss, he held me close, whispering, "You're going to be the death of me."

* * * * * * *

It's been two weeks since Botlhale came home. I told her about Neo; they talked and all seems well between them. Neo can't stop fussing over her little flower. Botlhale knows the truth, that Neo won't be with us for a long time. I don't hide stuff from her anymore, she's not a kid. I can't help but notice how she's been avoiding me ever since she came back home; she can't even look me in the eye nor hold a five-minute conversation with me. I'm worried. I'm really stressed about her. I've been having these hectic migraines now and again, but I guess it's nothing to worry about. I decided to take Botlhale out for lunch today so that I can talk to her and find out what her problem is. The drive to the restaurant is so dry and quiet; she even has her earphones on.

We arrive at the restaurant, get seated and order seafood; it's her favourite.

Me: "So... how's school?"

Botlhale: "Uhm. Good. I actually passed."

Me: "Oh. I thought you would've told me by now. When did your results come out?" I'm a tad disappointed by her behaviour.

Botlhale: "Last week Wednesday. Here you go." She gives me her phone and shows me her results. I'm overwhelmed with joy! My baby obtained three distinctions out of seven modules. I've never felt so proud!

Me: "Ngwana wa ko gae! Wow! Well done Tlhali wame! I'm so proud of you babys!" I'm on the verge of tears.

Botlhale: "Haha. You know me. Your future lawyer." At least she's showing some enthusiasm. "I'm still going to make you proud ausi wame. Watch the space."

I say nothing, stand up and give her a hug. She hugs me too. I go back to my seat and just look at her. She has grown up so much; she's even more beautiful. My baby! She just looks at me and continues eating her food.

Me: "And... your life?"

Botlhale: "What about my life?"

She's not even looking at me. I just wish she could be open with me, like in the old days.

Me: "You know... have you made any friends?" I'm crossing fingers here.

Botlhale: "Ausi I don't have a boyfriend, if that's what you are asking." She sounds and looks irritated.

"Oh." A sense of relief showers over me. The last thing I want is some lousy guy ruining my baby's future for some useless shit.

Botlhale: "But.." She starts talking again. She looks a bit scared. She's not even looking me in the eye.

Me: "Yes?" I'm kinda nervous about what she's about to tell me.

Botlhale: "I... I do have a girlfriend."

Me: "You mean..."

Botlhale: "Yes. I'm not into men, ausi Tlhalefo. I'm gay. I'm sorry."

To say I'm shocked would be an understatement. I didn't expect this from her. But I'm not hurt or anything. I don't even see a problem.

Me: "Sorry? What for?"

Botlhale: "Being a disappointment. I know you raised me better than that. I'm sorry." She says all of this while looking down, a tear escapes from her eye. I'm so hurt by all these thoughts of hers. I take her hand and hold it tightly.

Me: "No... No. You must never think like that. There's nothing wrong with being a homosexual. There's absolutely nothing wrong. You can never disappoint me, nana. Nothing has changed between us. Do you hear me?" I'm on the verge of tears again.

Botlhale: "Really? That means a lot my sister. Thank you for not judging me. That's why I've been kinda distant from you; I was scared of your reaction."

Me: "You can never disappoint me, Botlhale. Even if you try, you can never, my love. Okay?"

Botlhale: "Okay, sis." I see a smile curving on her lips.

Me: "Good. Now tell me, what's her name?" Kea di nyaka dikgang tse!

Botlhale: "Haha, come on ausi. Ayibongwe Mkhwanazi. She's Ndebele, twenty-one years old. She's studying Graphic Design. We met at the campus library; she approached me, and the rest was history." I can see her face and mood lightening up as she talks about her Ayibongwe.

Me: "Is she treating you well? Do you love her?"

Botlhale: "Yeahp she is, I also am. It's more than love, sister. And don't worry; I won't neglect my studies. Never in a million years." This is the sweet girl I know!

Me: "Please baby. I'm happy that you are happy. I love you so much, no matter what."

Botlhale: "I love you too ausi wame. Oh and how are you and abuti Tsebo? Is he still treating you well?"

Me: "Yeahp, baby. Nothing has changed."

Botlhale: "Good. Hella Bathong! O kae Rose le le india le lagwe?" She's laughing so hard.

Me: "Yhuuu that one. They are always away on vacation. She only comes to see us for two minutes and that's it. But she's happy though. Even though that guy of hers likes cracking some really bad jokes, like he tries so hard to be funny. You should see the way Rose laughs at his jokes. Eyyy new love! Re tla reng!"

Botlhale is laughing so hard, she's even struggling to breathe. It's so hilarious!

Botlhale: "Whuuu ausi. Tlogela go mpolaya hle!"

Me: "Okay. Okay. I'll stop." She has finally stopped laughing and is wiping off her tears.

Me: "Sooo. O akanya eng ka Neo? Be honest." I'm treading on thin ice here.

Botlhale: "Ahh what can I say? I can't say I've forgiven her because I was never really angry at her. She wasn't a constant thought in my life. You

171

were. You are the one and only mother I've ever known and loved and that's it. As for Neo, I have no problem with her, she's just another human being occupying Earth. It's just a pity that she's dying nje. But that's it, I've got no feelings for her." Her face is really emotionless, even her tone is cold. I guess that's it.

Me: "Okay baby. I love you."

That's all I can say.

Botlhale: "I love you too Mrs-Mogorosi-To-Be."

We share a good laugh and order dessert. I've missed this. I've missed her so much. She's back! And I'm happy!!!

CHAPTER ELEVEN

It's been a week and three days since that lunch with Botlhale. Thankfully, she's returned to her lively self, and it's a relief to see her smile again. But Neo... Neo has deteriorated from bad to worse, and I'm now closer to her than I ever imagined I would be. Loving her feels like both a blessing and a curse; the thought of losing her is almost unbearable. She's my mother, and though I've only just truly found her, she's already slipping away.

Four days ago, Neo was admitted to the hospital. Her body is so frail—her weight has dropped drastically, her veins stark against her skin. The doctors shaved her remaining hair, leaving her head bare, while her face has become hollowed, her cheekbones sharp under the sunken skin. Red patches now cover her body. Every day, I sit with her, telling her stories, massaging her hands, and staying even though she can't respond. But she hears me. I see it in the way her eyes move, barely blinking, staring into some distant space. She hasn't spoken since she was admitted, and her eyes are constantly wet, brimming with unspoken pain. I dread what lies ahead.

As I sit by her bedside, lost in thought, Dr. Radebe and Mr. Radebe enter. They look worn and drained, shadows of the people I knew.

"Ntokazi. How is she today?" Mr. Radebe asks quietly.

"Same," I reply, my eyes fixed on Neo as she blinks slowly, her gaze fixed on the ceiling.

"There's no hope," he murmurs, almost to himself.

"Don't say that," I protest, feeling anger rise in me, clinging to any shred of hope.

173

"Aii Tata. Suthetha ngalo hlobo," Dr. Radebe mutters, trying to steady her husband. But Mr. Radebe seems lost, holding Neo's hand, gently kissing her cracked forehead.

"Nkosikazi, go and rest. Hamba kak'hle, MaRadebe om'hle," he says, tears streaming down his cheeks.

"Don't you dare!" I shout, rising to my feet. "She's not ready for that!"

"Sisi..." Dr. Radebe tries to calm me.

"Shut up! Shut the hell up!" I scream, shaking as tears blur my vision. "She's not going anywhere, not now! In fact, get out—both of you!"

In that moment, I hear a faint whisper: "Tlha...le...fo..."

I freeze. My mother has spoken. Trembling, I sit beside her, holding her hand tight.

"Mama! I knew it! You're a fighter—you're not giving up!"

"Co...continue being the woman that you are," she says, her voice a fragile whisper. "Stay strong, no matter what. Thank you... for everything. Tell my flower that I love her."

"No, Mama, you'll tell her yourself. You're going to leave here with us! Please, don't leave me—please!" I cry, my heart pounding.

She looks at me, her eyes brimming with love. "My love, Noluntu... We shall meet again. Tlhalefo, I love you, and remember, you are stronger than you think. I love y—"

The machines beep sharply, and the line on the cardiogram flattens. Her grip weakens in my hand. Her eyes, wide open, are still, one last tear sliding down her cheek. She is gone.

The silence in the room presses down on me, but within seconds, Mr. Radebe's anguished cries fill the space. Still clutching her hand, I can't bring myself to let go.

"Mama... Mama..." I whisper, hoping for a response, praying for a miracle that doesn't come. And then reality crashes down. I scream, shaking her lifeless body, refusing to accept the truth. Dr. Radebe moves to hold me, her own grief mingling with mine as the doctors tend to the machines.

"Ma'am, would you like to cover her?" one of them asks gently.

Shaking, I reach out, closing her eyelids, her mouth, placing my hand on her heart—cold, still, empty. I lean down, pressing a final kiss to her forehead. "Goodbye, Ma." Then, numb, I leave, supported by Dr. Radebe as two doctors move in to assist me. One of them injects me with a sedative, and the darkness takes me.

****

When I open my eyes, I'm lying in a hospital bed. Tsebo sits beside me, looking hollow, his eyes red-rimmed.

"My love," he whispers, forcing a weak smile.

I reach for his hand, confused by the grief on his face. "They are gone," he says, voice breaking. His hands tremble as he looks away.

"Yes, I was there when she..." My voice trails off as his words sink in. "Wait. 'They'?

Tsebo's gaze is heavy. "Your mother, Tlhalefo. And... our baby. We were pregnant. He didn't make it—the shock, maybe. We lost him."

A raw, silent agony seizes my heart, so visceral it's like a wound tearing open. I lie still, silent, tears tracing down my face. I don't scream. I don't cry out. I just stare, letting my tears speak the grief I can't voice.

Rose and Botlhale come in, their faces mirrors of my pain.

"Ausi, I'm so sorry," Botlhale says, hugging me tight.

Rose's voice is a whisper. "I'm so sorry for your loss, for your baby, and your mother."

I can't respond. My body is numb, unfeeling as a stone. I wish someone would pinch me, hit me—anything to remind me that I'm still alive. I lie motionless, as still as my mother, as still as my baby.

Dr. Pillay, the young doctor, enters, her face solemn. "Ma'am, you went into shock because of Mrs. Radebe's passing. We had to sedate you. How are you feeling?"

I nod, barely hearing her.

"There's more, I'm afraid," she begins, but Tsebo interrupts.

"She knows," he says quietly.

"I'm so sorry, ma'am," Dr. Pillay continues. I feel Botlhale's grip tighten on my hand, a small lifeline.

"How long was I?" I finally manage.

"Nine weeks," Dr. Pillay replies. "Just over two months."

"And what happened?" I ask, voice empty.

"Shock, ma'am. After the news, you began bleeding. My colleague, Dr. Radebe, called us over. I'm deeply sorry."

She leaves, and Tsebo remains, holding me silently. After a moment, he lies beside me, cradling me as I release the grief pent up within, sobbing into his chest as he strokes my hair, whispering for me to sleep.

* * * * * * *

A week has passed and we are at the Radebe's preparing for Neo's funeral; it's tomorrow. It has been busy with everyone being here, Mr. Radebe's family, Noluntu's family, and Neo's friends and colleagues. Her family is nowhere to be seen. Mr. Radebe contacted them and told them about their daughter's passing and funeral details but not even one of them is in sight. But we are not stressing about that. Planning Neo's funeral has been keeping me busy and I prefer it this way, I don't want to just sit. I don't want to feel this pain. I just hope after tomorrow I'll get closure about everything, with Neo being laid to rest and me, having been cleansed at the hospital. My womb was cleansed, as Dr. Pillay said, and here at home, they performed a cleansing ceremony. I don't even sleep here; I only come in the morning and go home in the evening. But I'll have to sleep over tonight, as the funeral is early in the morning tomorrow.

Everyone is sleeping over at the Radebes; I'm talking about Botlhale, Rose, and Tsebo, much to their disapproval but it has to be done. Mr. Radebe is a walking zombie. One can tell that the poor man has no strength nor life left in him.

Neo's death really tore him apart; he's even losing weight. It's very sad to see a very strong man like him break down into pieces, bit by bit. Thing is, he has always been expecting Neo's death to happen, but he was never ready for it. I guess, nobody can ever be ready for death. Noluntu has been remaining strong and keeping everybody together; she's being the warm soul she's known to have. It's just a pity that she doesn't have a kid, even Neo didn't have any children. Apparently, Mr. Radebe cannot have kids, and he doesn't want to try the surrogacy or adoption route.

It's 5:00 p.m and the mortuary has brought Neo's casket to sleep overnight for the funeral tomorrow. I'm in the kitchen washing the dishes and I can hear people singing and humming outside. I continue with what I'm doing because I don't want to go outside, I'm scared. I'm lost in my thoughts when I can feel Tsebo holding my waist from behind, lies his head on my shoulder and kisses my ear lightly.

Tsebo: "My love, don't be scared; I'm here. Come outside."

As he says this, a tear escapes my eye and he wipes it with his thumb. I take his hand and follow his lead. The people are still humming, and Neo's casket is being brought in. Mpikayiboni, Mr. Radebe's older brother, is holding a branch of leaves, waving it at the casket and talks to Neo. Mr. Radebe and Noluntu follow his lead. I let go of Tsebo's hand, go and hold Botlhale's hand and we go walk to the other side of the casket. I'm not crying; I'm just swallowing hard and pray to the dear Lord to make me strong. We get into the house; they put the casket in her bedroom and the mortuary guys use their curtain blinds to surround the casket. Mpikayiboni opens the head of the casket, Mr. Radebe looks at me and signals for me to hold his hand. I go. I'm still holding Botlhale's hand. Botlhale only cried the first day and that was it. The three of us go and look at Neo. She looks so peaceful. She looks so well-rested. Mr. Radebe breaks down and his other brother, Mpiyakhe, takes him away.

Mpiyakhe: "Nqombimpi. Ku Lungile mfo." I didn't know that Mr. Radebe's name is Nqobimpi. Wow.

Botlhale looks at Mpikayiboni and nods, signalling that he can now close the casket. We go away and continue with our duties until nighttime arrives and we go to sleep. Honestly, I'm scared for tomorrow. While in bed, Tsebo disturbs my thoughts and calls out my name.

Tsebo: "Tlhalefo." He's lying on the bed, looking at the ceiling.

Me: "Yes?"

Tsebo: "You are still taking your pills, right?"

Me: "Yes, love. I won't stop, trust me." I'm being honest here.

Tsebo: "Good. I need you to promise me one thing."

Me: "Yes?"

Tsebo: "You will never turn to alcohol again, no matter what. You know that I'm here for you; I'm not going anywhere, okay?"

Me: "I promise. I know that you are my punching bag." I say while stroking his arm. He chuckles a bit then lies on his side then hugs me.

Tsebo: "Let's sleep, my love. It's gonna be a long day tomorrow."

Me: "Goodnight, Mogorosi. I love you."

Tsebo: "I love you. Now sleep."

We sleep and before we know it, our 5:30a.m alarm rings. I go to the room where Rose and Botlhale are sleeping and wake them up, then go and join Tsebo in the shower. The service will take place at Neo's church, AKA Mr.

Radebe's church, I still can't get used to the fact that he has a church and is a pastor...

We are given a chance to look at Neo for the last time and as I'm busy staring at her lifeless self, her words keep ringing in my head, *"remember, you are stronger than you think..."* After the service, we go to the cemetery to put her to her final resting place. All those shovels hitting the sand feel like a spear in my long-dead heart. They make it look and feel so final. I'm sitting with Botlhale and Noluntu while Tsebo and Mr. Radebe and his brothers are busy covering the grave with sand. While people are humming, Noluntu stands up and reads a poem that Neo apparently instructed her to read at her funeral. It's a poem by Christina Rossetti titled "Miss Me, But Let Me Go."

Miss me, but let me go
when I come to the end of the road
and the sun has set for me,
I want no rites in a gloom-filled room;why cry for a soul set free?

Miss me a little – but not too long and not with your head bowed lowed.
Remember the love that we once shared.

Miss me but let me go.

For this is a journey that we all must take and each must go alone.

It's all a part of the master's plan,
A step on the road to home. When you are lonely and sick of heart,
Go to the friends we know
and bury your sorrows in doing good deeds.
Miss me, but let me go.

As the words wash over me, I know she's at peace. And as the last line falls into silence, I close my eyes, holding onto her parting words, feeling her love hold me together in the midst of the pain.

CHAPTER TWELVE

A week had passed since the funeral. Botlhale had returned to university, and Rose, in her usual style, had disappeared off with her boyfriend again. Noluntu had been telling me about Mr. Radebe—how he had hit rock bottom after Neo's death. It seemed to have shattered him. As much as I hated to admit it, when Neo's coffin was lowered, it felt as if a part of me went with it. But it's something I'll have to live with.

As for Tsebo and me, we're just taking it one day at a time. I can tell he's hurting but trying to stay strong, probably for my sake. Losing our baby has hit him hard too. It's Wednesday today, and the Golden Awards are coming up this Saturday. Our outfits are ready, though it's a shame my sister and Rose won't be able to attend. I'm even second-guessing going myself.

Tonight, we're in bed early, settling back into the rhythm of work and daily life. Tsebo lies on his side, looking at me with such warmth that it makes me smile.

"Baby," I say, breaking the silence.

"Mmh?" he murmurs.

"I'm thinking of not going to the awards," I admit. "I'm just... not in the mood."

"Why? You think you won't win?" he asks, his voice soft but certain. "Tlhalefo, I've told you a million times that award is yours. You're a brilliant and powerful businesswoman. Even if you don't get that trophy, you'll always be my winner, okay?"

I smile, feeling the depth of his support. This man, my go-to, my rock. "What would I do without you, my love? Okay, we'll go. On Friday, we'll pick up our outfits from Leon."

"Alright. And I love you, okay?" he says, voice tender.

"Goodnight, my love."

He pulls me close, resting my head on his chest, his hand gently placed over my stomach. I feel him exhale deeply, his heart racing.

"Mogorosi?" I whisper.

"Yes?" His voice trembles slightly.

"Cry," I say, pressing myself closer to him.

His hands begin to tremble, and a moment later, I feel a warm tear trail down my forehead. He cries, releasing all the pain he's held back, and I whisper softly, "Cry, love, until the very last tear."

* * * * * * *

The next day, I find myself back at the office. It's been a strange return to routine, and as I settle in, my friend Themba bursts in.

"Hehake, girl! You're actually here? I thought you'd be working from home for good!" he exclaims. "I've hardly heard from you, just the odd email here and there. You're impossible to reach! What's up?"

"Yhuu motho, slow down! One question at a time," I laugh, but it's short-lived.

His face softens, concern etched in his brow. "You even have bags under your eyes, Tlhali. Are you okay?"

My resolve crumbles, and I look down, feeling the weight of everything that's happened. Without a word, I start crying. Themba rushes to close the door, then hops onto my desk, placing a comforting hand on my shoulder.

"Oh sana, speak to me. What's going on?"

"It's... it's been a lot, chomi. I don't even know where to start," I stammer.

"Then start at the beginning," he urges gently.

I take a deep breath. "It started last month... I found my mother. The woman who left me as a child. She was sick, with cancer. I was trying to get close to her, to understand her, but she passed away two weeks ago. And that same day... I found out I was pregnant and then... I lost the baby."

"Hayini, Tlhali! I'm so sorry. You should have called me!"

"My mind was all over the place, chomi," I reply. "But don't worry, I'll be okay."

Themba sighs. "Just because you're strong doesn't mean you deserve all this pain." His voice lightens a bit, trying to cheer me up. "By the way, I guess Valentine's Day wasn't on your radar?"

I laugh softly. "We even forgot about it. Where are we now, February what?"

"21st !" he exclaims, his excitement returning full force. "So, ready for Saturday?! Is your outfit ready? Shoes, makeup, speech? Also, sis, we need to fix that hair and nails!"

"Slow down before you collapse!" I laugh, shaking my head. "Yes, the gown is ready, shoes are bought, and I'm doing my own makeup. I'll hit the salon Saturday morning. As for the speech—if I win, I'll speak from the heart."

"Of course you'll win, duh," Themba declares, brightening my spirits.

Just then, Gugu, the HR manager, knocks and enters.

"Ms. Khama, I've been trying to reach you since the weekend," she says with her usual impatience.

"Was it urgent?"

"Yes. Brian from IT resigned and relocated. We have an opening."

I perk up at the mention of Brian. "Remember that Indian girl from the interviews? My favourite?"

Gugu rolls her eyes. "I'll contact her," she says shortly, noting my tired look. "By the way, you look like you haven't slept."

I flash her a smile. "Gugu, let me know if you want any fashion tips or makeup recs. I've got you, girl."

She huffs and leaves, and Themba and I break into laughter.

* * * * * * *

Later, I have a meeting with Mrs. Pauwels, a client. I arrive early and settle into her office. She's a poised older woman, dressed elegantly, her voice refined.

"Ms. Khama, it's great to finally meet you in person! My daughter Paula has been handling your account, right?" she asks.

"Yes, I was surprised when my PA said I'd be meeting you today. Will I be working with you from now on?"

"Yes," she says, a shadow crossing her face. "Paula is mourning her brother, Brian. He was... troubled. We weren't close."

183

I freeze. "Could I see a picture?"

She shows me a photo of him on her tablet. It's the same Brian who worked in our IT department. My shock is palpable. "This Brian used to work for me."

"Be glad you're safe," she says coldly. "He was violent, a genius with tech but dangerous. Shall we get back to business?"

After the meeting, I drive home, still shaken.

* * * * * *

It's finally Saturday. I'm at the salon, getting my hair and nails done. When I get home, I'm panicking about the time, but Tsebo calms me.

We dress in our elegant outfits—he in a black suit with a striped gold tie, and me in a black mermaid dress with lace sleeves. By the time we step onto the red carpet, it's almost 8: 00p.m. The camera flashes, the screams—it all feels surreal.

And for the first time in a long time, in the midst of grief and uncertainty, I feel like myself again.

The crowd roared as we stepped onto the red carpet, cameras flashing with an intensity that could blind you if you didn't stay focused. I wasn't sure if the shouts and applause were for Tsebo, for me, or just for the thrill of it all. Amid the dazzling lights, a journalist rushed up, smiling brightly.

"Mr. and Mrs. Mogorosi-to-be, congratulations on your engagement, and welcome to #Golden19!" His enthusiasm was undeniable.

"Thank you," I replied, feeling a bit of pride bubble up. Tsebo only nodded, his face serious as ever.

"You both look stunning!" the journalist continued, eyes wide with admiration. "The black and gold theme is to die for! Who are you wearing?"

"Thank you," I said, smiling warmly. "We're both wearing Leon Kay Gush." I couldn't help but return his excitement a little.

The journalist beamed, nodding approvingly. "Great choice! And Ms. Khama, you are a blooming sunflower in the marketing world. Congratulations on your nomination—I'm rooting for you! Mr. Mogorosi, the Golden Awards must feel like home to you. Any advice for your wife-to-be?"

Tsebo's eyes flashed with mischief. "I've told her everything she needs to know... at home," he replied, and I caught the flicker of disappointment on the journalist's face.

"Thank you for your time. Enjoy the rest of your evening," the journalist said, looking a bit deflated.

We thanked him and moved on, pausing to pose for the cameras. Tsebo wasn't thrilled, but he indulged me with a tight-lipped smile. After the photos, we were led into the grand hall. The venue was nothing short of spectacular—sophisticated, elegant, every detail polished to perfection. We took our seats, and I ordered a cocktail, while Tsebo opted for a whiskey.

The ceremony began with a captivating performance by Thee Legacy. Their smooth vocals and lively dance moves electrified the room, setting the perfect tone for the night. Soon after, the MC, a beautiful young woman named LaShanelle Smith-Brookes, took the stage. Her poise was magnetic, and her words stirred up the crowd's energy even further.

Eventually, she announced, "And now, to present the award for the Youngest Businesswoman of the Year, please welcome businesswoman and TV personality, Nicolette Shabangu!" A round of applause filled the room as Nicolette stepped up, beaming at the audience.

"Good evening, ladies and gentlemen," Nicolette said, her voice steady. "There's something incredible about seeing young women stand strong, claiming their space in the business world. Izimbokodo za ngempela! So, it's an honour to present the award for the Youngest Businesswoman of the Year. Here are your nominees…"

The room fell silent as the nominees were announced, each name flashing across the giant screen. My heart pounded as Tsebo squeezed my hand, a reassuring presence amid my nerves.

"Well," Nicolette said, building the suspense, "there you have it. It's a tough choice, but the Golden Award goes to… BUSINESSWOMAN & CEO OF NEW-AGE MARKETING INTELLECTS, MS. TLHALEFO KHAMA!!!"

The room erupted in cheers, and I felt myself drawn to my feet by the force of the moment. Tsebo hugged me, whispering, "Told you!" with a grin that finally cracked his usually stoic face. I made my way to the stage, the weight of the golden award in my hands grounding me. I took a deep breath before speaking.

"Wow. I don't even know what to say—thank you, everyone, who voted for me. To my family, friends, and especially my team at New-Age Marketing Intellects, this is ours. Thank you for all your hard work. To the incredible women nominated here tonight, we're all winners. Let's keep pushing forward. Remember, we are stronger than we think. Thank you!"

A loud cheer rose from the back. "Love you!" a woman shouted, and I laughed.

"Love you more!" I shouted back, sparking laughter and applause from the audience. As I looked out, I caught Tsebo in the crowd, clapping wildly and beaming—such a rare sight.

After a whirlwind of backstage photos and interviews, I returned to my seat beside Tsebo, who was clearly enjoying the night. The final awards wrapped up with Sho Madjozi performing, her energy pulling everyone to their feet.

The night was a perfect celebration, the cameras following us even as we slipped away to the hotel, still riding the high of the moment.

As soon as we reached our room, we changed into our after-party outfits. Tsebo looked effortlessly stylish in blue jeans, a black polo, and his favourite Nike kicks, with his silver Casio watch catching the light. I chose a short maroon velvet dress that hugged me in all the right places, paired with black heels and my engagement ring—the only accessory I needed.

"My love, I'm so proud of you," Tsebo said, pulling me close.

"Thank you, motho waka. Tonight, I'm getting pap drunk!" I laughed, already feeling the celebration in my veins.

We danced until morning, losing ourselves in the music and each other. Tsebo's dance moves took me by surprise; I'd never seen him let loose like this. We were in our own little world, a perfect night to remember.

* * * * * *

Monday morning came too soon, and I reluctantly dragged myself to the office, already dreading the end of such an amazing weekend. As I walked in, the building seemed eerily quiet.

"Surprise!" my team shouted, catching me off guard. They stood in the lobby, each holding a glass of champagne, their faces full of pride.

"Congratulations on your award, boss lady! You deserve it!" Themba said, handing me a glass.

"She does!" Everyone echoed, their smiles and cheers filling me with joy.

"Ncoah, thank you all so much," I said, feeling a surge of emotion. "This means everything to me. I wouldn't be here without each one of you."

They all raised their glasses, cheering, "To the future!" before heading back to their desks. Themba lingered, watching me with a knowing smile.

"Sana! You looked like a goddess on Saturday," he said, a bit starstruck. "I was glued to the TV!"

"Thanks, chomi," I laughed. "I really had an amazing time."

Before we could chat more, Pearl, the receptionist, walked in with a delivery. "Ma'am, there's someone here for you," she said.

I signed for the package, and when I opened it, I found a glittering snow globe with a photo of me inside. Inside the box was a note:

TO THE MOST WONDERFUL SISTER IN THE WORLD, I LOVE AND MISS YOU. CONGRATS ON YOUR ACHIEVEMENT, CONTINUE MAKING US PROUD. —TLHALI JUNIOR

I felt a warmth spread through me. My little sister hadn't forgotten after all. Themba eyed the snow globe with a sly grin.

"Ndiphe yona. I'll put my pic with Kagiso in it," he teased.

"Ha, don't get ideas!" I replied, laughing.

He rolled his eyes dramatically, then left my office. I picked up my phone and dialled my sister, who picked up almost immediately.

"If it isn't the best baby sis in the world!" I said.

"And if it isn't the best big sis!" she laughed back.

"Thank you for the gift, Botlhale. It's beautiful."

"Congrats on your award," she replied warmly. "You looked amazing, by the way."

I smiled, my heart full. "Thanks, sis. How's school?"

"It's tiring, but I'm managing," she said.

"Hang in there. Remember, you're stronger than you think," I told her, my words coming full circle.

As I ended the call, I sat back, taking in the moment. Winning the Golden Award was a reminder that my hard work mattered—that I was seen, valued, and celebrated. The weekend's joy lingered with me, a gentle balm to life's more challenging moments. For once, I allowed myself to savour happiness fully, a rare but treasured story of my life.

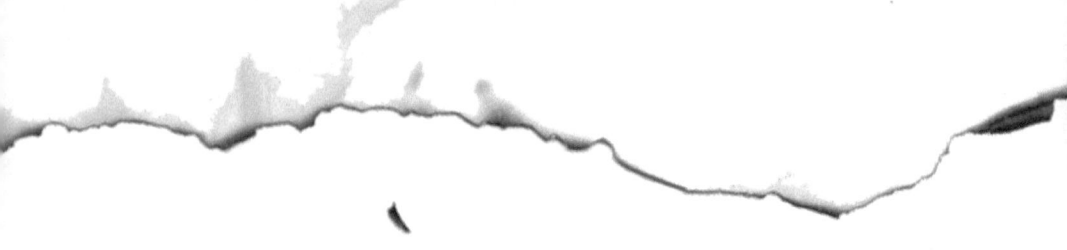

CHAPTER THIRTEEN

The early morning chill weighed on me as I sat, lost in thought. The past three months since the awards had felt like a blur. A cleansing ceremony for Botlhale and me had been done, but today I was about to face a different kind of cleansing. Today, I would confront my uncle.

The idea of it filled me with dread. My heart felt heavy, my nerves unsettled. I hadn't seen him in almost a decade—not since my father's funeral. Last I knew, he lived alone with his daughter, Reneilwe. She was four years older than me, and we never really got along. Now, I didn't know what to expect from him or if I'd even have the courage to face him.

"You sure you don't want me to go with you? Anything could happen," Tsebo said, breaking into my thoughts.

"I know," I replied. "But I need to do this alone. I'll be safe, my love."

"No, Tlhalefo. We can't risk it. I wouldn't forgive myself if anything happened to you. Besides, you don't have to go through this alone."

I tried to object, but Tsebo cut me off, saying, "No. I'm going with you, and that's that."

Eventually, I relented. "Alright. Let's go."

The drive felt endless. When we finally arrived in Rustenburg, we parked in front of my uncle's gate. Nothing had changed: the rusty gate, the familiar four-roomed house with chipped lime paint on the walls, and the broken handle on the door. I swallowed hard, feeling my heart hammer in my chest.

"You good?" Tsebo asked, giving me a reassuring look.

"Yes." I took a deep breath. "Let's go."

We walked to the door, and Tsebo knocked. Silence. He knocked again, harder this time.

A gruff, irritated voice barked from inside. "Argh fokof maan ketla!!"

It was him. My heart raced, but I clenched my fists and stayed firm. After what felt like forever, the door opened, revealing the familiar figure of my uncle. He looked the same, with a few more grey hairs, a large, untucked shirt, and a sour expression under his old glasses.

"Wena? What do you want here?" he sneered.

I opened my mouth to speak, but nothing came out. Tsebo stepped in. "She wants to talk to you," he said firmly.

"E le gore o mang o tlo nna makgakga fa?!" my uncle shot back.

"That doesn't matter. We want to talk to you, and we will." With that, Tsebo pushed him aside, taking my hand as we stepped inside. We sat down on the worn-out couches. My uncle slowly followed, looking at me with a hint of disdain.

"Tlhalefo. You're still alive," he remarked with a mocking grin.

I swallowed, feeling a surge of anger. "Why?" I finally managed to say, looking him dead in the eye.

"Wa reng?" he asked, his face blank.

"Why did you kill my father?"

He rolled his eyes. "Argh maan. You're still on about that? That's all in the past."

191

I felt the anger boil over. "Don't you dare tell me it's all in the past!" My voice was shaking. "That day changed my entire life! And to make things worse, you wanted to kill me too!"

He chuckled darkly. "Eyy mosetsana! You saw what happened. Your father promised me money but then changed his mind. I didn't kill him; his empty promises did."

I could feel the sting of tears in my eyes, but I pushed them down. "Oh, please. My father did everything for you and your daughter! He was tired of you. You were nothing but a leech, bleeding him dry."

My uncle scoffed, crossing his arms. "Well, maybe he shouldn't have made empty promises! I made a big bet that day, and because of your father, I lost it all. I lost my temper—it's normal. I'm only human. And you... you've grown into a disrespectful tramp."

"Hey! Watch it!" Tsebo's voice sliced through the tension. I looked over to see him pointing a gun at my uncle. Shock crossed my uncle's face, but I felt a dark satisfaction seeing him cower.

"You are going to apologise to her," Tsebo said, calm but menacing. "Not just for the insults, but for everything you put her through."

"Tsebo, put the gun down," I said softly, placing my hand on his arm. "We're not like him."

Tsebo hesitated, then lowered the gun. My uncle's face contorted with a mixture of fear and anger. He was about to say something when I heard a familiar, obnoxious laugh outside. My cousin, Reneilwe, sauntered into the room.

"Tlhali! Cuzzy!" She squealed, running over to hug me. She looked worn down, with a short denim skirt, a faded pink crop top, and a head of messy hair. "And who is this sexy hunk?" she added, eyeing Tsebo up and down.

"Aii, ska tlo phapha," I muttered, rolling my eyes. Tsebo just shook his head, amused.

My uncle grumbled under his breath, regaining his composure. "I'm not apologising for anything. It was never my fault, and it won't be now."

"Molato ga o bole," I said sharply, my voice cold.

He just laughed, shrugging. "Ha! You think those courts of yours will do anything? Ba ka se mpone molato."

"Who said I was planning on going to the courts?" I shot back, meeting his gaze with fire in my eyes. "But I *will* make you pay."

Tsebo took my hand and stood, tugging me gently. "We're wasting our time here."

We walked toward the door, my uncle's mocking laughter echoing behind us. As we reached the car, I finally broke down, burying my face in my hands.

"But... why? Why does it always have to be me?" I whispered, feeling the weight of everything crash down.

Tsebo pulled me into his arms. "Don't worry, my love. You will get justice. One way or another."

As we sat in the car, preparing to leave, Reneilwe appeared at my window, tapping eagerly.

"Hey! Is this your car? Give me your number so we can hang out sometime!" she chirped, giving me a big grin.

With a sigh, I took her phone and punched in my number. "Bye. I'll wait for your call. Tsebo, let's go."

Later that day, I found myself at home, quietly preparing lunch. I hadn't even realised Tsebo had left his phone on the counter, but it buzzed several times with messages from unknown numbers. I resisted the urge to look, but eventually, curiosity won out. As I skimmed the messages, my heart sank. Diamonds, copper, missing crates of weapons, dealings in the DRC—his life was far more dangerous than I'd realised.

> *Boss. We got the stuff. Diamonds complete. Copper complete. Just one crate of weapons missing.*

> *Leaving DRC. It's about to get messy. The soldiers spotted us earlier on but we managed to get out of their way. What are we supposed to do about the missing crate?*

> *Mabuza: Mogorosi. My order arrived. Pure diamonds, as always. I'll deposit the rest of the money first thing tomorrow morning. Always a pleasure doing business with you.*

> *Boss?*

> *Please hold on to our cocaine order at your hardware till further notice. The police are onto me. My house got raided two days back. Call me as soon as you get this.*

> *Sir, the Japanese requested a meeting with you on Tuesday next week. Apparently, they want to extend their contract with our farm. Can I confirm?*

Just as I was trying to make sense of it, Tsebo entered the kitchen, eyeing his phone on the counter.

"Do you know where I might've put my phone?" he asked casually.

"Nope. Haven't seen it," I lied, trying to hide my unease. He searched for it all around the lounge and kitchen, til he spotted it on the counter, right next to the cabbage I was chopping. I could feel his eyes on me but I just maintained mine on my cooking, I could hear him mumbling something as he scanned through the texts.

After a quiet lunch, he paced around the house, packing a bag. "I'll be gone for a few days," he said, his voice flat.

"Where are you going?" I pressed, feeling the familiar stirrings of panic.

"Somewhere," he replied curtly.

"Tsebo, that's not an answer. Where's 'somewhere'? And what's a few days?"

He sighed, looking frustrated. "Argh maan, I said I'll be back. I have something to take care of. Will you give me a hug, kgotsa jang?"

Knowing it was pointless to argue with him, I stood up and wrapped my arms around him. His embrace felt colder than usual, distant.

"Rose is coming. She'll be with you. I've also upgraded security, so don't be shocked when you see a lot of men in the compound," he informed me, his face unreadable.

"Promise me that you'll come back," I whispered, trying to catch his gaze.

He looked at me, his eyes dark and unreadable, then said, "I love you. Goodbye," before heading to the garage. I watched him leave, a gnawing worry twisting in my gut.

As soon as I heard the car start, I regretted ever opening those messages. I returned to the bedroom, helplessly replaying the last few minutes. I thought of calling him, but when I looked around, I saw his phone lying on the bed. He'd left without it. What was I supposed to do now?

Just then, I heard a voice from downstairs. "Hello? Tlhali?"

It was Rose. I went to meet her, hoping she'd know something that would calm me down.

"Hey, girl. Didn't think you'd get here so fast," I said as we hugged.

"Well, I didn't have much choice. Abuti told me to rush over because he's going away for a few days. Any idea what that's about?" Rose asked, her voice tinged with concern.

"Nothing at all. I was hoping you could enlighten me. I'm scared," I admitted, unable to mask my anxiety.

Rose gave me a sympathetic look. "I thought you'd be used to this by now."

"What do you mean?"

"Tlhali, this is the life he lives. There are times he just disappears, then comes back as if nothing happened. He's always been secretive, even growing up. I'm worried too, but I've learnt to accept it. All we can do is pray that he comes back safe, whenever that may be."

Her words only intensified my fear. "Wait. What do you mean, 'whenever that may be'?"

"He once disappeared for two full months, Tlhali."

"What?! I just hope that doesn't happen again!"

Rose shrugged, heading to the fridge. "Hope so too. Anyway, anything to snack on?"

I nodded, trying to gather myself. "There are nuggets and foldovers in the microwave."

She flashed me a grin. "Mmh... yummy!"

We chatted as she ate, her cheerful updates on her clothing brand and her boyfriend offering a temporary distraction from the worry gnawing at me.

The next morning, I tried to distract myself by following through on plans to take my cousin Reneilwe out. I arrived to pick her up, and as soon as she hopped into the car, her chatty, energetic presence filled the silence. Despite the awkwardness between us, I was grateful for her company.

By the time we reached Emperor's Palace and made it to the movies, Reneilwe's endless chatter and the silly comedy we watched had finally eased some of the tension I'd been holding onto since the day before. When the movie ended, we shared a few laughs about the characters and agreed it had been a solid pick.

Feeling somewhat lighter, I suggested, "Let's go to the spa? I could use some pampering."

She laughed, her voice bright. "Yes, please! I've always wanted to go to a spa. Money just never seemed to agree with my dreams."

The spa was everything I'd hoped for—a much-needed break from reality. For a while, I let myself sink into the peacefulness of the moment, pretending that my world wasn't on the brink of collapsing. But as we settled into the comfortable quiet, I felt a new determination rise within me. Whatever Tsebo was involved in, I'd be ready for whatever came next.

"Aren't you working? What's happening?" I asked, noticing the slight tension on Rene's face.

"I'll tell you everything during dinner," she replied, brushing it off with a faint smile that hinted at a story much longer than I had bargained for. I could feel it was going to be one of those conversations that unearth everything hidden under the surface. Rene was always the one with big dreams. What could have changed?

"Okay. We're here. Girl, let's get pampered!" I nudged her, trying to lighten the mood.

"Haha, let us!" she chuckled, her eyes lighting up as we walked into the spa, welcomed by a kind Chinese woman who led us into a room where we changed out of our clothes. The stress melted away as the gentle hands of the masseuse worked over my tired muscles. It was only then that I realised how much I had been carrying—emotionally, physically, mentally. All of it, it seemed, was catching up to me.

The masseuse commented, "Geez, ma'am. You were so tense. Wow."

"Yeah, I know, right?" I laughed, feeling lighter with each touch.

Rene turned to me with her usual candidness. "Hau Tlhali! How can you be so tense and have money? Nnyaa tlhe wena!"

"Rene," I replied, shaking my head, "not everything is about money. And when you say I have money, did you see it?"

"It's obvious," she continued without missing a beat. "I mean, I saw your man. I saw the car you drive, a whole Velar! And the clothes you wear. That's evidence enough."

This girl! I had almost forgotten how blunt she could be. "Alright, Reneilwe, can I just enjoy my massage in peace now?"

"And from today onwards, make sure you go to a spa at least twice a month," she declared.

Ignoring her, I let myself sink deeper into the relaxation, the weight of everything momentarily lifting. But as I lay there, I couldn't ignore a few scars I noticed on Rene's arms and legs. She hid them well, but something in her story still lingered unspoken. We moved on to manicures and pedicures after a rejuvenating facial, and when we left the spa hours later, I couldn't believe it was already 5:13 p.m.

"Cuzzy! I feel like a brand-new person! So refreshed and at peace," Rene gushed as we stepped outside.

"Same here. That was just what I needed," I agreed.

She glanced at me. "I'm starving. Let's go eat dinner. It's been ages since I ate at a restaurant."

"Which restaurant do you have in mind?" I asked, already suspecting she had a grand idea in mind.

After a few back-and-forth suggestions, we settled on Braza, a place we both knew would deliver both good food and the alcohol Rene would no doubt want. As we walked into Braza and got seated, I watched her take selfies and videos on my phone. She was in her element, enjoying every bit of the experience.

The food arrived, and I couldn't resist asking the question that had been on my mind. "Rene, what happened? Why do you want to be close to me now? We didn't exactly get along growing up."

She looked down for a moment before meeting my eyes. "Tlhali, I know I wasn't the best cousin to you. I didn't treat you well, and I was...disrespectful, especially to Rangwane. I regret it all. Life... life hasn't been kind to me."

I simply nodded, waiting as she found the words to continue. I could see the weight of her past settle on her shoulders, adding years to her young face.

Our main courses arrived just as Rene seemed ready to speak again. "I'm a single mother now," she said quietly. "I have one child, Nobuhle. She's fourteen, in Grade 7. Her father...he was abusive. I stayed with him for so long because he provided for us, but it was terrible, Tlhali. He...he would chase me outside, sometimes naked, strangle me...all in front of my child."

I listened, absorbing her words, the pain embedded in every syllable. "Rene, I... I'm so sorry."

She gave a weak smile, but her eyes betrayed the trauma. "I have to support my father too. He made me drop out in Matric, said a girl's place was at home. Since then, I've been...doing what I can to survive. Sometimes I go to the taverns. Sometimes I..." Her voice broke. "Some of the men, they hit me, for the smallest things."

She looked away, lost in thoughts too painful to voice aloud. I placed my hand over hers. "Where is Buhle now?" I asked softly. "She lives with her grandmother, her father's mother. But things are...bad." She trailed off.

We sat in silence for a moment, letting the noise of the restaurant fill the spaces between us. "I can help," I said finally, the decision firm. "I can pay for Buhle's education. And... I'll help you find a place to stay, a job. We can figure it out together."

Her eyes filled with tears. "You'd do that for me?"

I nodded. "Yes. You can take over with paying for her school once you're able to."

Her shoulders relaxed, and a small, hopeful smile returned to her face. For the first time, I saw the cousin I used to know beneath all the scars and the pain.

After dinner, I dropped Rene at her place, and as I drove home, thoughts of her weighed heavily on me. I found Rose at home, binge-watching cartoons. She glanced up with a grin. "Finally! The glamour girl is back!"

Laughing, I joined her, my heart a little lighter knowing I had been there for Rene.

Days passed, and I busied myself, managing to secure Rene an interview as a cleaner at a student residence where Themba's aunt works. It wasn't much, but it was a start. At home, Rose threw herself into preparing for her clothing line launch, but despite the progress, Tsebo's absence hung over us like a shadow.

One night, as Rose and I watched TV, I turned to her. "Sis, are you really, okay?"

She glanced away, her defences crumbling. "No, I'm not. I'm scared, frustrated… I don't even know if my brother is alive," she said, tears filling her eyes. I wrapped her in a hug, feeling her pain echoing through me.

"I know. But he'll come back. He always does," I whispered, both of us clinging to the fragile hope.

That night, I found it hard to sleep, memories and worries mingling in the silence. I tried to clear my mind, to relax, but just as I was about to drift off, my phone rang. A number I didn't recognise.

"Hello?" I answered.

"Please open up for me." The voice was calm, familiar.

"Tsebo?" I whispered, my heart racing.

"Yes. Please, open the door." Throwing the phone down, I raced downstairs. There he was, standing in the doorway.

"My love," he said, but I held back, feeling the anger, the hurt.

Without a word, I leave the door open, go to my bedroom and take my phone and I go and sleep in the guest bedroom. I can hear the door of our bedroom shutting, I take it he has gone to sleep. Few minutes later, he comes knocking in the guest bedroom. I don't respond. I don't have time for his lies and games. He opens the door and comes in. He sits on top of the bed, I turn my back on him and look the other side. I don't want to lie, when I heard his voice on the phone, a sigh of relief escaped from my body. At least now I know that he's alive. But I'm still angry at him.

Tsebo: "Allow me to explain.".

Me: "Ke batla go robala."

Tsebo: "Please. I'll explain everything. I won't even leave a single detail out."

Me: "Will explaining everything make up for all the time you were gone?! Will it make up for leaving Rose and me alone?! Will it make up for all the nights we stayed up not knowing what to expect?! Will it make up for all the misery you put us through for the past month?!" I'm now sitting up straight spitting fire. I am not able to maintain my calmness at all. He just looks down with his hands on his head and lets out a deep sigh.

Me: "Answer me! I'm talking to you!" At this point, I'm beyond frustrated!

Tsebo: "No. No, explaining everything won't make up for anything. But it's the least I can do. Please, Tlhalefo."

Me: "Please ya eng, Tsebo?! Or were you with the love of your life wherever you were, and you didn't want little irritating Tlhalefo to disturb your quality time?! Is that what was happening?"

Like usual, my tears betray me. I didn't want to cry. I hate being weak! He looks at me, shocked as ever.

Tsebo: "What?! How can you think that of me? You know I can never cheat on you, Tlhalefo. Never in a million years!"

Me: "At this point, I don't know what to believe."

Tsebo: "Anything but that, please." I just fold my arms and look away.

Tsebo: "I was in the DRC. I had to sort out some stuff. It was urgent."

Me: "An entire month?! An entire month, Tsebo?!"

Tsebo: "I was arrested. Things didn't really go according to plan. I was arrested for two weeks, but I got out, you know your man mos." He says attempting to cheer me up. I don't have time for that.

Me: "How did you get out?"

Tsebo: "I know a few soldiers and the captain of the police, so I had to pull off some strings. And I eventually got what I went there for. A crate of guns

202

and swords was missing from my delivery, so I had to get it. It's the crate I was carrying when I got here."

Me: "Geez. All of this for guns?"

Tsebo: "They are worth a fortune, my love. And I know it was stupid and selfish of me to go without telling you anything and not even staying in contact with you. I'm sorry."

Me: "Damn right it was stupid of you."

Tsebo: "And I accept that. I'm sorry. O kae Rose?".

Me: "In her room."

Tsebo: "I missed you." He thinks he's my buddy now.

Me: "Okay. Please close the door on your way out."

Tsebo: "But…"

Me: "Goodnight, Tsebo." He goes out and closes the door. Good. Thank God he's safe.

I'm sitting in a colourful garden on my own wearing a black dress. I'm able to see him, finally. He hasn't changed one bit, just a touch of grey hairs and beard here and there. He comes to sit next to me, wearing purely white clothes. He gives me white roses; they have blood stains on them. "pelo ya go e tsejwa ke wena le ramasedi wa go, mosetsana wame. Kgotso ya go e tsejwa ke wena. Botshelo le bokamoso ba go, bo ka matsogong a go, mosetsana wame. Moya wame o tsebile kgotso ka ntlha ya go. O intirile motlotlo, gontse. Tsohle ke di tlogelela matsogong a go. Tlotla le ramasedi wa go nako tsohle. O mofenyi, mosetsana wame".

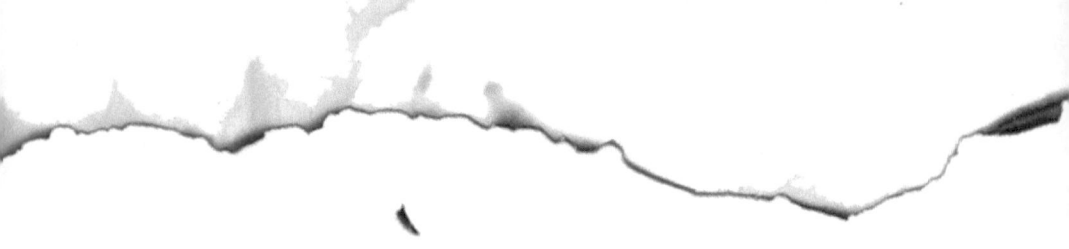

CHAPTER FOURTEEN

It had been two months since Tsebo came back, tail between his legs, from his AWOL disappearance. We weren't going to let him off easily. Silent treatments, one-word replies, cold shoulders—we gave him every weapon in our arsenal of resentment. Rose had left her place the day after he showed up, refusing to answer any of his calls or texts. She hadn't even invited him to her clothing line launch. And yet, typical of him, he still showed up.

Meanwhile, I pored myself into work and even took a weekend to visit Botlhale. At home, I slept in the guest bedroom for an entire month, but, as if that could faze him, Tsebo moved himself in there with me. All this suffering? It served him right. His selfishness had cost him dearly. But as the days wore on, my anger faded, turning into something close to pity. It wasn't funny anymore to see him so desperate for forgiveness. His apologies became a constant, so sincere that, eventually, Rose and I gave in. He promised, with all the fervour of a man making a final stand, to stop disappearing without explanation, to let me in on every detail that could endanger him or us. But I knew he was lying. His secrets were too deep, too dark. Love, after all, comes with its own sacrifices.

I was still mulling over his promises, seated at a café, when the anxiety hit. I had no idea why they'd called me here after so many years. Had they even remembered me? Every second that ticked by felt heavier than the last. And then, at last, I looked up. There, just beyond the café entrance, stood the twins—Uncle Rearabilwe and Uncle Kearabetswe. Age had changed them, but not their sameness: tall and slightly stooped, heads crowned with white hair, faces traced with white beards. They both have walking sticks. One wore a grey suit, the other a brown one.

They scanned the café, searching, until the one in brown spotted me. My heart stammered. He smiled. I knew immediately it was Uncle Rea, the warm one, the easy-going one. He pointed in my direction, nudging his brother. Uncle Kea glanced over, face still as stern as stone. I froze, unsure whether to wave, to smile, to stand. My nerves were a mess.

"Mosetsana! A ke wena motho o?!" Uncle Rea's voice was deep, familiar. I nodded, managing a small smile.

"Eya, Ramogolo. Ke nna." He pulled me into a tight hug, one that felt like a bridge back to my childhood, warm and comforting.

"Lady," Uncle Kea greeted, extending his hand. I took it. He was respectful, as he had always been and his handshake firm.

We sat down, and they ordered coffee and muffins, while I opted for a calming chamomile tea.

"You've grown," Uncle Kea noted after a beat of silence. He had softened, just a little, his voice mellow with age.

"Yes. Ke godile, ramogolo," I replied, chuckling nervously.

"Wa mmona mara? Ke gore o kgona le go buwa sekgowa. Yah maan!" Uncle Rea quipped, laughing at his own joke, and I couldn't help but join him.

Once the laughter died down, Uncle Kea's voice cut through the atmosphere, all business. "We received the letter. Are you ready to take such a big step?"

The letter? My heart missed a beat. "Uh... Ramogolo, I'm sorry, but you've lost me. What letter?"

He sighed, looking almost regretful for a moment. "The letter your fiancé wrote to us, asking for your hand in marriage. I take it this is the first time you're hearing of this?" His serious face didn't soften for a second.

"Oh," I said, taken aback. "He's already sent it?" I wasn't expecting this at all. "I didn't know, but we are engaged," I added, still reeling from the shock. Traditional customs weren't exactly my area of expertise.

Uncle Rea leaned in with a knowing smile. "A fa o go tshwere sentle?"

"Yes, Ramogolo. I'm happy with him," I reassured, blushing slightly.

"Good. But we need to meet with him before we start any negotiations," Uncle Kea insisted.

"Of course, I'll arrange it," I said, still trying to wrap my head around the entire situation.

"No, we'll handle that. We wanted to hear from you first, make sure you're happy," Uncle Kea asserted, the matter settled in his eyes.

My mind raced with questions I knew were best left unspoken, but curiosity won. "Rakgadi Gontse ene?" I asked before I could stop myself.

Uncle Kea's face turned hard. "She died long ago. Alcohol poisoning," he answered curtly. His tone warned me to drop the subject, but I couldn't help myself.

"And your brother?"

"Still alive," he replied dismissively. "But he doesn't matter."

I sipped my tea quietly, trying to gather myself. They reminded me so much of my father, especially Uncle Rea. My heart ached with his absence; with all the losses I'd felt.

Tsebo had been saying he'd send the letter, yet I hadn't imagined it would all unfold this soon. The conversation eventually wound down, leaving only

Uncle Rea to fill the silence with his cheerful banter. I couldn't wait to wrap up, find an excuse to leave, and head to work.

"Bagolo, it was great *meeting* up with you. I have to get to work," I finally said, relieved to break free.

"Where do you work?" Uncle Kea asked with a curious tilt.

"At a marketing agency," I replied, standing. "Lo tla sala sentle," I added, waving goodbye.

"Goodbye," they said in unison, and with a sigh of relief, I left the café and headed to work.

Once I arrived, Themba barely looked up from his computer. "Your to-do list is on your desk, and a delivery came in for you. I signed for it," he muttered, not a hint of his usual warmth.

"E tswa ko mang?" I asked.

"I didn't check," he said curtly.

My heart sank a little at his coldness. "Themba, a o siame?" I asked gently, hoping he'd open up.

After a pause, he looked at me, his face dark. "Kagiso's father found out he's gay. Now he's threatening to take everything and kick him out of the family business."

"Oh no, chomi. Where is he now?" I asked, worry tightening my throat.

"He's at my place. Doesn't want to go outside," he said.

"Go and be with him. I'll manage here," I urged.

He looked at me, grateful. "Thank you so much, Tlhali."

I hugged him tightly. "Everything will be alright, chomi."

Later, I walked into my office, greeted by a bouquet of red and white roses and a box of chocolates. The note, in Tsebo's familiar handwriting, read:

"To the most beautiful fiancé in the whole world. I just wanted to remind you how much you mean to me. You are loved, Mme Mogorosi."

I couldn't help but smile, cheeks warm with a deep flush. I dialled his number immediately.

"My babbbbyyyy!" I gushed when he picked up.

"Haha, my loooooove!" he replied, his laughter infectious.

"I got the flowers and chocolates! What are you doing to me!?"

He laughed again. "You know I'll never lose my touch."

The rest of the day was filled with that warm feeling of his affection.

By the time I got home, it was 7:30 p.m, and the aroma of a home-cooked meal greeted me. Tsebo met me at the door, apron on, his arms ready for a hug.

"Welcome home, my love," he murmured, kissing me softly.

I melted into him, forgetting the doubts, the secrets, the fears. Right now, it was just us, laughter filling the kitchen and the warmth of his embrace wrapping around me like a shield. For now, I'd leave the questions for another day.

Me: "You send me roses at work and now I find you cooking. What are you feeling guilty about, Mogorosi?" You can't blame me for being suspicious.

Tsebo: "Can't I spoil my lady without anybody accusing me of anything?" I can see he's getting really annoyed.

Me: "Mmmhh... smells good. What did you cook?"

Tsebo: "Greek salad, mashed potatoes, and fried pork."

Me: "Smells nice! I can't wait to dig in!"

"And I can't wait to eat my dessert…" He says while squeezing my bum… butterflies in my stomach!!

Me: "Ohhh! You will enjoy every second of it!"

Tsebo: "Let's take this to the bedroom." He looks at me with those seductive eyes. I can't resist…

Me: "I want to eat my food nna Mogorosi."

Tsebo: "After dinner it is then, besides, I wouldn't want my effort to go to waste." He takes my laptop bag, takes off my blazer and puts them on the couch then he comes and opens the chair for me so that I can get seated.

Tsebo: "Love of my life, dinner is served. Prepared by yours truly." I can't help but laugh.

Me: "You should consider being a waiter, you know." I say this and wink at him. He laughs out loud.

Tsebo: "It is in one of my options, my love. Wine, madam?"

"Yes please." I'm even surprised he offered me alcohol. The minute I dig in, I'm taken to a world of whatchamacallit!!!

Me: "Baby! This is… wow!" I mean it.

Tsebo: "I told you never to underestimate me." We dine, conversate and laugh together. I feel so complete when I'm with this guy. I've never felt so comfortable with anyone. I don't think I'll ever love anyone the way I love this man right here. Everything comes to a stop when I'm with him.

"Let me go wash the dishes." I say as I stand up. Tsebo stands up, picks me up and he carries me up the stairs. He throws me on top of the bed, gets on top of me and kisses me passionately. I immediately feel hot.

"I've been waiting for this moment all day long." He says while taking breaks during the kiss, breathing heavily. He takes my dress off, rips off my underwear. I take off his shirt and pants. He's still on top of me, we are both naked. His body feels warm. I feel protected. I'm in a safe place. He breathes on my neck and inserts his manhood deep inside of me. I can feel the butterflies playing around in my stomach. I can feel my heart beating faster. My mind is going in circles. I can feel my thighs tightening. My toes curling. My womanly juices flowing inside my beautiful, majestic temple. I'm as wet as a waterfall. His strokes take me to neverland. I find myself screaming and moaning words I never even thought existed in this world we are living in. One hand on my waist, another tightly holding my hair, he groans on top of me like a wild animal none ever knew existed. I can never get used to him. I can never get used to this feeling. I always find myself lost in a secret world of unknown pleasure...

* * * * * *

I open my eyes and find myself wrapped in the arms of the love of my life. He's looking at me with those hazel brown eyes that I get lost in every second of my being.

"Morning, beautiful." He says in that husky, erotic voice of his. Once again, I lose myself. I'm blushing. I can't help but bury my face in his beloved chest. He laughs.

"What a night that was! Can never get enough of you." - Tsebo. I'm honestly at a loss for words. My cheeks keep betraying me. I'm a hundred percent sure they are red as hell right now. He's not even moving his eyes away from me.

Me: "Is that why you've been communicating with my uncles behind my back?" He laughs out loud. It doesn't even shock me anymore. I've gotten used to and accepted his mental condition.

Tsebo: "My love. You don't need to know every little thing I do." He caresses my back with his fingers. Heaven knows I'm trying so hard to look as normal as possible.

Me: "Even if it involves me?"

Tsbeo: "Yes, my love. Even if it involves you. Wa se itsi setso sa rone."

Me: "Ha.a Mogorosi. As your wife-to-be, you should update me on each and every detail. And I mean it." I'm willing to stand my ground today. He sighs. He even has the nerve to roll his eyes at me!

Tsebo: "Okay. I'm meeting with your uncles today."

Me: "Both of them?"

Tsebo: "All three of them."

Me: "Argh. So that bastard will be there."

Tsebo: "Worry not. I can handle him. It's your other uncle I'm worried about. He sounded a bit tense on the phone. Are they both like that?"

Me: "Ramogolo Kearabetswe. O ntse yalo. They are way different. Ramogolo Rearabilwe o siame. To be honest, I'm also scared of Ramogolo Kea, I've always been scared of him."

Tsebo: "I'm sure I can also handle him."

Me: "Aren't you scared? Anxious?"

Tsebi: "No." Ne nka makala. He never admits to being scared or anything like that. But I know that deep down, he is a little scared. He is human, after all.

Me: "Mmh. If you say so..."

211

"Ebile let me start getting ready. The meeting is only in a few hours." He says as he gets out of bed.

Me: "I'll start on breakfast then."

Tsebo: "Cool."

While Tsebo is getting ready, I decide to call Rene. Maybe she knows something about the meeting. Actually, there's no way Rene can never know about the meeting, o rata dikgang motho o!

Rene: "My sugar pie pie!"

Me: "Hahaha Dumela Reneilwe. How are you?"

Rene: "Ke siame nnake. Plus our new place is treating us well and I've even made some friends at work."

Me: "Mmh. I'm glad you are happy. But be careful about 'friends' at work, it might not even end well. There's always politics where those people are involved. Anyway, Tsebo is meeting le bo Ramogolo kgompieno. Do you know anything about that?" Crossing fingers…

Rene: "Oh thanks for the tip. Yeah I know about the meeting. That's why I'm on my way home. Papa said I must be there to host. Ga o itsi ke tenegile gore!"

Me: "Oh. So meeting o ko geno?" I wasn't expecting this.

Rene: "Yeahp. I'm so lazy. I wish the day could end already. I'm not in the mood for papa le ramogolo Kea. Tsebo le ramogolo Rea are better, I can even host them the whole day!" She says then laughs. That was weird. But I'll let it slide.

Me: "Mmh. Bona ha, you'll update me akere? I don't know what to expect. Wa ba itsi bo ramogolo ba gago."

Rene: "Yeah sure. Worry not. I got your back, cuzzy!"

Me: "Sure. Bye."

Rene: "Bye bye sweet thingy."

I hang up, wear my gown then head to the kitchen to make breakfast. Nothing hectic, just eggs, bacon, cheese, toasted bread and orange juice. Tsebo comes down just on time because I've just finished setting the table. He's wearing brown cargo shorts and a black golfer with black kicks. That German cut of his makes him even fresher. He looks so yummy.

"Smells nice!" He says as he comes down the stairs.

"Right on time! Anyway, I'm going to shower. Enjoy your breakfast." I say as I move up the stairs.

"Hau. You're not joining me for breakfast?" He says as he pulls me closer to him by my waist and gives me a deep kiss.

Me: "Nope. I also wanna feel fresh."

Tsebo: "Whatever…" spanking me on my bum. I burst into laughter.

I go to the bedroom, make the bed, and choose my outfit for the day. Today I'm rocking my red boob-tube maxi dress with black sandals. I go into the shower, and have the time of my life while singing, screaming, rather, Celine Dion's 'Love Doesn't Ask Why.'

"LOVE DOESN'T ASK WHY

IT SPEAKS FROM THE HEART AND NEVER EXPLAINS

DON'T YOU KNOW THAT LOVE DOESN'T THINK TWICE

IT CAN COME ALL AT ONCE OR WHISPER FROM A DISTANCE

*DON'T ASK ME IF THIS FEELING IS RIGHT OR WRONG IT
DOESN'T HAVE TO MAKE MUCH SENSE*

IT JUST HAS TO BE THIS STRONG

*'CAUSE WHEN YOU ARE IN MY ARMS I UNDERSTAND WE DON'T
TRY TO HAVE A VOICE*

WHEN OUR HEARTS MAKE THE CHOICES

THERE'S NO PLAN

IT'S IN OUR HANDS"

After a few good minutes, I'm out of the shower, applying my lotion and getting dressed. I look hella cute! I've plaited my hair in a plain straight back hairstyle with blonde hairpiece. I head downstairs only to find Tsebo preparing to leave.

Tsebo: "Baby. Were you singing in the shower?"

Me: "Yah. Why?"

Tsebo: "Yoh. I was even scared to enter our bedroom. I thought there was a goat dying."

"Wa thoma akere." I'm irritated by this stupid comment of his. He laughs out loud. Mxm!

Tsebo: "Askies my love."

Me: "Just go already."

Tsebo: "Suna papa?"

I throw the dishwashing cloth at him. He gives up and heads to the door.

Tsebo: "Bye." I keep quiet and eat my breakfast. I don't have time for nonsense.

214

I spend most of my day lazying around the house and I've just started with the book Ayibongwe, Botlhale's girlfriend, bought me. It's a novel by my favourite author, Chimamanda Ngozi Adichie titled *Half of a Yellow Sun.'* I've just started reading it and I'm already hooked! There's just something about African Literature. It doesn't only captivate your mind, but also captivates all of your senses, your body, and your soul. In simple terms, it hijacks all of your being. I believe that those African authors, especially women, are the voice of the unheard and voiceless. They are the ones who were courageous enough to break not only the stigma against Africa but also the stigma questioning the capabilities of women. They are the ones who are brave enough to demolish the "single story" people all over the world have about this beautiful continent of ours.

It's been hours since Tsebo left, and I haven't heard anything from Rene. I call her and it goes to voicemail. I send her a Whatsapp text message.

> *What's going on?*

> *Tsohle di apere tshiamo.*

> *So why aren't you updating me, as promised earlier on?*

> *Ke busy. Talk later.*

And just like that, she's offline. I wonder what's keeping her so busy that she can't even sit down and focus on her phone. It's not like she's part of the meeting. Her job is just to make beverages and snacks and that's it mos. But keh, ke tla reng? It's already 6:00 p.m so I decide to start on supper. As soon as I put the rice on the stove, Tsebo enters.

"Finally! Go neng!" I say as I hug him.

215

Tsebo: "I know right."

Me: "How did it go?"

Tsebo: "It was hectic at first but things eased up as time went by. Your uncles are pretty cool waitsi. You know who the problem is."

Me: "That old bastard. What did he do?"

Tsebo: "He just made things quite difficult for me, like I'm in some sort of interview or something. Even let everyone know that I once came with a gun to his house and pointed it at him. Acted like the innocent party all the damn time."

Me: "Bathong. What happened then?" I'm actually not surprised by that man's behaviour, I expected him to act like the bastard that he is.

Tsebo: "I sorted it out."

Me: "Mmh."

He goes down to sit on the couch, switches the TV on and goes to the rugby channel. I join him.

Me: "As long as everything went well, then. When are the negotiations starting?"

Tsebo: "We decided on the 24th of August, this month. I just have to inform bo Radebe and Ntate Masenya, some man I work with, I asked him to be part of the negotiations."

Me: "That's like... two weeks from now. That was quick."

Tsebo: "Yebo my baby."

Tsebo: "Eyy that cousin of yours maan."

Me: "Rene? O entseng?"

Tsebo: "She was wearing some tight short skirt and some skimpy top that was barely there. Ke gore, ne a sa fele mo thoko ga ka. She kept coming and offering me tea all the damn time. She paid too much attention to me maan. O ke o mmotse go re a apare sentle maan" Wow! I can't believe this. That's what she was "busy" with the whole day!? Was she trying to seduce my man or something like that!? Let me not try to overthink the situation.

Me: "Mmh. Ke tla mmolella." I've never been this disgusted.

Tsebo: "Good. Things are coming together, my love. I can't wait to make you my wife."

Me: "Yeah. Me too." My mood has suddenly dropped.

"What are you reading? Chimamanda? I should have known." He says taking my book from the table.

Me: "You know me too well."

I'm trying so hard to think about Rene trying her slutty moves on Tsebo. Maybe that's how she is, she wasn't even making moves on him. Maybe that's how she usually dresses. I'm really trying so hard not to imagine this whole situation but my mind is just...

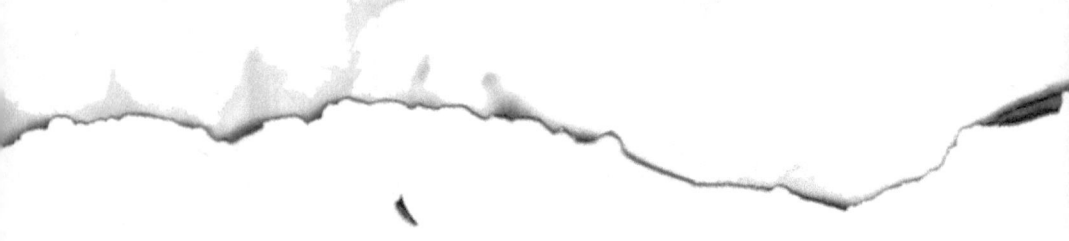

CHAPTER FIFTEEN

It's Makgadi day and I've never been so nervous. We are at Rene's home, much to my discomfort. I'm with my usual squad, Botlhale, Rose, and Rene. It's only 5:30a.m and we are already up. Rene is the one who has been telling us the dos and don'ts because she's the one who has more traditional knowledge than us. We are all in our dresses and doeks. It's been two days since I saw Tsebo and I miss him so much, talking with him on the phone is just not the same as being with him. I just want to finish with these negotiations, get out of this creepy house, be with my man and start planning for my wedding! It's gonna be such a great time!

"There! There they are!" Botlhale says peeping through the curtain. One can see clearly what's happening at the gate from Rene's room. I go and peep through the curtain. I see Mr. Radebe, he's so thin, his brother, Mpikayiboni and one old man I don't know; it must be the man Tsebo was talking about from his workplace. I don't see Tsebo.

Me: "Bathong. Tsebo is not here mos."

Rene: "He's not supposed to be here." She sounds irritated. She's been giving me some bad vibes lately. Maybe it's just my imagination.

Rose: "Oh they should just open up for them already. They've been shouting for a while now, even though we can't hear what they are saying."

I see Mr. Radebe is holding a Johnny Walker Blue Scotch Whiskey. Uncle Rearabilwe walks towards the gate and he talks about something with them; finally, he opens the gate and they come in.

As I'm busy stressing, a phone call from Tsebo comes in. "My love. O ko kae?"

Him: "My love. I'm inside the car, down the road."

Me: "Mmh. They've just opened up for them.". He laughs. "I know."

I'm not even going to ask.

Me: "I miss you."

Tsebo: "Only a few hours then we'll be together. Worry not." Just hearing his voice drives me crazy. I hang up.

Rose: "Abuti?"

Me: "Yeahp. It was him."

Rene: "O re o ko kae?"

Me: "Down the road…"

Rene: "Mmh. Should I go check him up on him?"

Me: "What for?" I snap. This girl o tlo ntena straight!

Rene: "Tjo! Tlogela." She even has an attitude.

Botlhale and Rose look at each other. I decide to keep quiet and let things be, just for the sake of peace and besides, I have bigger things to worry about. We can hear people talking from the sitting room, but they are inaudible.

Me: "I can't hear anything. I wonder what's going on." I swear I'm a nervous wreck right now.

Rose: "Me neither. But let's just take it as a sign of peace. Since we can't hear anything, that means everyone is still calm." I guess she has a point. We just spend the first few minutes pacing up and down in this bedroom, trying to eavesdrop on the conversations taking place in the sitting room, all in vain. Out of the blue, we hear a loud bang. It sounds like somebody just banged the table.

"That little rubbish in the bedroom has always been troublesome. Re mo godisitse boima a ntse a sasanka ha. Ka mo that bastard fiancé of hers is disrespectful! What you are offering us doesn't make up for all those troublesome years we've been raising that little trash!" It can only be one person—Rene's father. Hearing those words about me just breaks my heart into pieces.

Uncle Kea: "Motho wa Modimo! Tlogela go aka maarn! And there's truly no reason for you to be fuming like this. It's called negotiating for a reason!"

The Bastard: "I'm not lying maarn. That trash has always been a spoilt brat. Now that her father is dead, she expects us to be soft on her? Never! We don't have time for that nonsense. We are not the ones who said her father must die and leave her miserable ass behind."

I'm heartbroken and fuming at the same time. How heartless can one be? I'm on the verge of bursting right now and I won't tolerate that old man spreading lies about me and calling me names. Just as I'm heading to the door, Botlhale blocks my way.

Botlhale: "Ausi. He's not worth it!"

Me: "Botlhale, get out of my way! I can't have that excuse of a man spreading lies about me, calling me names and talking about our father as though he was nothing! I won't tolerate it!"

Botlhale: "You know he's like that. Please ausi, pay no attention to him. Don't let him get the better of you, cos that's what he wants. Please, ausi."

"She's right, Tlhali. This is your day, don't let him ruin it for you." Rose says as she grabs my hand and leads me to the bed. I'm on the verge of tears but I manage to fight the tears.

Botlhale: "I think they've calmed down. Ga ke utlwi sepe yanong."

Before we can respond, there's a knock on the door. It's uncle Rea.

Uncle Rea: "Reneilwe, Tlhalefo le wene Botlhale, put your blankets on and come to the sitting room. You know what to do."

Me: "Go siame, ramogolo." We put on our blankets, fully covered, head to the sitting room and sit on the floor.

"Gentlemen. Here are our beautiful flowers of the family. Do you know who you came here for?" It can only be Mr. English, Uncle Kea.

Mr. Radebe: "Ewe, siyamazi."

Uncle Kea: "All good, then. You can point your bride out." I hear whispers among the men.

Mr. Radebe: "O semaphakathini. Nguye u makoti wethu." Damn! He got it wrong! I'm the first one from the left. The one in the middle is Botlhale.

Uncle Kea: "Lady in the middle. You may reveal yourself."

I take it Botlhale uncovers herself from the blanket. I can hear Mr. Radebe expressing a sigh of disappointment.

Uncle Kea: "Mosetsana. Do you know these people?"

Botlhale: "Nnyaa, Ramogolo."

Uncle Kea: "Ladies. You also may reveal yourselves." We do as he says.

"Lady. Do you know these people?" Uncle Kea asks looking at Rene. She takes a long time before answering.

Rene: "Nnyaa. Ga ke ba itsi."

Uncle Kea: "Gentlemen. It seems you landed at the wrong house."

Mr. Radebe: "Aba phelelanga nje."

Uncle Rea: "A ba phelelanga bo mang? Lo hlopile mosadi o eseng ene, ebile ga le itse. Mosetsana, wa ba itsi batho bantseng ha?" I'm looking down but I can feel his eyes on me. I look up at him, then I look down again.

Me: "Ee, Ramogolo. Ke a ba itsi."

Uncle Kea: "Like we already said, you got your bride wrong, meaning you don't know her. We will welcome a fine of R3550, not open for negotiation. Ladies, you may go back to the bedroom, thank you."

We do as he says and go to the bedroom.

Me: "Bathong! R3550 for a fine. Nyaa hle, Ramogolo Kearabetswe ga iri tsone!"

Botlhale: "Wena. Nnyaa it was too much shem!"

Rose: "Keng na? They picked out the wrong woman?"

Me: "Yeahp. Botlhale." Rose laughs out loud. We all can't help but burst out in laughter.

Me: "Don't laugh maarn, Rose."

Rose: "So they fined them R3550?! That's a lot!"

Me: "Imagine!"

My phone rings... it's Tsebo. I hope everything is okay. He seems to know more about what's happening in this house than I do.

Me: "Mogorosi."

Tsebo: "Baby. Brace yourself. I'm on my way there. Tsohle di apere tshiamo."

Me: "Ba heditse?"

Tsebo: "Yebo."

Me: "So ba duetse bo kae for makgadi a me?"

Tsebo: "I can't tell you that information."

Me: "Come on. Hint nyana."

Tsebo: "No. my love."

Me: "Okay then. I guess we'll wait for them to call us. Oh my God, I can't wait to see you, motho wa ka!"

Tsebo: "Few seconds, my love."

Me: "They are done. Tsebo says everything went well." I'm trying so hard to hide my excitement. I want to save all this excitement for when I see my man!

Rose: "E le gore how does he know all of this?"

Me: "Search me..." Again, There's a knock on the door. He comes in even though nobody instructed him to. It's Ramogolo Rea.

"My meisie. It is done! Re heditse! Come on and help us welcome your in-laws." He says while playing with my cheeks. I can't help but blush. We all go to the sitting room. There he is. My man. Mogorosi wa me. He's at the door. I can't hold back the tears. I scream and run to him.

Uncle Rea: "Seems like you've already been welcomed. Nonetheless, welcome to the family, monna Mogorosi le ba lusika lwago."

Uncle Kea: "Indeed. Welcome to the family. What a union. And again, thank you for this beautiful whiskey. We hope there's more where that came from; alcohol is forever welcome here at the Khama household." So unlike him.

Mpikayiboni: "We'll keep that in mind. And thank you for the not-so-warm welcome."

Uncle Rea: "Whether it was warm, cold, lukewarm, hot, extra hot, it doesn't matter. As long as it was a welcome." We are stitched with laughter. I'm even struggling to breathe!

Tsebo: "Re emoga ka ditebogo, ba ga Khama. Palesa e le re fileng yone, re tla e hlokomela." My man finally speaks. Butterflies… butterflies…

"As if it will last." Rene's father. We all keep quiet. Ramogolo Rea breaks the awkwardness, as usual.

Uncle Rea: "Good people. What are we waiting for? Let us have a feast, eat the good food that has been prepared for us, mingle and finally, drink the one thing that is very close to our hearts, alcohol."

We head to the dining room, have a feast, converse and have a good time. I'm sitting next to the love of my life, and I've never been happier. That old bastard is sitting on the chair at the corner busy looking at everyone as if he's disgusted and irritated. No one is even paying attention to him.

"Ntate Mogorosi. A o siame ka chakalaka?" Rene says to Tsebo.

Uncle Rea: "Batho ba Modimo!" He's as shocked as everyone.

"My love, ke kopa o intsholele chakalaka." Tsebo says looking at me. I snatch the bowl from Rene's hand and dish up for my man. She sits down, embarrassed. I swear I'm up to here with this trash but I won't let her get to me. This is my day, and it must stay like that.

The day goes on and on and everybody starts dispersing.

Tsebo: "Babe. Let's go."

Me: "Nnyaa. I'll find you at home."

Tsebo: "E le gore o nyaka go sala o irang?" I don't like his tone.

Me: "I wanna take Rene to her place. It's late. She can't take taxis."

Tsebo: "Tlhalefo. O ikemiseditse go irang?" He even looks at me suspiciously.

"Bathong. Nothing. I'm just looking out for my cousin. Mogorosi, I'll find you at home. Bye." I say and leave him standing there.

I see Rene at the gate, and I rush to her.

Me: "Reneilwe!"

Reneilwe: "Tlhalefo."

Me: "Where are you going?"

Rene: "To the taxis. It's late. Ke tla go bona."

Me: "Let me give you a lift."

Rene: "Mmh okay. O tla be o inthusitse. Let's go." We get into the car and the drive is so awkward. She can't look me in the eye. I told myself that I'll handle the situation in a calm manner. I'm hoping to achieve that.

"Congratulations for makgadi." Rene says, looking outside the window.

Me: "Kea leboga."

Rene: "Mmh."

Me: "Why?"

"Why eng!?" Rene snaps.

Me: "Why are you doing this? What is it that you are trying to achieve?" I'm not looking at her. I'm looking at the road ahead.

Rene: "Doing what exactly!? Aii ska nyaka go ntena maan! Sentle sentle you think you are better than everyone and you can have it all, neh!?" I can feel that she's now looking at me. I'm fuming inside. I still manage to maintain my cool.

Me: "O ra go reng?"

Rene: "Aii fokof maarn! Take a turn at the first corner ke tswe fa."

Me: "I know where you stay, Reneilwe."

She keeps quiet and looks out the window again. I also keep quiet. We arrive outside her flat; she just storms out of the car and slams the door. That banging sound of the door goes straight to the core of my heart.

"Reneilwe." I say as I open my window while she's passing through the gate.

Rene: "Keng!?"

Me: "O dumedise Buhle."

Rene: "Okay."

The drive back home is somewhat awkward. I feel so angry at Reneilwe. Has her father poisoned her against me? Did I do something to her unaware? I thought we were working on becoming close. Another part of me is excited because I'm driving home to the love of my life, my husband. After a bittersweet day it has been, there's one thing that makes me content, I'm Mogorosi's wife. I get home in an hour and so and I find Tsebo driving out the gate.

"I was on my way to you. Waitsi gore ga ke rate kgang e yago ya go driver bosigo." Tsebo says as he opens his door. I also get out of my car.

Me: "But babe I told you gore I took Rene to her place mos."

Tsebo: "One can never be too sure about you, Tlhalefo; I didn't even know what you were going to do to her."

Me: "Bathong! What do you mean? Do I have any reason to do something to her?"

Tsebo: "Don't act dumb. You saw what she was trying to do earlier on."

Me: "What was she trying to do?"

Tsebo: "You know what? Let's just drive the cars in. I ordered pizza and ribs. They should be here any minute."

Me: "Yummy!" I swear my love for ribs is out of this world! Tsebo just rolls his eyes, shakes his head and gets in his car and drives it to the garage. I do the same.

We get inside and I go straight to the bedroom to change into my pyjama onesie. As I walk down the stairs, Tsebo is sitting on the couch busy with his phone. He looks up to me and chuckles a little bit.

Me: "What's funny?"

Tsebo: "You look like a bunny." He's back at his phone again.

"I know." I say as I sit next to him. I'm trying so hard not to blush.

Tsebo: "Eh. You've grown neh, wifey."

Me: "Why?"

Tsebo: "I expected you to tell me off or hit me with something. Phela we both know you are the violent one, my love." He's still chuckling.

Me: "Mogorosi stop lying. I'm not violent. Ke no kgalemela lenyatso sometimes." He laughs out loud; I can't help but laugh too.

Tsebo: "Sooo mosadi wa Mogorosi, a o ile wa kgalemela lenyatso kgompieno?"

Me: "Nope. Why?"

Tsebo: "Why did you take Rene home?"

Me: "You are still there? I thought we talked about this."

Tsebo: "Tlhalefo."

Me: "What do you think her plan is?"

Tsebo: "It's pretty obvious that she wants me. I mean, all the signs are there. She even got my numbers."

Me: "What?! O mo file tsone?" I can't believe this!

Tsebo: "Nuh. She just texted me, telling me she congratulates me."

Me: "Wow!"

Tsebo: "Relax, my love. I will handle this."

Me: "Don't tell me that you will handle this meanwhile you are so calm! Keng? Wa mmatla le wene?"

Tsebo: "What?! How can you say that?! Look. When I say I will sort this out, I mean I will sort it out. What does my calmness have to do with anything? Now I must wear soldier uniforms and carry grenades to show that I will sort this out?!" His mood has changed all of a sudden.

Me: "You don't have to be so rude."

Tsebo: "My love. I'm yours and yours only. No one will take me away from you. Rest assured."

Me: "Okay. If you say so. I love you, husby!"

Tsebo: "I love you more, wifey. Haha. Come here and give me a kiss." I lean in and kiss him. Just as we're having a moment, the doorbell rings. What a party pooper!

"Eish! Must be the food delivery." Tsebo says as he stands up to attend the door.

As he's busy talking to the guy, his phone beeps on the couch. I check it only to find a message from an unsaved number.

Gudnyt, ntate mogorosi...

It can only be one person. I manage to keep my cool and put the phone back on the couch.

Tsebo: "And supper is served!"

Me: "Finally! Let me fetch the plates."

I go to the kitchen to fetch the plates and when I come back to the sitting room, I find Tsebo staring at his phone, his face is a little tense. He must've seen the message.

Me: "O sharp?"

Tsebo: "Yeah. Look, I have to go and sort out some crisis. I'll be back now."

Me: "Bathong! O ya kae?"

Tsebo: "Some work stuff. I'll be back." He stands up and heads to the garage and drives off. I wait for a few minutes then get into the X6 and follow him. He would easily spot me if I used my own car. I have trouble catching up with him because he's ridiculously speeding but I'm not losing him. He's going exactly where I thought he was, to Rene's place. I can feel my head spinning but I'm not going to let my overthinking get to me. We finally arrive at Rene's street and I can see his car parked at the gate. I park at the corner down the road, get out of the car and walk. He gets out of the car and makes a call. After what seems like a minute, the gate opens up and he walks in. I hurry as I plan to jump the gate because it's closed but fortunately, they are standing inside. I stand outside and I can perfectly hear them talking.

Tsebo: "Mosetsana! Nare wa tsenwa?! What is it that you are trying to do?!" He's shouting.

Rene: "Dumela le wene, ntate Mogorosi. O buwa ka eng?" She sounds so calm.

Tsebo: "Tlogela go itira semaumau! Listen here, you are going to stop this nonsense right now!"

Rene: "But I can't help how I feel. I didn't tell my heart to choose you. And stop fighting it, you know very well that you want me."

Tsebo: "Pssh. You not even my type. Have you seen my wife?"

Rene: "Mxm. O go jisitse moloi ola. But that doesn't change the fact that I love you." This slut!

Tsebo: "What is that you are teaching your daughter, ge o ntse o le maratha yana?"

Rene: "Buhle? Suka! O tla gola a iponela botshelo gore bontse yang." How can she say that about her own child?

Tsebo: "Retsa ha. If you care about your life, you'll stay the hell away from me and go find some trash at the tavern you can mess around with. I'm warning you."

Rene: "Whoa. Are you threatening me?"

Tsebo: "No. I'm promising you. The worst."

I'm five to losing it so I run back to the car and drive off. My mind is about to explode. I keep asking myself questions I don't even have answers to. Could Tsebo know that I was following him, and he decided to act innocent? Or maybe he was being genuine during their confrontation? I honestly have no idea. I don't know what to think. I don't know what not to think. I arrive home, quickly dish up for myself and switch on the television. He arrives after what seems like twenty minutes.

Me: "Crisis solved?"

Tsebo: "Yes. Hopefully."

Me: "Mmh. Let me dish up for you."

He sits beside me on the couch and switches the television off.

Tsebo: "I was with your cousin. This is deeper than we thought. Mosetsana o la wa tsenwa."

Me: "Hau? What did she say?"

Tsebo: "A bunch of rubbish. I managed to put her in her place. I hope she heard me loud and clear."

Me: "I hope so too."

Tsebo: "I have to ask you this. And please, my love, do not be offended."

Okay he's scaring now.

Me: "Mmh?"

Tsebo: "Is there any history of mental illness in your family that you know of? And understand me; I'm not saying you are crazy." I keep quiet and look away.

Tsebo: "Tlhalefo."

Me: "Eish. Yah. Our great grandmother, our grandfather. But I didn't inherit it. You know the cause of my mental state."

Why am I so defensive?

Tsebo: "Yeah, I know. But do you think…"

Me: "Wait… Rene?" He nods.

Mc: "Uh-huh Mogorosi. Not possible."

Tsebo: "You should've seen her. You should've heard the things she said. Not normal at all."

Me: "Well, if that's the case. She must just go and be crazy elsewhere. Not in my marriage!" I'm suddenly fuming up.

Tsebo: "Tlhalefo! I said I sorted this out!"

Me: "Okay. I heard you! Let's eat geh."

I dish up for him and switch on the television. He pays no attention to me and eats his food.

Me: "While you are busy ignoring me like I don't exist, don't forget that we only have a month to plan our wedding."

He just keeps quiet and focuses on the television. Ouch.

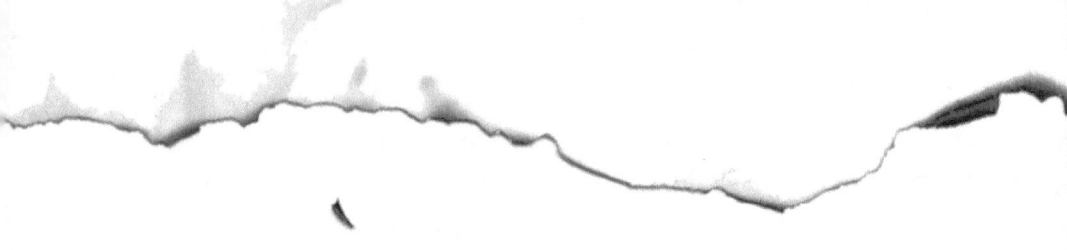

CHAPTER SIXTEEN

It's Thursday, the 19th of September, two days before our big day. Everybody has been busy going up and down during the course of the month helping me prepare for my wedding. This must have been the busiest time of my life! If there's one person who can't wait for this wedding, it has to be Botlhale. She has been raving about it since forever began! I'm excited because I'll finally get to meet her girlfriend, Ayibongwe, as she's also coming to the wedding.

Reneilwe has been distant since the day of the confrontation, and she hasn't involved herself in any of the wedding preparations. I don't care. I'm a nervous wreck right now and I think I'm starting to get cold feet.

Rose has organised a mini bridal shower for me at her place and it's a vibe! Dr. Radebe, Botlhale, Rose, Pranav's sister, some of Rose's friends and a few ladies from my workplace are also here. There's great music playing, champagne popping and the theme, believe it or not, is lingerie wear! I'm wearing a black and red chemise with red stilletos and the makeup is on another level! I swear we all look like strippers at this party! There's pole dancing, karaoke and some male strippers entertaining us. I heard that Tsebo's business associates are holding a bachelor's party for him, but I didn't ask him anything. I just want to enjoy my day and not bother anyone. I feel a little tipsy and I'm having such a great time! All the nerves are gone and I'm carefree.

I'm woken up by Botlhale who is busy poking me like crazy. I have a banging headache, and I feel nauseous. Rose is sleeping on the couch opposite the one Botlhale and I were sleeping on.

Me: "Botlhale! Keng?"

Botlhale: "Yoh ausi. I have a banging headache!"

Me: "Bathong wena! Le nna I have a hangover. Akere we all drank alcohol maobane? O batla ke ire eng, Botlhale?"

Botlhale: "Do something!"

Me: "Aii Botlhale ema nyana." I swear I can feel my head spinning like crazy!

It's so heavy!

"Hahaha! Niyabona utywala buyenza i-nonsense?" Dr. Radebe says as she's coming down the stairs. She looks so sober; she's even wearing a gown.

Botlhale: "Yoh. Don't you feel sick? You look fresh."

Dr. Radebe: "Haibo. Mna sana I know when to limit. Imagine what would've happened if we were all drunk as hell. I've even just finished taking a shower."

Botlhale: "Nnyaa hle Doc. My head is heavy, and I feel so sick. Please make a plan or something." Dr. Radebe laughs out loud.

Me: "Geez! So loud!"

Dr. Radebe: "Aii aii andik'thumanga etywaleni mna. Let me prepare you drunkards a remedy."

Botlhale: "Pleeeeasse do."

Me: "Aii marn Botlhale wa rasa! Doc, what happened to the other people?"

"I chased them away, even those strippers. I told them we wanted to sleep and that the neighbours were starting to complain. I told you that I took care of everything. Kusele thina qha." Dr. Radebe says as she's busy mixing some vegetables and syrup in the blender.

Me: "I hope that's not for us."

Dr. Radebe: "Unfortunately, it's yours. Imbi lento but you have to drink it. Well, if you want to get better. Andithi niyizi dakwa nina. Futhi nantsi, I'm done."

She's rubbing it in so bad. I tell Botlhale to give me my glass. I can't stand the smell of this thing! Yhuuu it smells so bad!

Botlhale: "Nnyaa hle Doc do we really have to drink this?"

Dr. Radebe: "Bethuna. You said you want something that will get rid of the hangover, and I made you a quick fix. Nantsi ke. And please go sleep upstairs; I wanna clean up here."

"3-2-1-go!" Me and Botlhale say simultaneously before we drink this horrible thing.

Botlhale: "Eeeuuuuwww!!!! This thing must be from hell! Yoh!"

Rose: "Yoh! Yoh! Why are you guys making so much noise!? Uh-huh maarn!"

Dr. Radebe: "Oh! She's alive!"

Me: "Come. Let's go upstairs."

Botlhale, Rose, and I go up the stairs. We can't even walk properly, annnnnddd we are still wearing lingerie! Dr. Radebe is stitched with laughter. I swear if laughing could kill, she'd be dead by now! When we get to the bedroom, Rose throws herself on top of the bed. She looks like a zombie right now.

Me: "Any better?"

Botlhale: "Yeah. Just a little. The headache is not that hectic anymore, but the nausea is still there."

Me: "Same. Bona, go and pour Rose a glass of Doc's remedy. She's five to dying."

Botlhale: "Mara you should've told me while we were still downstairs mos…"

Me: "Ska tlo mphaphela wene. Just go."

She rolls her eyes and goes out of the room. The nerve to be giving me an attitude! Mxm. I so wanna laugh at Rose but I'm scared my headache is gonna come back, so I decide to go to the bathroom to run Botlhale a bubble bath. I'll use the shower. Botlhale comes back, wakes Rose up and gives her that horrible thing. The look on Rose's face!

Me: "Come, let's go and bath. I ran you a bath."

Botlhale: "Bathong! So, we are gonna be using the same bathtub?" This child seems to be forgetting that we used to do everything together and she wouldn't mind. Now that she's at varsity and dating, she thinks she's 'little miss privacy'!

Me: "I'll use the shower maan Botlhale."

Botlhale: "Ohh that's better." Rose chuckles a bit. We both take off our lingeries, wrap ourselves in towels and head to the bedroom.

Botlhale: "Whuuu a bubble bath! O re ke go ratela eng?" I just laugh and get into the shower.

The water is so nice and hot, especially when it hits my back. The steam in the shower is giving me so much well-deserved peace. I've never been this relaxed since the planning of the wedding. It's the first time I feel that everything is falling into place. The headache is gone and the only thing I'm feeling now is hunger. My stomach is growling. I get out of the shower after a while but I can't see my towel. Botlhale is still enjoying her bubble bath.

Me: "Baby girl, where's my towel?"

Botlhale: "I don't... whoa!"

Me: "Keng?"

Botlhale: "You look thicker. And why is your stomach like that? It looks bloated."

Me: "Hau yeah. You know I'm always gaining weight. And obviously my stomach is gonna look bloated."

Botlhale: "And that line? Heee ausi when last did you get your period?"

Me: "What line? Eish! Botlhale you know that I have an irregular period. Waitsi keng? I'm taking your towel. Bye?" I take the towel, wrap myself and go back to the bedroom. I don't have time for weird people and their tactics. Rose is sitting up on the bed busy with her phone.

Me: "Tsamaya o hlapa.".

Rose: "Aii yoh. I'm lazy." I keep quiet, take off my towel and apply my lotion.

Rose: "Bathong wena! You are such a secret keeper! How many months?" I ignore her and quickly put on my dress then head downstairs. I'm so hurt by their remarks and I can feel myself getting emotional.

Dr. Radebe: "Breakfast is ready. You'll... ohh sana! Yinton' ngoku?" The tears are already flowing down my cheeks. She runs to give me a hug.

Me: "Doc I... I know that I'm fat but there really was no reason for them to rub it in."

Dr, Radebe: "But I don't see anything wrong with you. You are beautiful sisi."

Me: "I honestly don't wanna look fat on my wedding day. It's only tomorrow. Even at my last fitting, my designer asked me if I was pregnant. It hurts."

Dr. Radebe: "You are going to be the world's most beautiful bride sisi. You have nothing to worry about. Trust me."

Me: "Really?"

Dr. Radebe: "Ewe sana, ma nyan nyan. Now come and eat your breakfast."

She dishes up for me and we sit at the kitchen table eating our breakfast. She's telling me how Mr. Radebe asked her out the very first time they met, and I've never laughed like this! Turns out the infamous Mr. Radebe has always been a ladies' man and as Doc says, ubhut'wendawo! I'm having such a good time, but the wedding nerves are back as she's narrating about her wedding day. So many things went wrong, from rain and thunder, to the rings getting lost, to Mr. Radebe's exes wanting to stop the wedding. Shuuu! It was hectic. I really hope none of those things happen on my big day.

Dr. Radebe: "Yeahp. That's how my wedding unfolded sana. But suba muncu maan, none of that will happen tomorrow. U Likhaya ngumntu onesizotha, uziphethe kak'hle. Akafani na lo wam.' Anyway, ready for tomorrow?

Me: "Everything is set. Venue. Catering. Security. The guest list is done; obviously, you are the one who took care of that. My makeup artist will be there first thing in the morning. Today I'm going to get my nails and hair done. Oh and also fetch my dress."

Dr. Radebe: "Seems like everything is in order then."

Me: "Where's my phone? I even forgot that I have a phone."

Dr. Radebe: "On top of the fridge."

Me: "Oh thanks. I thought I lost it yesterday."

I get three missed calls from Tsebo and an SMS:

> *Can't wait to take you as my wife tomorrow. Counting the hours down. You are loved by me.*

I'm pretty sure my cheeks look like fireballs right now!

Dr. Radebe: "Somebody is blushing…"

Me: "Just a sweet message from a very sweet someone in my life."

Dr. Radebe: "I don't even wanna know."

We both burst out in laughter and just as I'm having the best moment of my life, these two bullies come down the stairs. My moment is ruined. They are busy talking and laughing their lungs out.

Dr. Radebe: "I hope niyashesha ukudla. We have to go and fetch Tlhali's dress and go check if everything is perfect at the venue."

Botlhale: "Oh yah. We'll hurry up."

Rose: "Have you spoken to abuti kgompieno, Tlhali?"

Me: "Yeah. He says he also had a great time yesterday. I just can't wait to see him tomorrow!"

Rose: "Haha. Don't worry. You'll see him when you guys say your 'I dos' tomorrow."

Botlhale: "Ohhh ausi I just remembered. I can't go with you to fetch your dress today. I have to go and fetch Ayibongwe at the airport when she arrives."

Me: "Does she have a car?"

Botlhale: "Nope. We'll request a cab."

Me: "No. We'll fetch her later together. What time is she boarding the plane?"

Botlhale: "She has already boarded. She says I must make my way to the airport now because wa theokga in a few minutes."

Me: "Come let's go to the airport. You'll eat when we come back."

Botlhale: "My sister! My sister! The best I've ever had!"

I can't help but laugh. I just can't stay angry at my little sister for long. One would swear I'm under a spell. She is my first-born, after all. We make our way to the airport, leaving Rose and Doc to breakfast. I'm sooo excited! I can't wait to meet the person who makes my sister happy and has her heart! Botlhale and I are busy singing out loud to our favourite songs by Sjava while driving. I can feel the excitement in her soul. My little sister is beautiful shame! She has let her pitch black long relaxed hair that she highlighted with red at the split end down. She has big, brown eyes and her crisp golden skin just glows in the rays of the sun, her body is that of an African queen, voluptuous! In my eyes, she gets more beautiful every second of the day and I love it!

We arrive at the airport, and I keep looking around for the person I always see from the pictures my sister is forever posting. My eyes can't locate her. All of a sudden, Botlhale screams and runs in the opposite direction and hops on the person who has the world's most beautiful smile. She's of a medium height, has caramel skin full of beautiful freckles; she kinda has a trainer body, one would not believe she is a girl and she has a blonde-dyed German cut. She's wearing a white vest tucked in boyfriend jeans, a checked oversized shirt and white Nike sneakers. I walk towards them, and they both look my way, holding hands.

Ayibongwe: "Lotshani." She hands her hand out for a handshake. I shake her hand.

Me: "Dumela, Ayibongwe." She has a crystal smile.

Ayibongwe: "You must be uSis Tlhalefo. No questions asked." I laugh out loud.

Me: "In the flesh. It's great to finally meet my sister's heart's keeper."

Ayibongwe: "Haha! And it's great to finally meet my girlfriend's heart's keeper. Congratulations on your marriage. I can't wait for tomorrow, it's been a while since I attended a wedding."

Me: "Thank you so much. I promise you; you will have a great time."

Botlhale: "O-kay okay. Now that the two most important people in my life have met each other, I'm happy. We have to get going; we don't wanna be late."

Ayibongwe: "Where are we going?"

Me: "Fetch my dress, check the venue, do our hair and nails."

Ayibongwe: "Oh. Then offfffff we shall go."

Botlhale: "Offfffff we go!" They look at each other for a second and burst into laughter. Okay, I must have missed something. Must have been an inside joke. Botlhale sees my confusion.

Botlhale: "You won't understand. Let's just go."

Me: "Aii. Let's go vele."

We go to the car, Ayibongwe puts her bags in the boot and off we drive... I'm sitting alone at the front. The passenger seat is empty as Botlhale is sitting at the back with Ayibongwe; they are holding hands and busy giggling non-stop. I don't blame them; I know the feeling of being madly in love, especially when it's still the honeymoon phase. We arrive at Rose's place, and everyone is so happy to meet Ayi. Rose is busy asking the poor kid a million questions about her life and their relationship; I have to save her because I know a conversation with Rose never ends.

Me: "Uhm good people, we have no time. We should get going; we have a lot to do today."

Dr. Radebe: "Yeah. Let's get going. Where are we starting?"

241

Me: "We are starting at the Garden Venue to check if all is in order; we'll find the décor staff there. Then we go to the catering staff for food and cake tasting. They said they'll deliver the food and cake tomorrow morning, then we are off to fetch my wedding dress and lastly, we are off to do our nails, hair and full body massages." The ladies fetched their dresses on Wednesday and Tsebo is fetching his suit today from his designer, minus one problem.

Ayi: "I'm looking forward to the food tasting and massages." We all burst into laughter.

Dr. Radebe: "We all are, hey."

Botlhale: "And Abuti's attire? Your makeup? What time should we be at the venue tomorrow?"

Me: "Uhm.. he's fetching it today, I just don't know what time. My makeup lady will arrive first thing in the morning. And just to avoid chaos, we are sleeping at the venue tonight, as it has a hotel. And yes, the guys are also sleeping there, but worry not, we won't see each other before the wedding."

Doc: "Really? I don't trust you *no* Likhaya."

Me: "Haha. Don't worry, Doc, we'll behave. Let's go."

Just as we are heading to the door, Rene comes in. I had even forgotten about her existence.

Rene: "Uhmm.. I hope I'm not late."

Everybody just keeps quiet and looks at each other. It's so awkward.

Me: "You aren't. Wanna tag along?"

Rene: "Yeah…"

Me: "Okay. Ga re tsamayeng."

Botlhale: "Wait. Are we all gonna fit in one car?"

I can see she's irritated; she doesn't want Rene to come with us. As I'm about to respond, Doc saves the day.

Doc: "No. Rose, you'll drive with Reneilwe, Botlhale no Ayibongwe. I'll drive with Tlhalefo." Botlhale rolls her eyes.

Rose: "No problem. Let's get going."

As planned, the four get into Rose's car and I ride with Doc in her Audi A7; it feels so comfortable and smells so fresh. We are the ones leading the way, with Rose driving behind us.

Doc: "Be careful with her."

Me: "Who?"

Doc: "Reneilwe." She's looking at the road ahead.

Me: "She's no threat to me. And Tsebo doesn't want her. She's just being crazy."

Doc: "It all starts like that. You won't know how serious she is. You don't know how far she might take this. It's always the ones we undermine who defeat us when we least expect it."

Me: "Talking from experience?" She nods and lets out a deep sigh.

Me: "Neoentle?"

Doc: "Ewe. See, the thing about Neo, may her soul rest in peace, is that I never saw her coming. Frankly, I didn't see your mother as a threat at first because I thought I knew my husband. I thought I knew the type he usually goes for and Neo never fell into that category, little did I know how wrong I was." She still hasn't looked at me.

Me: "So Ntate Radebe ended up falling for her?"

Doc: "He loved her. Wayyy more than me. Even in death, he still does. And it took me time to accept that. I had become second best to the one who held my heart. Never underestimate the power of the underdog."

Me: "So...what should I do? Chase her away from attending the wedding?"

Doc: "No. Not necessary at all. Just be careful, Tlhalefo. You are a kind and welcoming person. That's a very good quality to have, but there should be boundaries. Too much kindness invites disrespect. There are some things you have to be heartless whilst protecting them. Like... your marriage."

Me: "I hear you, Doc. I hear you."

Doc: "I'm not telling you all of these to scare you. This is real talk. U ya emendweni ngoku, Nkosazana yami. You have to know this stuff. Iskhathi sokudlala asisekho. I'm just being honest with you, sisi." I see a tear escaping from her eye. She quickly wipes it off.

Me: "And I thank you for that."

Doc: "You remind me of myself. I saw myself in you the very first time I saw you at the hospital. I don't always say this, kodwa, you are like the daughter I never had. Ndiyak'thanda sisi." I can't help but shed a tear or two. I suddenly feel so emotional.

Me: "I love you too, Mme. More than you'll ever know."

Doc: "Your parents must be so proud of you, wherever they are."

Me: "I'd like to believe so."

Doc: "Oh. jonga, sifikile. But we are not done; we still have a lot to talk about, yeva sisi?"

Me: "Go siame, Doc." We drive through the entrance and park at the parking lot. Rose does the same. We are welcomed by a beautiful young lady who has been taking care of my enquiries regarding the venue, Gontla.

Gontla: "If it isn't the lovely bride and her family."

Me: "Hahaha. You know us too well. Everything in order?"

Gontla: "Yes. The décor staff have been here for a few hours, and they are still busy prepping. Come, let's go through."

Botlhale: "Whuuu. I can't wait to see."

Gontla: "Trust me, you'll love every bit of it. They haven't even finished but it looks wonderful already!"

I can't believe my eyes! We can only see half of the décor but it's so beautiful. It's like heaven on earth! I'm not having a full white wedding, it's a mixture of a traditional seTswana wedding and a white wedding, so the theme is sparkly crystal blue and white. It's a garden wedding; at the garden, they are setting up transparent tifanny chairs. At the front, there's a transparent pulpit and fresh white flowers with small blue glitters set up where we are gonna be saying our vows. Instead of a red carpet, I opted for a white carpet and it looks so refreshing. We go inside to see how far they are with setting up the reception, and as expected, heaven on earth! There are two long train transparent tables with white serviettes and sparkly blue centrepieces with white fresh flowers in them. The chairs are like the ones outside, transparent tiffany chairs. Our main table is also transparent with sparkly blue serviettes and a transparent centrepiece with white fresh flowers inside and a silver MR & MRS frame.

There's two long white princess chairs. I sit on one of the chairs and I've never felt so much comfort in my whole life!

Décor lady: "Comfy, right?"

Me: "Soooo comfy! I love your work."

Décor lady: "We are not finished. We still have to put chandeliers at the ceiling. There's gonna be a variety of transparent chandeliers with blue lights and blue chandeliers with white lights. Oh, and we are yet to put a blue carpet from the door to your main table. You said you wanted pure white walls and there you have it. It's gonna look so magical in here!"

Me: "It already looks magical. I can't wait to see the final product tomorrow!"

Décor lady: "We'll be here first thing tomorrow morning for a few touch-ups and we'll bring your bouquet with."

Doc: "It looks magical, indeed. Kudos to you and your team. And please don't be late tomorrow; we don't want any mistakes."

Décor lady: "Worry not, madam. 'Punctual' is my second name."

Botlhale: "So who is gonna take care of the guest list and make sure that only the people who were invited and RSVP'd have access? We don't want any gatecrashers."

Gontla: "We have a team that…"

Me: "Uhm.. Tsebo said he's gonna bring his own security team."

Gontla: "I guess it's sorted then."

Me: "Thank you so much. I love everything here! So we've made our booking for tonight, right?"

Gontla: "Yeahp you did. I noted it down. Three rooms at Unit five for you ladies and three rooms at Unit two for the gentlemen."

Doc: "Great. We'll see you in the evening."

Gontla: "I take it you are going to Food Loves Us caterers for your food and cake tasting down the road?"

Rose: "Yeahp that's correct. Can we leave our cars here as we'll just walk?"

Gontla: "No problem at all, dear."

Rose: "Sharp. Thank you!"

We go down the road for our food tasting, and we are welcomed by the chief chef, Beatrice. She looks a lot like Gontla, but we are not here for that.

Beatrice: "Right on time, ladies. Welcome back!"

Me: "We are always on time when it comes to food." She laughs and leads us to the dining room. The food she prepared looks so colourful and fresh; it smells nice too!

Beatrice: "Chilly and regular samosas with mini strawberry and vanilla shakes for starters." We dish up for ourselves and the taste is out of this world! These ain't no regular samosa!

"MAGNIFICENT, MY DARLING. Shaya la!" Ayi says as she fist-bumps Beatrice. We are all dead with laughter.

Rose: "I like the chilly ones more."

Me: "Me too. They have that kick!"

Doc: "Ewe. Izidakwa zithetha kanje." We all burst out in laughter I nearly choked.

Rene: "The shakes aren't that bad."

Botlhale: "Nobody asked for your opinion. Not even a single soul." Rene looks at Botlhale and rolls her eyes. It's getting awkward again.

"Uhmm... so what's next, Mrs Chef?" Ayi slices the awkwardness. Thank God.

Beatrice: "For the main course, we made ting, samp, fried rice, grilled chicken, beef stew, fried wors, chakalaka, potato salad, pumpkin and sweet and sour veggie gravy with chutney. We made a variety of foods for people with different diets and preferences."

Me: "Oh. Makes a lot of sense. Let's dig in." We all dish up different dishes with different menus. I only dished up fried rice, chakalaka, potato salad and fried wors. Everything tastes so great! The others agree on the menus they dished up for themselves.

Me: "Aii nor! This tastes awesome!"

Botlhale: "Right? All of it! What's for dessert?"

Beatrice: "We made Blueberry mousse with mirror glazes. And dessert is on the house, free of charge. It's our way of congratulating the beloved couple on their blessed union."

Me: "Nchoa thank you so much. That really means a lot, Beatrice."

Beatrice: "Always a pleasure, ma'am. Now you can dig in for some heavenly taste!" I only have a spoon and as Beatrice said, there is some heavenly taste to it!

Doc: "Wow! I've never eaten this before. Yam'nandi into!"

Beatrice: "Thank you, ma'am. Now if you ladies are done, I can bring the cake for you to see and the cake samples for you to taste."

Botlhale: "You can do so, ausi."

She calls for some guys to bring it and whoa! Pure bliss!!! It's a pure white three-tier cake with sparkling blue roses on the top cake. The two small side cakes are also white with blue glitters all over them. The cake is soooo beautiful.

Everyone: "Wooooow!"

Me: "Beautiful neh?"

Botlhale and Doc: "So beautiful."

Ayi: "I don't even know what to say."

Rose: "This cake must be framed and put for decoration. It must just not be eaten, never! What are the flavours?"

Beatrice: "Vanilla on the first side cake and Pistachio nut on the other side cake... For the main cake, we have Lemon on the bottom cake, the middle cake is Tiramisu flavoured and Red velvet at the top cake. All these flavours blend so well together. Again, heavenly taste! Here are the cake samples."

I only eat the pistachio and red velvet and it's a tick for me. I'm already full.

Everybody approves of all the cake flavours.

Me: "Great job, Beatrice. I hope you don't forget the open bar tomorrow."

Beatrice: "Don't worry, my darling"

Me: "We'll see you in the morning. Thank you, once again."

Beatrice: "Pleasure. Tomorrow it is, then."

We go and fetch our cars from the Gardens Venue.

Rose: "Where are you fetching your dress?"

Me: "My designer's office is three blocks away from here and a street away from his office, there's a mall where we'll go to a spa and there's a salon opposite it."

Rose: "Okay. I'll drive behind you then."

We are jamming to jazz music in the car with Doc and the atmosphere is so relaxed. While I'm still relaxing, I get a phone call from Tsebo.

Me: "Baby."

Tsebo: "How's my beautiful bride doing? I miss you so much."

Me: "I miss you more. I've just been to the venue, it's so beautiful. Don't you wanna see it? Now I'm on my way to get my hair done and fetch my dress. Have you fetched your suit?"

Tsebo: "Whoa. One question at a time. I'll see the venue tomorrow, besides, I trust your judgement. We fetched our suits in the morning, and I got my haircut done on my way back."

Me: "So le ira eng yanong?"

Tsebo: "Uhm. We are watching TV."

Me: "Stop lying. I know that wherever there's you, there's alcohol involved. Just don't drink too much, the last thing I want is a hungover groom tomorrow. And send me pictures of your suit."

Tsebo: "Okay... Okay... just two beers. Worry not, my love. I can handle my alcohol. I'll send you the pictures in a few hours. Can't wait to see you tomorrow!" He thinks he's clever this one. I'll let it pass.

Me: "Can't wait to see you too, my baby. I'll call you before I sleep tonight. What time will you guys be at the hotel?"

Tsebo: "We'll leave here at 6 p.m. And no, I'll call you, sweetheart." Hearing his voice makes me miss him even more. I'm starting to get emotional.

Me: "Okay. I love you."

Tsebo: "I love you. A thousand times and beyond." Hearing him say that just makes me even more emotional, but I'll be strong. He hangs up and a tear escapes my eye.

Doc: "Ohh sisi. You'll see him ngomso."

Me: "I know. I just miss him so much."

Doc: "Only a few hours to go."

Me: "Yeah, I guess. Park at the yellow building. That's where we are going."

Doc: "Alrightee."

We get out of the car and make our way to Leon's office. We find him busy with a sketch and he looks tired! Pink nose, eyebags, pale skin, the works!

Me: "Aow bathong darling. You look tired."

Leon: "Tell me about it! That dress of yours took up 100% of my time and life!"

Me: "Hahaha, askies my skaat. But i-job i-job. I've come to collect it."

Leon: "Okey-dokey. Here it is. Go and wear it for the last time inside a designer's room."

He unzips it from the bag and my heart skips a beat! You know, I've been tracking the progress of this dress every forthnight but it always looks amazing and out of this world every time I see it.

Ayi: "Oh my word! That's like a dress from an ice movie! Magnificent!"

Botlhale: "I know right? Told you my sis is stylish!"

Me: "Yippee. Let me go and fit it."

Doc: "Let me come and help you." We make our way to the fitting room and she helps me put it on. This dress is practically like my second skin! It is a white lace mermaid dress with very subtle blue glitters all over the dress. It exposes my cleavage and hips very boldly, yass! It has sleeves with subtle glitters all over it. It hugs my body very tightly and has a long train that is also full of sparkles. The thing I like about this dress is that it has that modern seTswana style plus a Western touch to it. The veil is long and pure white.

Doc: "Wow! I have no words, angel…"

Me: "Haha I'll take that as a compliment. Let's go and show the others. I wonder if they are going to be impressed or not…"

Doc: "I'm pretty sure they are gonna be left speechless, just like me!"

We go out to show the others the dress. Leon is busy telling them about one of the stories about his 'glamorous life', as usual. The second I walk out of the fitting room, there's silence in the room.

Botlhale: "Whoa! You look… wow! Ausi!"

Ayi: "I did say you are going to be an Ice Queen! Geez!"

Rene: "You look beautiful, Tlhali."

251

Rose: "She does, right!"

Leon: "Ice Queen indeed! Talk about a lady of high class!"

Me: "Thank you guys. I really appreciate it. And Leon, I knew you wouldn't disappoint. You are the best in your field. Thank you."

Leon: "I'm flattered, my darling. The pleasure is all mine."

Me: "What time is it?"

Botlhale: "2:30p.m."

Me: "Whoa. Time is flying! Let me take this dress off so we can go." I go back to the fitting room to take the dress off and Leon puts it back into the bag for me. We get into the cars and head straight to the mall; it's only a street away from Leon's office. We park the cars and hurry to the spa to get our massages.

Everybody looks so relaxed; I'm relaxed too but I keep thinking about tomorrow. The nerves are starting to get the better of me, but I'll try and ignore them.

Rose: "I've never felt so relaxed! That massage did me good."

Rene: "These ladies really know their job. They are good at what they do."

Me: "Time to go get our hair and nails done."

Ayi: "Mina ngi grand sisters. I got my hair cut and nails groomed last week."

Doc: "Even I plaited my dreadlocks last week. I'll just do my nails."

Me: "Alrightie then. Let's go."

In two hours, we are done at the spa and we head to the salon, just opposite the spa. Luckily, there are three hairdressers who are free and two free nail technicians. Doc and Rene start with their nails while Rose, Botlhale and I start with our hair. Ayibongwe is just sitting comfortably on the couches while busy on her phone.

Me: "Please straighten my hair, apply gel and put on an extensive long curly ponytail. But it must not be too simple, be creative."

Stylist: "Uhmm, lemme see... Okay, I know what I'm going to do. You'll love it!"

Me: "Hope so."

Stylist: "Worry not, my darling. You've got only the best in me. I like your hair; it has so much volume."

Me: "Thank you. But Afro hair is no joke hey; it requires patience. And the products are so expensive! I don't know how many times I've thought of relaxing my hair or even doing the big chop."

Stylist: "I know right? I tried having an Afro but it was just too painful and expensive to maintain. I ended up relaxing because wow."

Me: "Haha I know."

I look at Botlhale and Rose and they are being plaited freehand straightbacks, I think they are going to put on weaves on top because I heard Botlhale saying something about Peruvian hair. I check the time and it's already 5: 00p.m! But I'm not stressing because I'm only left to do my nails after they are done with my hair. This lady really knows what she's doing. Her hands are so soft and smooth, and she handles my hair with so much care. Since I have nothing to do, I decide to call Themba because I last spoke to him two days ago and I kinda miss him.

Themba: "Hey girlfriend!"

Me: "*Mei chomi*!"

Themba: "How's the beautiful bride doing? Everything going well?"

Me: "Yeahp! Tsohle di apere tshiamo. I'm just waiting for tomorrow."

Themba: "I can't wait to see you tomorrow. I know everything will be perfect. You never disappoint when it comes to style and class!"

Me: "You know me too well, my friend. I'll see you tomorrow neh chomi."

Themba: "Bye makoti!" Haha this one, he is such a mood activator!

As I'm busy browsing through my social media, I receive a WhatsApp text from Botlhale.

Ausi. The rings?

They are in my bag at Rose's place. I'll give them to you when we get there.

Oh alright. I thought we forgot to fetch them.

Nuh. Which hairstyle are you doing?

A Peruvian Pixie weave, it has a purple highlight at the front. Rose is having a 28-inch curly Brazilian weave. Wena?

A curly ponytail, mara ke extension. I'm having my hair straightened.

Okay. Why did you allow Reneilwe to come with us?

We can't shut her out.

I wonder what kind of nails she's doing. I'm even scared to see what hairstyle she'll get.

LOL! I hope it's got nothing to do with orange. I don't want her ruining my theme!

LOL! Let's just wait and see.

In what seems like an hour and a few minutes, Rose and Botlhale are done with their hair and start with their nails. Rene has long started with her hair; it looks like she's also about to finish. She got a haircut and dyed with maroon; she also went for maroon nails. That's better. The lady who is doing my hair really got creative. She plaited one line in the middle and put a medium-sized silver jewellery that overlaps a little on my forehead, straightened and applied gel on my hair. The edges she created are out of this world! Now she's implanting the curly ponytail I asked for. She's done in a good fifteen minutes, and I love it!

Me: "Wow! I knew you wouldn't disappoint! I love it!"

Stylist: "You look really beautiful. Pleasure."

After finishing with my hair, I go straight to do my nails. I opt for nude long nails with silver décor on the index fingers.

Doc: "Reneilwe. Uphi umntwana?"

Rene: "I left her at my place."

Doc: "Masim'lande. She'll sleep with us at the hotel."

Rene: "Cool. Plus I also had bought her a dress and shoes and got her hair done."

Doc: "Nizas'fumana kwa Rose."

Me: "Okay. No problem." Ayibongwe stands up and goes with them. I guess she got tired of just sitting and doing nothing.

Botlhale and Rose are done with their nails and wait for me at the couches. They both opted for baby pink long nails.

After what seems like forty-five minutes, I'm also done with my nails. Rose helps me settle the bill and off we drive. We arrive at Rose's place in less than an hour and we start packing for what we'll need right away. I give Botlhale the rings for safekeeping. We all make our way to the Garden Hotel, and we get there after a few minutes past nine. Apparently, Tsebo and his crew really did arrive here at 6:00p.m, Rose spoke to him. He's with Mr. Radebe and his brothers, two people from his workplace and my twin uncles. We are all starving and very tired, so we request room service so that we can eat and sleep. It's gonna be a long day tomorrow...

Room service arrives with the platters we requested, we are busy eating while chatting and playing music. It's such a chilled vibe. Doc signals for me to go to the balcony; I do so, and she follows me.

Doc: "You ready for tomorrow?"

Me: "I think so."

Doc: "Listen. From tomorrow, you must know that you are someone's wife. It's you and your husband against the world. Some things will have to change in your life. It's not gonna be smooth sailing all the way; you will meet some obstacles along the way. You just have to be strong. Umfazi ukubekezela, kodwa, unga bekezeli amanyala. Don't be like myself and all the other women who were told ukuba masibekezele. As women, we are also human; we have feelings; we are not made of steel. When we say 'through thick and thin', we are talking about staying together and conquering whatever life may throw at you as a couple, be it illness, poverty, death, and all those things. We are not talking about infidelity, disrespect, and unfaithfulness. Jonga sisi, if you feel that love, loyalty, care, attention and respect are no longer being served at the table, move away. I'm not going to stand here and lie to you ndithi bekezela ude uyofa because I know how painful that can get. You can feel demeaned and dehumanised uloku ubekezela amanyala womntu. Marriage is a give and take, all efforts must be met halfway. As a woman, you must be the pillar of your own home. Ube yi Ntsikayomzi. Respect your husband. Love your husband.

Build and protect your home. Never broadcast your problems. You might think people care, kanti they are desperately waiting for your downfall. Most importantly, be happy in your marriage. Have a fruitful marriage. Enjoy each and every second of your being. Lobomi, ngobakho."

Everything she just said has been mind-blowing and eye-opening for me. I needed to hear that.

Me: "I hear you, Doc. Thank you. Thank you so much."

Doc: "No need to thank me; that's what I'm here for." I just smile and give her a tight hug.

Doc: "But… you know that it is possible, right?" She has lost me.

Me: "Uhm… what is possible?"

Doc: "For you to be carrying a little one without being aware, especially after a miscarriage."

Me: "Ahh Doc, not you too. I'm not pregnant. I've just gained weight."

Doc: "Tlhalefo, unomzimba. So it obviously won't be that visible for the first few months."

Me: "You know what? I'll go and get tested after the wedding. But I'm telling you, there's nothing here."

Doc: "Okay-Okay. If you say so. Let me go and sleep, you should sleep too."

Me: "I will, goodnight, MaRadebe."

Doc: "Goodnight, MaMogorosi. Best wishes."

Me: "Thank you."

She goes inside and just as I'm also about to go back inside, I get a phone call from Tsebo. My heart lightens up.

Me: "My Love."

Tsebo: "My love. Are you sleeping?"

Me: "I was about to."

Tsebo: "Oh, good. Let's meet at my car for a quickie. It's been long since I had you."

Me: "Aii, Mogorosi. I thought you called me to tell me sweet nothings."

Tsebo: "Hau. These are sweet nothings, my love. Please."

Me: "No, Mogorosi. Have sex with your hand. I'm sleeping. I love you."

Tsebo: "But…" I quickly hang up before he can finish his sentence. I get an SMS from him.

> *I love you too. I'm going to show you hell tomorrow night…*

I ignore this stupid message of his and go to my bedroom to sleep. The nerves are back again…

* * * * * * *

It's 8:00a.m and everybody is busy getting ready. Botlhale, Rose, and Rene are done bathing and getting dressed and the makeup staff is busy pampering them in the sitting room. Doc and I have just finished bathing and now she's helping me get into my dress. As promised, the décor lady brought my bouquet and did a few touch-ups here and there. My bouquet is a mixture of white fresh roses and blue tulips; it looks so cute. Doc is also done getting dressed and she said she's gonna do her own makeup. My makeup artist arrives and finds me in the bedroom and she starts working. She's done the cat-eye look with gold eyeshadow and brown lipstick, with a slight bronze blush and my eyebrows are on fleek! I go to the sitting room to join the others and everybody looks so beautiful! Ayibongwe is sitting on the couch and putting her shoes on. She's wearing a suit.

Botlhale: "You look so beautiful, my sister. You look like an angel."

Me: "Thank you, ngwana ko gae. You look magical too. And everybody else looks amazing."

Rose: "Are you okay? You sound a little... down..."

Me: "Yeah I'm okay. I just... I just wish my father was here, you know." My voice is breaking and my eyes are now full of tears. I can't hold them back.

Doc: "I know, my baby. He's here with us, in spirit."

Botlhale: "And I'm pretty sure he's very proud of you."

It has always been my dream, from a young age, for my father to witness everything I do. I wish he was there when I got accepted at varsity. I wish he was there when I graduated. I wish he was there when my little sister matriculated. I wish he was there when I got my first job, started my own business. I wish he was here to meet the love of my life and walk me down the aisle. There's not a single night that I go to sleep and don't wish I can wake up in the morning and find him in the kitchen making breakfast and listening to jazz music. I miss his laughter, his voice, his jokes, his strictness, his games, his hugs and kisses. I miss everything about him. He should have been the first person to see me in this dress and grant me his blessing. I don't want him to be with me in spirit; I want him here, beside me. I want him to touch me and squeeze my hand. I want my father.

I can see they are also shedding a tear or two.

Botlhale: "You'll ruin your makeup, ausi."

Me: "Yeah. Haha. Let me stop with the tears."

Makeup lady: "Let me fix you up really quick."

Rose: "So who is gonna walk you down the aisle?"

Me: "Ramogolo Rearabilwe. He should be making his way to our room."

Rose: "Alright."

Doc: "I just called the catering company. They'll be here in an hour."

Me: "Re tla be re simollotse by then. You'll go and check up on them, right?"

Doc: "Yeahp."

There's a knock on the door, Ayi opens up and it's Uncle Rea.

Uncle Rea: "The beauty in this room! mosetsana wami, you look like an angel."

Me: "Kea leboga, ramogolo."

Botlhale: "Let's go and sit with the guests so we can welcome ausi." They all go to the garden, and I'm left with ramogolo.

Uncle Rea: "Goitsimang o tshwanetse go nna motlotlo ka wene." He says while holding both my hands; I can see him getting a bit emotional.

Uncle Rea: "Emoga, mosetsana wame. The people are waiting."

I stand up and he covers my face with my veil and hands me my bouquet. There won't be any bridesmaids and groomsmen. I only have a Maid of Honour, Botlhale and Tsebo has a best man, Mpikayiboni. Buhle is the flower girl. We go and he's holding me by my hand. There's a band playing some sweet instrumentals. The second I step on the white carpet, people stand up and look at me in awe. I can see him. He's standing there with his hands in his pockets. He's wearing a blue and white Chinese collar blazer with white pants. I never thought I'd see the day Tsebo Likhayalimile Mogorosi sheds tears in front of people. He's trying to hold them back, but they just keep flowing. I love this. At least I managed not to cry; I can only smile with a heart full of joy. We get to the front and Ramogolo hands me over to Mogorosi.

Uncle Rea: "Take care of her. You break her heart; I break your bones."

I can't help but chuckle.

Tsebo: "I promise you I'll do no harm to her, sir."

Ramogolo goes and sits down, and I'm left standing with Tsebo. We are facing each other. Mr. Radebe comes and stands at the pulpit; he's a pastor after all. He looks better than the last time I saw him. I take it he's starting to accept Neo's absence in his life. Good for him.

Mr. Radebe: "Good morning, beautiful ladies and handsome gentlemen. I trust you are all well. To bless this beloved union, may we all bow our heads and pray."

Everybody does as he says. Tsebo and I are left looking at each other and smiling. He has stopped crying, but I can still see the emotion in his eyes. My heart is full of joy.

Mr. Radebe: "Amen. Thank you all for coming. Nam'hla sizawudibanisa Labantu abahle abame phamb'kwethu. We are here to witness the union of two families into one, ba kwa Mogorosi na ba kwa Khama. We are here to witness the union of two souls to become one. Liyatsho izwi lithi, 'He who finds a wife, finds a good thing'. A man without a significant other can be considered redundant. Love is a beautiful thing; we all should be proud to witness it with our very own eyes today. The beautiful couple has told me that they will say their vows coming from deep down in their hearts. May we have the rings?"

Botlhale stands up and comes with the rings. I give her my bouquet. Mr. Radebe prays for them and Tsebo takes my ring and inserts it on my finger while saying his vows.

Tsebo: "MmeKhama. You look beautiful, as always, my angel. With this ring, I promise to love you, care for you, protect you and serve you for the days of my life. I'm proud to say that our fate had already been jotted down. I knew the second I found you, that I found a good thing. I thank you for loving me when I thought it was impossible for one to love a man like myself. Thank you for being the pillar of strength in my life. Thank you for being my light at the end of the tunnel. I appreciate your patience with me. I appreciate the love and care you've shown me. Thank you for taming me; I know I'm not perfect, but you love me with my imperfections. Through thick and thin, for better or for worse, I will always remain by your side. Again, I promise to love, care, cherish and protect you with my life. I love you with all of my being, MmeKhama. Til' death do us apart.". A tear escapes from his eye. The melodies from the band are making us so emotional.

Me: "Ntate Mogorosi. I don't even know where to start."

Tsebo: "At the beginning." Everybody laughs.

Me: "I always thought I will go through this thing called life alone. I always thought I was destined to go solo for all the days of my life. Until you came along, you became my pillar of strength, my shoulder to cry on. You helped me carry my load. We've been through a lot together, but we are still standing, may that be the case even when we are married. The love, care, attention, and protection you've shown me, I cannot express in words. With this ring, I promise to love you, care for you, in health and in sickness, protect you and respect you. Through thick and thin, for better and for worse, I will remain by your side. I love you with all of my being, Ntate Mogorosi. Til' death do us apart."

Mr. Radebe: "Beautiful indeed! Tsebo Likhayalimile Mogorosi, do you take Tlhalefo Khama as your lawfully wedded wife?"

Tsebo: "I do, with no doubt!"

262

Mr. Radebe: "Tlhalefo Khama, do you take Tsebo Likhayalimile Mogorosi as your lawfully wedded husband?"

Me: "Definitely, I do!"

Mr. Radebe: "Is there anyone who is against the union of the bride and groom standing before us? Tell us now or forever hold your peace?" This is the part I hate with all of my heart when it comes to weddings. There's silence amongst the guests. After a few seconds, Reneilwe stands up, everybody is amazed. She looks at the people, then Mr. Radebe, then us. I can see Tsebo is ready to strike, I squeeze his hand tightly. By the look of things, Botlhale is waiting for one word to come out of Reneilwe's mouth and only God knows what's going to happen.

"Uhm... I need the bathroom..." Rene says and rushes to the bathroom. Everybody sighs. No words can describe the level of disgust I'm feeling right now! That stunt she just pulled will have consequences, I can assure her.

Mr. Radebe: "With no further ado, manene na manenekazi, as I see our groom is getting impatient for the part we've all been waiting for. Mr. Mogorosi, you may kiss your bride!"

Tsebo opens the veil, looks me in the eyes, holds me by my neck and deep kisses me. For a moment, I forget about the world and think it is just him and me in paradise. I hear screams from the ladies and whistles from the guys. I softly pull away from him; I know he can go on the whole day this one.

Mr. Radebe: "That was a kiss and a half! Ladies and gentlemen, I give you Mr. and Mrs. Mogorosi!" Everybody screams and claps and some are busy taking videos and pictures. We sign our marriage certificate. I saw the photographer arriving when I got out of my room le Ramogolo. Good, he was on time. Doc stands up and addresses the people.

Doc: "Good morning, beautiful persons. While our bride and groom are taking pictures, may we all go to the reception area, it's just behind you, where there are glass doors." Everybody stands up and does as she says.

The pictures are taken at the Garden Venue still. There's a beautiful park with all kinds of flowers and fresh grass; it even has a fountain. It's so beautiful. The photographer takes us pictures as a family, as a couple, the ladies only, the gents only, myself only and Tsebo alone. We are done in about forty-five minutes and everybody goes to join the others in the reception. When we get into the reception, the band is still playing some chilled, sweet harmonies and Tsebo and I are led by Buhle, who is scattering white roses on the blue carpet. Everyone is up on their feet welcoming us. We finally get to our main table, and I can see the entire hall in its entirety. Everything looks so beautiful. The décor is so magical. I'm just glad that everybody adhered to the wedding theme. The last thing I would have wanted was colour-blocking on my wedding day. The cake is on the mini table next to our table and the food warmers are at the far left of the venue. As promised, I see that the tables have the champagne that I ordered and the guests are being served starters. It's time for the speeches.

Doc is first in line.

Doc: "Likhaya. Ukhulile nyan! I'm very proud of the man you've grown to be. I admire your strength and confidence. Your will to protect those you love and go the extra mile for them. Usisi, inoba uyazidla ngawe lapho ekhona. Tlhalefo. I appreciate your presence in our lives. The pillar you've become for all of us, the love and care you carry inside your heart. I wish you all the best in your marriage, my people. May your love grow, and may it conquer everything, just like it has already done. Best wishes. For those of you who don't know me, I'm the aunt of the groom, and the MC of this wonderful event. Next up, can we have Botlhale Khama."

Everybody claps their hands and Botlhale comes to the front. Did I mention that my little sister is beautiful?

Botlhale: "Hi everybody, I'm Botlhale Khama. The younger sister of the beautiful bride. Ausi, thank you, for everything. To be honest, I don't take you as my sister. I see you as my mother. You took care of me from the moment I arrived on this Earth, even when our parents were still alive. You took care of me even after Papa's death and you were still so young. Honestly, I've never felt and seen myself as an orphan, not even once, because I knew I had you. I never envied other kids who had parents because I knew I had you. I love the way you love me, even though I can be a bully sometimes. I love the way you are overprotective of me, even if it can get too much at times. I love the way you are always willing to go the extra mile for me, no matter how silly my request is. My heart is not heavy to see you getting married. I'm not sad. I do not have mixed feelings. I am happy. All because I know that I'm not losing you; I will never lose you. You've never turned your back on me. You are my mother. You are my father. And I wish you all the best in this life-changing journey you are taking. I know you've got this, you always do. You never fail at anything. All the best, abuti. I love you both, a lot!"

I tried to remain strong but her words just brought tears to my eyes. These are tears of joy. When I think of everything we've had to go through. She was so little, and now she has fully grown. I'm proud. It has been a long journey, a long fruitful journey. Next up is Themba. I'm even scared to hear what he will say!

Themba: "San'bonani! I'm Themba, Tlhalefo's very productive PA and best friend! Chomi, when you told me that this day would come a year ago, I would have laughed at you! We both know ukuthi nje wena into ekuthiwa yindoda uyayisaba! But look at you now, sitting with the love of your life. You are a true definition of the word 'strong', chomi. No matter what life throws at you, you always come out on top! I appreciate all the talks, cries, laughter, crazy moments and fights we've had in the office, coz at the end of the day, that's what makes our friendship strong. You are beautiful chom'am. Both on the inside and outside. I'm so happy for you that you've

265

found a man who loves and cherishes you. May your marriage conquer against all odds. Mandihlale phansi!"

Everybody burst into laughter when he mentioned that I was scared of men. Themba can be an embarrassment when he likes waitsi.

Doc: "And now, can we have Mr. Masenya to address the lovely couple."

I now recognise him, he's the man who works with Tsebo and was part of my makgadi negotiations.

Mr. Masenya: "Good day. I'm Lehlogonolo Masenya, friend and business associate of the very serious groom. Monna Mogorosi, I know that you have been waiting for this day all of your life. The day when you seal the deal with the woman you love the most. The woman who respects you and loves you just as much. That day has arrived. I don't have much to say, my friend, all I can say is that you have made it. You have arrived at your destination. And I'm marking that as your greatest life achievement. Tsela tshweu, Ntate le Mme Mogorosi."

Doc: "So many words of wisdom. And now, for the grand moment. Our bride and groom will address us."

The band stands us up with a sweet harmony. I go first.

Me: "Uhm.. Dumelang bagaeso. Re emoga ka ditebogo ka ntlha ya thekgo le lorato lwa lone. We thank you so much for making time to celebrate our big day with us and for being so beautiful. Indeed you all have helped me in achieving my dream wedding. We thank you so much."

Tsebo: "Like my wife, Mme Mogorosi said, we appreciate your presence. Thank you." I knew he was gonna be brief.

Me: "You may go and eat, beautiful people, the food is at the left side of the hall. The caterers will be helping you dish up. Dessert will be served after the main course and there's a mini bar just after the food table. Have fun and rejoice! Thank you, once again."

Everybody stands up and goes to get their food, Botlhale has dished up for Tsebo and me; she's such an angel.

Tsebo: "You look beautiful, Mrs. Mogorosi."

Me: "Thank you. You look handsome, Mr. Mogorosi."

Tsebo: "I have a surprise for you."

Me: "Yes?"

He takes out some pieces of paper from his pocket and hands them over to me.

Me: "Whoa! Tickets to Bali! And the flight is tonight at 8:00p.m!"

Tsebo: "Yeahp. That's where our honeymoon will be. I know you've always wanted to go to Bali. We are going away for two weeks, my love."

Me: "My word! I can't wait! Thank you so much, husby!" The level of excitement I'm at right now is unmatched.

Tsebo: "Let's eat our food so we can pack and get out of here."

Me: "Let us!!!" I tell Doc and my squad what my husband has surprised me with and they are all so excited for me, well, except one person, of course.

Tsebo and I eat and have a few drinks while conversating. I check the time, it's already 4:00p.m! We still have a lot to do. We have to take our stuff at the hotel and go back to our house for some stuff then off to the airport. While he accompanies me to pack my stuff in my hotel room, we have a little quickie and it feels like heaven on earth! It's been long since we had each other; you can't blame us. We make our way to our house, pick up a few stuff; we both change into jeans and vests and off to the airport we go. Luckily, we are on time for our flight.

I can't wait to spend a full two weeks with my husband, unbothered and at peace. It all feels so right...

267

CHAPTER SEVENTEEN

It's November the 21ˢᵗ, two months since I became Mrs Mogorosi. This time, life has been fair to Tlhalefo Mogorosi, N-AMI is growing in ways I've never imagined! Business is popping and we have managed to bag some international clients! Tsebo and I had the best days of our lives in Bali, Indonesia during our honeymoon. We got some well-deserved rest and had some quality time with no interruptions at all. And yes, everybody was right. We went for a scan and it turned out I am now five months pregnant with a baby boy. Tsebo was so over the moon. He was ecstatic!!! I'm also happy but I'm still shocked at how the pregnancy hid itself. I thought it was just normal weight gain here and there; nothing has changed. My sleeping patterns haven't changed; my eating and appetite patterns haven't changed either. The only thing that has changed is my complexion. I've gotten a lot lighter and my nose is as shiny as a mirror! I am happy about this pregnancy but I can't help worrying. I don't want to lose my baby again. That would totally break me. I don't think I'd be able to handle it this time around.

Botlhale has just finished her semester exams and she's coming home tomorrow. I'm so excited; two months is a lot of time for me to not see my sister. I can't wait to tell her that she's going to be an aunt!

Rose and her boyfriend, believe it or not, have decided to move permanently to New York. She said she feels that her clothing line will be most successful in New York, and she has decided to be a full-time designer, so she left her job in finance. It was convenient for them because Pranav has a lot of businesses that side. Rose told me that she won't ever get married or have kids with any man, hence she has blocked her tubes, without Pranav knowing. She has always been one for adoption and all that philanthropy stuff. Tsebo, as hard as it was, had no choice but to let go of Rose. She is a woman who can make her own decisions and take care of herself. He doesn't even like Pranav; he always asks me why Rose would go for an Indian man when there are Tswana men all over this world. At the end of the day, it was not his decision to make.

I was not shocked when I received a phone call from Dr. Radebe telling me that she's divorcing Mr. Radebe. She wasn't always the happy wife. Even before Neoentle got married to her husband, she said she didn't feel she was loved and cared for enough. After Neoentle's death, the situation became worse, she said. It was as if she was non-existent to her husband, except when they were in public. I think it is fair enough for her to follow her own advice and move away from the table if all those important aspects of a happy marriage are no longer served.

The problem that is called "Reneilwe" still persists. She has been busy sending my husband good morning and goodnight texts, half-naked and nude pictures of herself and has taken it as far as showing up in his workplace. She has blocked me on all social media platforms and blacklisted my phone calls. Tsebo has done the same to her but she keeps coming back with different numbers. We really thought this dizziness of hers would end as time goes but it only seems to be getting worse. Tsebo has confronted her several times; she would not hear the end of it. I have confronted her several times and she still wouldn't hear the end of it. Apparently, she's always taking her frustrations out on Buhle. Beating her up, swearing at her and enslaving her with house chores. It is time for me to take care of this situation, permanently so.

It's Thursday and it is my last day at work. I'll be working from home until January. I did say I'm more productive at home than in the office. I'll only go to the office when I have meetings. I get home at 7:30p.m and I find Tsebo busy in the kitchen with the pots.

Me: "Baby. I was going to cook, hey."

Tsebo: "Don't worry, I got this. And besides, I wouldn't want the mother of my children getting overworked. You must get enough rest. You know very well I don't like this thing of your knocking off at night."

Me: "I wanted to get most things done today. I'll be starting to work from home tomorrow. What are you cooking?"

Tsebo: "Come here." He pulls me closer to him and holds me by my waist, kissing my neck. That relaxing feeling...

"Pap, spinach and wors." He whispers in my ear while breathing on my neck.

Me: "Mmh..."

Tsebo: "O ntse yang boy-boy?" He's now brushing my belly. "He's growing. He's starting to get heavy. My back hurts."

"Up for a massage later?" He's still busy with my neck. I'm starting to lose myself in him.

Me: "A full body massage..."

Tsebo: "A full body massage it is then. Come, let me take you upstairs and run you a bubble bath." He carries me up the stairs, throws me on top of the bed and goes to the bathroom to run me a bath. I could live like this forever...

Tsebo: "I'll call you when supper is ready. I didn't make dessert though."

Me: "I have an idea of what dessert could be tonight." I say in my most seductive voice. He finally gets me.

Tsebo: "Ohhhh. Exactly what I had in mind." I laugh out loud. He comes to the bed and gives me a deep kiss.

Tsebo: "I'll see you at supper, ma'am."

Me: "Okay baby." He goes downstairs and I take off my clothes and head to the bathroom. The bubble bath is soooo relaxing. I keep looking at my big belly and I still can't believe I wasn't aware all this time. How could I not have felt my bundle of joy growing inside me? I can't wait to hold him in my arms. I hope he comes out looking like me. It just wouldn't be fair if he looks like his Tsebo. I mean, I'm the one who is going to carry him for nine months and the least he could do is come out looking like his cute mother. End of story. I get out of the bath after a few minutes and head to the bedroom, put on my g-string and silk maroon gown then head downstairs to join my lovely husband.

Tsebo: "I was about to call you. Supper is ready." I join him at the dining table.

Me: "The food tastes great. Thank you for cooking, my love."

Tsebo: "Always a pleasure. Boy-boy must be healthy, like his father."

Me: "No. Like his mother. Plus he's gonna look like me."

Tsebo: "What a joke, my darling. He's going to look like his father, that's quite obvious." He can be full of himself. Let me drag him down.

Me: "Yoh aii, that means he's going to be ugly, then."

Tsebo: "Whoa, lover! Have you seen me?"

Me: "Yeah I have. And I would recommend plastic surgery." He laughs out loud.

Tsebo: "I guess you love me like that, right?"

Me: "Whatever." He suddenly becomes serious.

Tsebo: "You know, I still can't believe that Noluntu is divorcing Radebe."

Me: "It was bound to happen, Mogorosi."

Tsebo: "What do you mean?"

Me: "She wasn't happy at all, Tsebo."

Tsebo: "But they made vows… and vows are meant to be kept."

Me: "No, not if you are no longer in it to win it."

Tsebo: "I disagree but let's just leave it there before it turns into something unnecessarily big."

Me: "Yeah. Let's leave it once. When last did you talk to Rose?"

"Yesterday morning…" He rolls his eyes.

Me: "Come on, Tsebo. She made her choice hle. It's about time you made peace with it."

Tsebo: "Let's go to our bedroom. I'm craving for you." He's changing the subject. Before I can say anything, he takes me from my chair and carries me upstairs. He gently throws me on top of the bed, takes off my gown and g-string.

Me: "Be gentle…"

He slowly slides it in and lets out a loud sigh. I moan with a high note of pleasure. We are both lost in a world of pleasure…

* * * * * *

We've been in bed most of the day today but we finally get up as I'm going for my check-up with our doctor. My appointment is at 3:30 p.m and thereafter, we are off to fetch Botlhale at the airport as she said she'll spend a week with us before going to have some quality time with herself at "her place," that being my old apartment.

Tsebo: "Nare what time is your appointment?"

272

Me: "At 3:30p.m."

Tsebo: "We should get ready then; I mean, it's already past 2:00p.m and we still have to fetch Botlhale. We don't want to keep her waiting at the airport when she arrives."

Me: "Okay, you can go and shower first. I'll make the bed in the mean-time."

Tsebo: "Hau. I thought we'll get into the shower together." He says so caressing my thigh. I jump out of the bed.

Me: "No. you know very well we take the whole day in the shower when we shower together."

Tsebo: "We won't do anything mos." He's lying. He always does this.

Me: "No no, Mogorosi. I'll shower after you."

He finally gives up and goes to shower. He's done in fifteen minutes, and I get into the shower. I'm also done in a few minutes. I put on my maxi boob-tubed floral dress with brown sandals and just fix my braids into a doughnut bun. I feel so big. Tsebo is wearing his white cargo shorts, black golfer shirt and black sneakers. We make our way to the doctor; even though we are an hour late, he attends us; that's what we pay him for anyway. The doctor confirms that everything is okay with the baby and me. He says boy-boy is growing really well and fast. You can feel how strong he is by just the kick, one might swear he's playing soccer inside his mother's womb. It's just not fair that he kicks mostly when he hears his father's voice. When we are alone, it's just mini turns here and there. What can we say though? Sons and their fathers...

It's already 5:30 p.m, a whole thirty minutes since Botlhale landed and we are on our way to fetch her at the airport.

"Told you that we are gonna be late. Now we are not gonna hear the end of it." Tsebo says while driving.

Me: "Aii Tsebo. I was hungry, what was I supposed to do?"

Tsebo: "We could have bought something along the way."

Me: "No. I was craving eggs. Specifically made by me." He just keeps quiet and shakes his head. I also keep quiet and look outside the window. Out of the blue, he just smiles and sings 'Buy Me a Rose' by Luther Vandross. He's busy singing with that beautiful bass of his while looking at the road ahead. I find myself smiling while looking outside the window. As I anticipated, the little one gives out massive kicks inside me.

Me: "See? You've woken him up. Now he's busy playing soccer again." I say while taking his hand and placing it on my belly. He looks at me and smiles with those crystal teeth of his.

Tsebo: "He's not playing soccer. He's dancing to the sweet melodies song by his handsome daddy. Right, boy-boy?" He kicks harder and Tsebo laughs out loud. It's like they have this special way of communicating. I just shake my head and smile at the window.

We arrive at the airport and find Botlhale sitting on the benches busy with her phone. I just hope she's not too angry. I poke her on her shoulder.

Botlhale: "You really took... whoa!!! And then?!" I take it my belly took her by surprise.

Me: "And then eng?"

Tsebo: "Guess who's gonna be an aunt?!"

Botlhale: "Oh my word! There's a little bun in the oven????"

Me: "Yeahp. Got that right. Five months." She screams and jumps around.

"And you hid it from me? Even you abuti? I thought we were loyal gossip buddies." She says patting Tsebo's arm. He laughs out loud and holds me by my waist.

Tsebo: "Oh I see. Now that Rose is gone, you wanna use me again? No ma'am, I've got my very own gossip buddy right beside me."

Me: "You heard that, right?"

Botlhale: "Whatever." We all burst out into laughter, Tsebo takes Botlhale's bags and we drive off. It's already dark outside.

Botlhale: "So do you guys know the gender ya baby nyana?"

Tsebo: "Yeah. A baby boy. A full Mogorosi."

Botlhale: "Ncoah. But I wanted a baby girl though."

Me: "Then make yours." Tsebo bursts out in laughter.

Botlhale: "Nnya ausi. You know that what's yours is mine and what's mine is mine. And besides, I don't want any kids. I just want to have lots and lots of money and flourish!". This one is crazy.

Me: "Whatever babes."

We finally arrive home and Botlhale and I start preparing dinner. There's still some leftover dumbling; it will be enough for all of us. I make beef stew and spinach. Botlhale makes the beetroot and chakalaka. We are done in three hours and I'm tired as hell.

Me: "Can I take a shower first then we can have supper?"

Botlhale: "Yeah sure. No problem. I'll watch TV in the meantime."

I go to the bedroom and Tsebo's is not there, but his phone is on the bed. I find him at the balcony, smoking.

Me: "Oh. This is where you are hiding."

Tsebo: "Yeah. Akere you and Botlhale made me feel like I didn't exist."

Me: "Mmh. Okay. I'm taking a shower neh."

"Do you want me to join you?" He says looking at me seductively.

Me: "Don't start."

Tsebo: "Mxm. Ke tsebile."

I go back to the bedroom and just as I'm about to take off my clothes, his phone keeps beeping on the bed. I take it, only to find several messages from an unsaved number.

> *You know you want me. All of me.*

> *It's only a matter of time before you find peace in between my legs.*

> *I can't get you out of my mind.*

> *Horny as hell right now.*

> *Mogorosi.*

Together with the messages, there's three nude pictures. I've had enough of this bitch. It's time to take matters into my own hands. I go to the bathroom, lock the door and message this bitch back using Tsebo's phone.

> *You know what? You are right. I've been denying this feeling for too long.*

> *Finally. I told you I'll be patient with you.*

> *We can't talk about this on the phone though...*

> *You can come to my place baby.*

> *This time? Isn't your child there?*

> *She's sleeping. I want you. I want you right now.*

> *What will I tell my wife?*

> *Forget about her. Just come.*

> *Cool. On my way. Wear something sexy.*

> *You won't be disappointed sweetheart. I'll buzz you in.*

> *Cool.*

I wear my tracksuits, take Tsebo's phone and open the safe and take his gun with me and head downstairs.

Me: "Botlhale. I'm going to my office to fetch something important. Tell Tsebo I'll be back."

Botlhale: "But ausi it's..." I don't wait for her to finish. I go to the garage and drive off. I can't allow this to go on. I won't be disrespected while I'm sitting comfortably in my home by some slut who is bored and doesn't know what to do with her miserable life. I arrive at the gate.

> *I'm here.*

> *I've buzzed you in. Room 2314.*

I drive through, take the elevator and go to her room. I find the door unlocked and I get in. The room is dark, but I can see her. She's even wearing lingerie, sitting on the couch. She's not even looking at me.

Rene: "Finally."

Me: "Yeah. Finally." She hears my voice and jumps off the couch.

Rene: "Tlhalefo!" The look in her eyes right now! She even spills the wine she was drinking.

Me: "Keng? Who were you expecting? My husband?" I haven't taken the gun out yet.

Rene: "No... I... Uhm..."

Me: "You are even wearing cheap lingerie. Yesses maan! Why are you trying to seduce my man? Don't you get the idea? He doesn't want you!"

Rene: "It's... it's not what you think. I was just trying to have some harmless fun." I laugh out loud.

Me: "Harmless fun with whose husband?"

Rene: "Waitsi keng Tlhalefo. You can't have it all. Not everything belongs to you. Stop being greedy." I see she has gained some strength.

Me: "What do you mean?"

Rene: "You want everything to be yours, Tlhalefo. Beauty, brains, riches, a handsome and rich husband, a multi-million company, a luxurious mansion, I'm not even going to talk about the cars you drive because wow. You want all the glory and recognition. You want it all!" This woman is crazy.

Me: "Mosetsana. Of course I want everything to belong to me because I worked so damn hard for it! Nare wa tsenwa? What did you want me to do? Sit back and watch as life defeats me like you? Wa tsenwa maan."

Rene: "You know, papa was right. You think you are smart. You think the world revolves around you."

Me: "Oh. I see where you got the stupidity from."

Rene: "Don't talk about my father like that."

Me: "Haha! The same father who I had to save you from? The same father I had to save your daughter from? Okay, daddy's girl."

Rene: "At least he's real. He's not a wolf in sheep skin, like someone I know."

Me: "What do you want from my husband?"

Rene: "Everything he gives you."

Me: "Wa tsenwa." I pull out my gun. She gasps.

Rene: "Tlhalefo!!!"

Me: "I'm tired of everybody taking away things and people I care about. Don't I deserve to be happy? Everybody mistakes my kindness for weakness. It's about time I stop that nonsense. I'm tired. I'm tired of having to fight for everything in my life. Ebile wene o worse. After everything I've done for you, Reneilwe? I looked beyond our differences when we were growing up. I looked past your harsh treatment towards my sister and me. I took you out of poverty, you bastard! I snatched you from the clutches of those million men who were abusing you and were a threat to your daughter. Got you a job, got you a decent place to stay. Took your daughter to the best school anybody could ever wish for and this is how you thank me? With a bucket full of trash! You people tend to forget how crazy I can get. I'm a maniac, remember? You are gonna regret it. Oh, remember that little stunt you pulled on my wedding day, you are going to pay for it!"

Rene: "You can't shoot me. Everybody will hear. You are gonna give birth in jail and rot in jail! Buhle will hate you with all her heart!"

Me: "Oh don't worry sweetheart. See, this gun has a silencer. It's really not like those guns that belong to those tavern boyfriends of yours. So everything will go nice and smooth."

Rene: "Please don't do this. I'm begging you."

Me: "Argh. I'm not even gonna use it. But it's up to you, though."

Rene: "What do you mean?"

Me: "It's either I call Buhle to come and witness the death of her mother... or you and I just head off to the balcony and you do your magic."

Rene: "Please. Please don't involve Buhle in this. I'm begging you."

Me: "Psssh. Stop acting like you care about her. She'll survive; I survived too, when your dearest daddy killed my father in front of me, remember? Like I said, it's entirely up to you babes."

She starts crying. Gosh! I don't have time for this.

"To the balcony, then. Let's go. Don't waste my time." I'm still pointing the gun at her. She does as I say and we end up at the balcony.

Rene: "I'm sorry. I'm really sorry. I'll stop it. I'll stop everything."

Me: "I don't need your sorry. And yes, you are gonna stop. Jump."

Rene: "What?!"

Me: "Fly, superwoman. Fly. Or would you rather have a bullet in your head?"

Rene: "Tlhalefo, please..."

Me: "Eyy mosetsana. I have a husband waiting for me back home. Stop wasting my time." I get closer and closer to her. She's finally balancing with the short balcony wall.

Me: "Climb the wall. Then jump. And I am not going to repeat myself."

She doesn't really give me a hard time. She climbs on the wall. She's crying so hard, but I just don't feel nothing. I want to get this over and done with.

I count down from three and she jumps. I hear a loud crash coming from down. I look down the wall and indeed… Reneilwe Khama… is gone, she 'committed suicide'…

* * * * * * *

Tsebo: "Where the hell have you been? You are even sweating! And o mo tseile kae Buhle?" He's fuming.

Me: "She called me using her mother's phone because Reneilwe is missing, so I had to fetch her."

Botlhale: "Reneilwe is missing!? Ausi, are you sure that everything is okay?"

Me: "Oh trust me, everything is perfect. Family, let us eat and rejoice in peace. Buhle, sit down and eat, my baby."

I can feel Tsebo's eyes moving with me, lies never work with him. I think he has already picked out what's happening. I look at him, his look feels so cold.

Tsebo: "Tlhalefo, bedroom. Now." I do as he says and follow him to the bedroom.

Tsebo: "What the hell did you do?" He's calm. He's looking at the horse painting on the wall.

"I… I did what I should have done a long time ago." My voice is breaking and a tear escapes my eye. He turns to look at me. He comes closer to me, holds my hand and puts my head on his chest. He says nothing; All I do is weep…

281

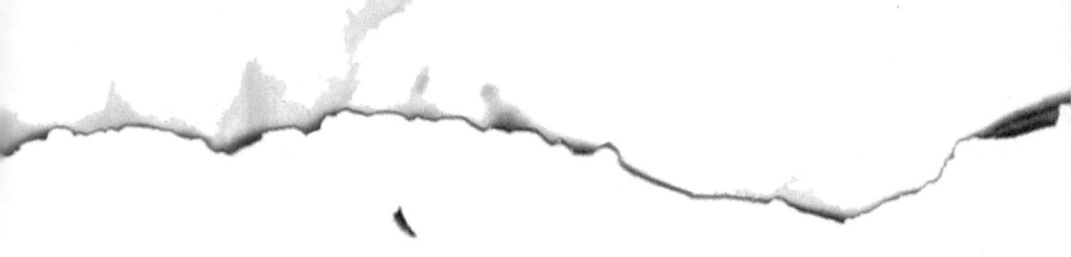

FIVE YEARS LATER

I'm busy in the kitchen, pulling together the last few snacks for my son's fifth birthday lunch. Mmusi Jongikhaya Mogorosi—our little handful. Five years old, and already he's the spitting image of his father. He's got Tsebo's face, his laugh, his charm—and his knack for trouble. Sometimes I think that mischievous grin of his could melt even the iciest heart. Not mine, though. I know his tricks.

Botlhale and Rose are in the dining room setting up the table, laughing together as they arrange the plates. I hear Nobuhle, my daughter, humming beside me as she slices vegetables for the platters. She's nineteen now, just starting college, and she's got this glow about her, this contentment. Every time I look at her, I remember how broken she was the day we told her about her mother. They all believe Reneilwe jumped from her balcony. And for Nobuhle's sake, I let them believe that story. She didn't need the whole truth, and honestly, I was more than ready to close that chapter.

I still remember Nobuhle's 15th birthday—the day we made it official and adopted her. She's blossomed in these four years, grown into a beautiful, vibrant young woman, with Tsebo and Mmusi as her pillars. She's always loved drama, and now, she's chasing her dream at a top college. It warms me to see her so close to Tsebo and her little brother; they're her family now.

Reneilwe's funeral was everything you'd expect for someone as notorious as she was. Packed to the brim with faces I didn't recognise. I let them mourn her how they saw fit, and I even gave her the dignity of a proper funeral. May she rest, wherever she ended up.

And life, as always, moves on. Botlhale has a year under her belt now as a qualified junior attorney, still in love and still steady with Ayibongwe, her fiancé. Then there's Rose. She split with Pranav and landed right on her feet. Now she's dating Steve Ban, a white billionaire geologist who dabbles in music production. Leave it to Rose to level up like that.

Of course, not everyone's adjusted so well. Reneilwe's father—he didn't take her death quietly. He's been a shadow of himself, drifting around like a ghost. It might sound cruel, but I needed him to feel that emptiness, that ache. When I told him the truth, every twisted detail, I watched him crumble. He's just as helpless as I was, feeling the same pain I've known for too long.

As for me and Tsebo, our marriage is stronger than ever. We've found a peace that I didn't know was possible, a peace that feels invincible. I'm three months pregnant with our third, though we haven't found out the gender yet. And N-AMI—what started as a little agency has grown into something global, something that keeps me busy and proud. Tsebo and I even opened a restaurant and a hotel together. Life is…sweet, in every sense.

Doc—my friend who once had it all—finally went through with her divorce. Now, she's out there living her best life, travelling the world, and leaving medicine behind.

But then, there's me—the woman I am now. The woman I had to become. I look at myself sometimes and see glimpses of someone I swore I'd never be—someone like Reneilwe's father. The pain, the betrayal—it changed me. Maybe I let my anger get the best of me, maybe I crossed lines that can't be uncrossed, but I don't regret a thing. If protecting what's mine, if keeping my family safe, means getting blood on my hands—then so be it. I've done it once, and I'd do it again without hesitation.

This is who Tlhalefo Mogorosi is now. Not just a murderer, not just a woman wrestling with bipolar disorder, but a sister to Botlhale, a wife to Tsebo, a mother to Nobuhle and Mmusi. I am someone willing to fight, to do whatever it takes, to keep what's mine. I'm prepared to face whatever consequences come my way. When that reckoning arrives, I'll be right here, waiting.

> We all have a dark side, It just takes an intriguing experience for one to discover hers. After all, pain becomes a part of our being. But... there's always a whisper of hope beyond the brokenness. —Rosi Molefe

www.ingramcontent.com/pod-product-compliance
Lightning Source LLC
Chambersburg PA
CBHW020544020726
47494CB00006B/1912